THE SCRIBING IBIS

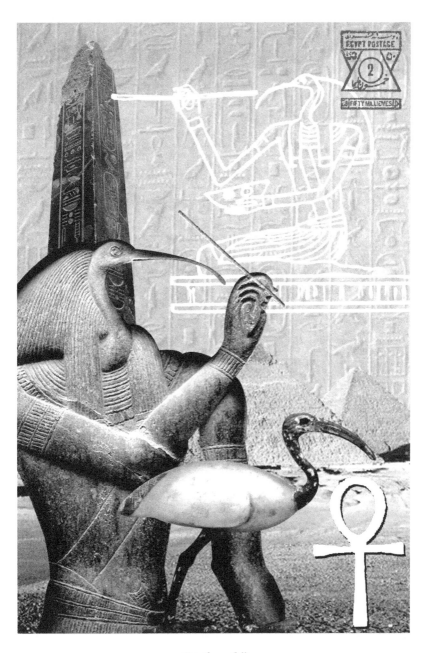

"Thoth"

by K.S. Roy

The Scribing Ibis

An Anthology of Pagan Fiction in Honor of Thoth

Edited by Rebecca Buchanan

Foreword by Inanna Gabriel

BIBLIOTHECA ALEXANDRINA

Dedication

She was known as the Eye of Re and, once upon a time, that wrathful Goddess abandoned the heavens and came to Earth. She took refuge in the burning deserts of the south, Her breath boiling away oasi and setting animals to flight. But Ra needed His wrath, His eye of justice and righteous vengeance. And so He sent clever Thoth to retrieve Her.

Feathers wilting before Her great heat, sweet-tongued Thoth sat down upon the scorching sands and wove stories for the Goddess: tales of magic and horror, wonder and misery, lust and honor, princes and bakers and thieves, Gods and heroes and villains. Charmed, homesick, reminded of Her place and power and responsibilities as the Eye of Ra, the Goddess agreed to return to the House of Life. Order was restored.

And so it is to Him that we dedicate this collection of tales – Thoth, Thout, Tetu, Techu, Zehuti, <u>Tehuti, Djehuty</u>. <u>The Scribe of Ma'at. The Lunar Librarian. Lord of Divine Words. Creation's First Storyteller.</u>

The Fires of Thoth

by Teresita Garcia

I hear the sound of words
rising from a great bonfire
and I am ready to receive
them with imperious
humility, for it is love that
wills the gaze of an ibis
by the immortal tongue
of Ra.

The heavens and earth
shift with pleasing
geometry, marking a
sacred space that shows
itself in silence, residing
in the poetry of one's
intentions, alive with
tradition.

I make my home under
the happening of the moon,
where the cypress weighs
the souls of the dead in
intricate scents lost to
measure. Here, the dogwood
and the dandelions stand firm
under the smoke

that drifts beneath leaves, in
a small mountain temple,
where there is order in
the observances, and divine
dominion, ruled in moderation.

Table of Contents

Foreword: Blessed Be the Mythmakers

by Inanna Gabriel

As modern Pagans, many of our spiritualities revolve around the gods and goddesses first recognized by ancient cultures. We study the myths of those cultures the way followers of many monotheistic faiths pore over their own holy books. Myths are a means of describing and explaining the gods, and of coming to know and understand them while at the same time gaining a better understanding of the world around us and our experiences and circumstances.

Myths are stories. That may seem a ridiculous thing to have to point out, but stay with me. Long ago, mythology, the lore of the gods and of their heroes and champions, was the backbone of many cultures. These are the cultures whose religions, based on those myths, many modern Pagans work to reconstruct in their practices today. Many more at least draw from the beliefs, practices, and stories of those ancient cultures in newer traditions that, for them, better suit their own lives and times. But regardless of the approach, reconstructionist or syncretic, the ancient myths almost always play an important role in the beliefs of today's modern Pagans.

Mythology, however, is not, by definition, restricted to the stories of our ancient ancestors. Any story that attempts to explain something, whether directly or via symbol and allegory, is a myth. Any *group* of such stories is, therefore, a mythology. That means that, really, *any* work of fiction qualifies as a myth. Some are more potent than others, most certainly, but they all qualify. Mythology was once the core of religious belief, but it has evolved to be more the center of pop culture. Not a bad thing, really; I enjoy Star Wars too, after all, and I defy you to find a bigger Harry Potter fan. But myth as religious tale? That seems to have all but left us completely.

I can't say, honestly, why this is so. We seem, as a community at large, to have shifted our focus more to a mix of poetry and nonfiction. Why, when our religious heritage was born of stories, are we no longer writing stories?

I won't deny that much of why this is important to me is because I write fiction, and because I don't particularly like poetry. For a very long time, these facts distracted me from the simple realization that fiction is at the *heart* of our religious history, and yet is all but absent in our religious *present*.

The book you hold in your hands is a step towards reestablishing this missing element in our continuing body of religious writings. I'm currently editing a volume of Pagan fiction as well, which will likely be published around the same time as this one. Rebecca Buchanan's website *Eternal Haunted*

Summer is yet another contribution towards reclaiming our title as Mythmakers. Because that's what our ancestors were, and by choosing to follow a Pagan path, and by honoring the figures of ancient myth, we have accepted the challenge to carry on the tradition of bringing the gods into the world. I, for one, am proud and excited to be a part of it.

*[Inanna Gabriel is co-Owner of **Misanthrope Press**, co-Editor in Chief of **Title Goes Here:**, a fiction magazine, and a published author of several short stories and (so far) one novel. She has also followed a very Wiccan-flavored eclectic Pagan path for the past 17 years. She has recently begun an attempt to marry these two very important things in her life, fiction and Paganism. She is co-editor of **Etched Offerings: Voices From the Cauldron of Story**, with C. Bryan Brown, and also has a story included in that collection. She maintains a fiction-related blog at www.inanna-gabriel.com.]*

Introduction

by Rebecca Buchanan

The first stories were Pagan.

Or, to use another, perhaps more accurate *p* word: polytheist.

By the middle of the twenty-second century BCE, residents of the Fertile Crescent were swapping tales of a mighty warrior king named Gilgamesh, and his encounters with monsters, demons, Gods and Goddesses – and one Goddess in particular: Ishtar. Go back even further, another century or more, and we find that the world's first poems were religious hymns. And not just any hymns, but songs in praise of Gods and Goddesses such as the heavenly An, the lunar Nanna, and ferocious Inanna (aka Ishtar). Go back even further, to 2400 BCE, and we find the oldest known writing in the world: the *Pyramid Texts*. Carved into the walls and sarcophagi at Saqqara, the *Pyramid Texts* invoked such Deities as the ithyphallic Min, creatrix Neith, green-skinned Osiris and mysterious Nephthys to guard the Pharaoh in the afterlife and lead him to glory. Travel further east, and we find the world's oldest, continuously-used sacred text, *The RigVeda*. This collection of more than a thousand hymns was being sung by devotees of Indra, Agni and Aditi as early as 1700 BCE – and those hymns are still being sung in temples today.

Polytheism – and therefore polytheist literature – remained dominant through most of the world down through the present. In Europe, the Middle East, and parts of Africa, however, monotheistic traditions rose to power. Unknown numbers of poems, satires, dramas, novels, hymns, stories, songs, rituals and myths were lost due to neglect, apathy, and active persecution and destruction. A fraction survived: as fragments (see Sappho's poems), within a text of the new status quo (see Celsus' *On the True Doctrine*), buried in ruins (see *The Epic of Gilgamesh*), or because they somehow proved useful to the new order (see *The Aeneid*), or because someone, somewhere, secretly loved them.

In the new monotheistic literature, which began its rise to prominence around the third century of the Common Era, the Gods and Goddesses of ancient days were demonized, sanctified, reduced in power to bit players on the cosmic stage, or mocked, or declared to be nothing more than projections of our inner lusts and fears. See, for example, Augustine's *City of God*, the hagiographies of Saints such as Christopher and Brigit, any original edition of *Grimms' Fairy Tales*, and superficial discussions of Jung and Campbell.

It was a very, very long time before that began to change – and, even then, the return of the Gods and Goddesses in literature was sporadic and inconsistent. Christine de Pizan, devoutly Catholic, wrote glowingly of

Minerva and Ceres and Isis, but considered them to be real women wrongly deified. Just over a century later, though, poets such as Pernette de Guillet wrote just as glowingly of Apollo and the Muses, but without the euhemeristic surtext.

In artwork, Their return was even more colorful, tantalizing, wondrous – Botticelli, Gossaert, Titian, Velazquez, Rubens, Poussin, Cranach – and utterly impossible to ignore.

The trickle became a flood. The mockery turned to admiration (John Keats in *On First Looking into Chapman's Homer*) to ecstatic devotion (Percy Bysshe Shelley raised an altar to Pan in 1821). Poetry and fiction and drama gave rise to scholarly works: Jacob Grimm's *German Mythology* (1854), Thomas Bulfinch's *The Age of Fable* (1855), Frazer's *The Golden Bough* (1890) and *The God of the Witches* (1931) by Margaret Murray; which, in turn, helped lay the groundwork for a rebirth of Paganism in the twentieth century.

In its own small way, the volume you hold in your hands is part of that rebirth. These are not ancient tales, but modern stories. Here, the Gods are not figments of the imagination or demons, but Powers to be experienced and honored and loved and feared.

The first stories were Pagan. They were tales and songs in honor of Gods of sky and justice and death and love. The Gods are still here, and we are beginning to remember Them, to see Them, to hear Them, to know Them again. Listen, read, and rejoice.

Recommended Reading

Obviously, any texts mentioned above, as well as those in *Appendix D: Select Timeline of Pagan and Polytheist Literature and Related Texts*. Also:

An Anthology of Sacred Texts By and About Women, edited by Serinity Young
Goddesses and Wise Women: The Literature of Feminist Spirituality 1980-1992: An Annotated Bibliography by Anne Carson
Humming the Blues: Inspired by Nin-Me-Sar-Ra, Enheduanna's Song to Inanna by Cass Dalglish
The Mirror of the Gods: How Renaissance Artists Rediscovered the Pagan Gods by Malcolm Bull
Women Writers of the Renaissance and Reformation, edited by Katharina M Wilson
A World Full of Gods: An Inquiry into Polytheism by John Michael Greer

Birth

by Erynn Rowan Laurie

I t didn't feel like he expected it to. It didn't feel like anything, really. Sand against the tips of his fingers. Linen. The slick, wet skin of an abdju-fish, wriggling. The smooth lapis senet-piece he placed on the board for his winning move. It shimmered under his palm as it parted.

His hand slid into it. Pulling. It was pulling at him. His long, slender beak rattled in surprise. Tricky, this Forever stuff. His fingers flexed and it took a firmer grip, irresistible. He pulled back against it. "Open, damn it," he grumbled. He pushed another hand in.

The feathers on the back of his neck rose with the feel of it trickling into him. It was like lightning behind his eyes, flickering images playing in his mind. Seductive. Terrifying. Illuminating. Everything expanded, receding away into infinite distance around him.

Everything.

Everywhen.

Like the Nile, he drowned in it, roiled in it, wrapped in it, steeped in it. The scent of it permeated his flesh and feathers. He opened his mouth and the cries of baboons echoed down its corridors.

He was here for a purposepurposepurpose.

Sparkling light fell from one hand, rolled, stopped. Damn Ra anyway. He didn't have a deal with old Hawk-beak. Nut was a sisterfriend and Khonsu was gullible and light exploded, expanding in the space he'd opened in Forever. His head spun with it, speeding, the Boat of Millions of Years flashing through spacetimeaeonsnightnow.

Everynow, and the earth cooled under the light of a star, melting as the star expanded the universe flashed and faded and flashed and…

Blinking, he pushed, spread his arms, flexed the fabric of Forever around him, opening the wasiswillbe with a great, agonized cry. Coelacanths spun through the sea. Sand pulsed like blood over the face of a continent as the earth groaned and moved, landmasses parting and slamming together, raising mountain ranges. Off in the distance, a city vaporized in an instant of light as millions of shadows burned into sidewalks and ragged brick walls.

Not now. It's not yet. The Boat of Millions of Years hasn't made that journey. Muscles rippled in his shoulders as light fell from his hand, blossoming like a fertile egg blooming into human form. Have to teach those monkeys to read. Writing. That needed to come first.

First? Hadn't he done that five million years from now already? Growth and decay slid along his skin like sparks in the sky, like stars raining down the circle of night. Light burst from his flesh as Nut cried out in her birth-pangs. How many was that, anyway? He'd win light for this. Had won it. One finger shifted in Forever and Khonsu's sticks sent his piece to the Waters of Chaos. He felt himself laughing as he snatched it from the senet board. He took a breathbreathbreath.

Music hummed and shifted and shook, pulsing beats of intention in cities and fields and human throats and the space between stars as the children of Gods left the planet. They fell, burning, rose like Phoenixes, flew between worlds in their shining chariots. The universe pulsed with them. Violins echoed in the hollow of his beak; high, whining notes and the bass boom of cannons and flares in the sky in hues like the colors of creation, sparkling, falling, rising with a long, drawn-out ooooooh. A sistrum rattled behind one ear and he blinked one round, black eye.

Crocodiles rose from rippling water, snapping at his long, black toes. Almost there. He heard the cries of infant Gods, echoing backwards with indrawn breaths. In the sky, cindered stars sparked back into light. The Boat of Millions of Years sailed the heavens, sucking its wake into its reed body. He felt Forever pushing against him, trying to close the gap around his thin, feathered body. I could really use a mocha. He pushed harder, chest expanding as he gasped with his effort. His fingers tightened around tendrils of moments. Push.

Nut wailed and Geb laughed and he felt the dark, cutting eyes of Ra on his back as he shuddered with the effort of the opening. Light flashed around him, pouring from his bones in gouts like the inundation, rising about his knees, his chest, his nostrils. It swirled, whirlwind, carrying the sound of his baboon-cries as the orange globe of the sun burst at the edge of the horizon, blinding.

With a gasp, he let go. Screaming, he fell and Forever pushed him out of its body, limp and panting on the wet verge of the river. Reeds surrounded him and the scent of lotus filled his burning lungs. Five days. He could feel it, how they'd leeched from his light, bird-bone marrow with the light he'd won from Khonsu. Love was more important than Order, after all, and he couldn't very well let Gods die in the womb. He heard their voices in the distance, excited and chattering.

Thoth smiled.

Persephone's Travels
by John Drury

G ood afternoon your majesty" said the shriveled figure. "It is always a pleasure to serve."

She regarded the stick of a figure before her with some mild disgust. Skin and bones really, with that toothy smile that masked a black heart. How he knew the time of day here was beyond her. After all, the man never saw the surface of the earth. Then again, somewhere in the world it was surely afternoon. But his greeting was not the same every time. Sometimes it was good morning, sometimes good evening, or just 'good day.' She wondered if he did this just to amuse himself.

Or shut out the wailing.

"Step carefully m'lady, the boat is narrow."

Well of course it was, and it wasn't like she hadn't stepped in this blasted barque before. Her daily trips across this wretched river weren't exactly infrequent. So many places to visit in the world, so much work to do. Today, however, it was a special day. And this, the trip down, was the herald of a special time.

She paused as the shadows clawed at her, literally supplicating to her. They had no form of course, and simply melted into puddles around her feet and legs. Shapes of hands, arms, faces, kicked away like smoke with the slightest movement of her feet. So many of them now, so very many. Ever since Yahweh had made his promise oh those many years ago, a promise to bring the gods and the people closer together. If only the other gods would trust him, he promised, things would be better. So her uncle agreed on their behalf, to let this other step up and try his grand experiment, which had failed on so many levels. The results were here for her to see, souls stuck on this side of the Styx. That blasted stick figure Charon was dark of heart, and would not let them pass either. It was his job after all.

But the agreement was coming to an end, and already things were changing. Those first few in the vanguard, brave souls (or fools she thought), working to restore what was lost. Don Quixote would be proud of some of them. But they were trying at least, and it was good to hear them speak again. The voices had never really stopped, even down through the centuries, at least for them. For some gods the voices were never gone, for other gods the voices were nearly lost. But now, the chorus for all was growing, if ever so slowly....

"Step to the end m'lady, be careful! The river is no place for a queen! We must allow our passengers room to board."

[3]

Such a sniveling way of saying it, she thought. But of course he was only doing his job. And while this trip was normally a solitary one for her, today there were two escorts. Ahh, Zeus's boys, Castor and Polydeuces. Normally they were either here standing watch with her beloved one day, or wandering the earth or sitting with their father upon high the next day. But for two days in the year, they were her companions, her guardians, her heralds, going between both worlds. Such pomp and circumstance. Her husband insisted on it, his realm's grip not to be dismissed lightly, lest anyone forget.

And how she longed to fall into his arms when this day was done. Not that she had been long absent. Humans, in their folly, imagined her here only for a certain period of time during the year. But they forgot, or did not know, that when the northern latitudes became cold, the southern latitudes warmed. Her mother decamped to this area, and they supped together many days, with many gods. Of course those places near the center of the world never felt their absence. At the same time, those far northern and southern reaches of the earth rarely saw them. Such cold, so forbidding. They left it to the ice and snow gods who ruled those realms all of the time, only occasionally venturing there to touch them, however briefly. But with their travels around the world, they were absent from some areas only for awhile. Thus, she often spent much time with her mother in the world where it was warm and lush. However, she also returned regularly to be with her husband.

Far from the brute many feared, Hades had shown such kindness and tenderness to her over the years. She was happy in her role, and happy to be surrounded by those that loved her, both here and above on the earth, and upon high.

Cloaked in these thoughts, oblivious to the wailing souls in the river, and with her escorts silent behind her, Persephone, Queen of the Underworld, drifted as the boat neared the other side of the river.

Already it had been a busy day. In the southern latitudes the spring equinox had already come some months ago. Her visits there had cheered her mother, allowing the area to warm and become verdant again. On this day Castor and Polydeuces had mounted their steeds and ridden out before her into the world, horns blowing, announcing her semi-permanent return to these lands for the next few precious months. As they traveled, with her twin guardians and her mother, fair Demeter, they were greeted and welcomed in many places. They dined with Wollunqua, Nokhubulwane, and Wendeunk, celebrating the warmth and the growing season which was so clearly and strongly occurring in these latitudes.

Now, however, such feasting was done for the day, at least for Persephone. With her mother remaining behind as a guest, she was returned here, ready to prepare her husband for his ride to the surface of the earth, for this one night in the northern latitudes.

For tonight, Hades would lead the dead to the surface, and they would walk the earth this eve.

Other such nights occurred of course, in various places. Dionysos would lead a contingent of his own in a few months, and various other places had their appointed times. For this evening, however, the largest such movement would occur. And it was time to prepare.

"Step carefully your highness, and make sure...." She ignored Charon's words as she stepped off and ran down the corridor, and found her beloved in the great hall seated upon his throne. She embraced him with a fierce passion, and marveled again at how strong he looked this day.

"Hello my love, I hope that your mother is doing well."

"She is doing fine. I gave to her your regards, as I always do, and always her smile faded just a bit. I doubt she'll ever warm to you completely, but she is happy nevertheless with our arrangement."

"Good, good. Oh, I see your escorts are here again."

"Hail Hades," said Castor, finally catching up. "We have ridden long today, but the journey has been good."

"Indeed it has," said Polydeuces. "However, tonight is an even larger journey. Are you ready, Uncle?"

"Almost," said Hades. "Just some final touches that await my wife's presence. We shall ride out immediately after she has performed her magic. Wait here, white colts of Zeus, and we will return shortly."

Hades and Persephone retired to their bed chambers. She brought out his most magnificent cloak, dark but shimmering in the torchlight, and placed on his shoulders. She retrieved his staff, polished, dark, twisted, and strong, and set it near him. Next she took out a crown, woven of sheaves of wheat and colored cock feathers, and blessed it, speaking words only intelligible to her. Placing it upon his head, she stood back and looked at him.

"Magnificent, if I do say so myself," she said.

"You have the touch, my love, and only you could make this night and day as special as it is," he said. "Let us go now, and do as we must."

They stepped out and walked to the great hall first, and then towards the river. The multitude of souls welled up from everywhere in this place, stepping aside and bowing as the royal couple passed, and then surging behind them. They continued to walk down to the riverside, with Castor and Polydeuces leading the way. At the river, Charon had prepared a special passage, allowing both the king and queen and their escorts, and the surging host behind them, to pass over the river. On the other side, after the crossing, they came to a magnificent chariot pulled by two black steeds. Next to them were the two white colts of the Dioskouroi, who mounted in silence as Hades and Persephone climbed into the chariot. Behind them, legions of the dead had crossed, and were waiting.

"Castor, Polydeuces, lead us to the surface," said Hades. Thus they began the procession, slowly at first, rapidly gaining speed, until they burst out of the cave in this northern part of the world. The dead poured out behind them, scattering to various places, with Castor and Polydeuces blowing horns as they rode off. Hades sat and stared at the starry night sky. Breathing in the night air, he waited until another figure approached, and turned to him. "Hermes, please make sure that the dead have returned after this night. Most know that they must, but please ensure that those reluctant to return do so."

"Of course Hades, I shall," said Hermes. "Some will take time to return, and others remain despite our pleas and actions, but I pledge to have them returned in good order." Hades nodded his ascent, and Hermes retired into the shadows.

"Even if we only do this twice a year, as we will in six months in the southern latitudes, it is wonderful to spend this piece of the night here with you, my darling," said Persephone.

"All too quick I'm afraid," said Hades. "Were I to stay too long, my realm would be in chaos and my presence here would create havoc as well. But it is good to be here with you by my side, for this important night." He breathed in the cool clean air, with his beautiful queen shining as brightly as the stars above. For a time he lingered, taking in the sounds of the earth, now sleeping here. He watched as the souls of the dead moved to their places for the night. At last he sighed, and turned to his wife. "Let us return now," he said "and let the dead do as they will."

Accompanied now by only the Dioskouroi, Hades and Persephone returned to the Underworld, to a night of intense lovemaking as the dead walked the earth.

The Story of Philemon and Baukis
by Amanda Sioux Blake

One of my favorite tales featuring Hermes is the story of Philemon and Baukis. You see, the Gods would sometimes disguise themselves as human beings and walk among men, in order to investigate crimes, help heroes, or see how a person would treat them when they didn't know they were a God. One day, Zeus and Hermes, the Gods who enforced the Law of Hospitality, came to Phrygia. They pretended to be road-weary travelers looking for a place to stay the night. It was the duty of every Greek to offer hospitality to strangers. First they went to the palace to ask to stay the night, but the guards simply laughed at them. The two disguised Gods went to a several more houses, indeed most of the houses in the capital city. Ovid numbers as many as a thousand households. Each time they were turned away.

Finally, on the very outskirts of town, a household did let them in. It was obvious from the first glance that it was owned by very poor people. It was built of mud, thatch and reeds, and looked like it was beginning to collapse. When Hermes and Zeus knocked on the door, an elderly couple answered and immediately ushered the two travelers in. The old lady, Baukis, apologizing for their poverty, took out a chuck of bacon that the couple had been saving and made a stew for their guests. Her husband, Philemon, used their last firewood to make a roaring fire to warm their guests. He then went into the garden to get all of the few fruits and vegetables that they had, to add to his wife's stew. They brought the Gods water so they could wash up. They brought out their best blankets to put on the dilapidated couch, trying to make the travelers feel welcome in their home.

Baukis set out all the food they had: eggs, fruit, a little cheese, fresh veggies, and of course the stew. She brought out the only wine they had, and when the meal was finished she offered their guest honey and nuts, berries and apples. She was afraid that the guests would still be hungry and thirsty, but there was nothing left in the house. Then she realized that the wine pitcher was still full, even though by now they had surely drunk it all. Realizing that only a God to cause such a miracle, the couple fell to their knees, and prayed that the Gods would not be angered by such a poor, small meal.

Philemon decided to kill their goose, so the Gods could have meat. The poor old goose did not like this idea, and he ran inside and hid in the lap of great Zeus himself. "Do not kill your faithful guard," Zeus tells Philemon. "And do not stay here any longer. We intend to take vengeance on the people who turned us away and violated the Law of Hospitality, but you deserve to live. Climb up the mountain with us, and do not look back till you reach the stop."

As you can probably imagine, it took the elderly couple a long time to reach the summit. When they did, they looked around and saw that the whole country had been flooded. Everything was washed away. All that still stood was the couple's little shack. But it was no longer their tiny home. It had been transformed into a glorious temple of marble with a golden roof.

Zeus offered Philemon and Baukis any gift they wanted. The elderly couple merely asked to serve Zeus as his priest and priestess, and also that when it was time for them to die it would be at the same moment, so neither would have to grieve for the other.

Zeus was only too happy to grant the pious couple's wish, and they faithfully served him for many years.

One day they were standing in front of the temple, when they realized that they couldn't walk. Their feet stuck to the ground and grew roots which shot deep into the earth. Their hair became leaves. Their arms which had been wrapped around each other became intertwining branches. Zeus had turned Philemon into a oak tree and Baukis into a linden tree, so that the couple could live on after their human years had ended, still embracing each other. Ever since then, whenever a traveler passes by that particular temple of Zeus, they hang wreaths on the trees in remembrance.

The Gallisenae

by Jhenah Telyndru

"One calls them Gallisenae: they claim to calm by their songs and the singularities of their artifices the seas in storms and the winds, and to take the shape of animals which they want. They can cure what by others is incurable and to predict what must arrive."

- Pomponius Mela, Roman Geographer

M y leather clad feet had walked this path countless times these past two years, but never with as much purpose – never with as much intention. It seemed the winds themselves strained to work against me this night, their fingers prying loose long strands of hair from the plait I had woven extra tightly, whipping hair into my face as if to deliberately obscure my vision. It was already difficult enough to see in the gloaming, now that the waning half moon had slipped below the horizon. We were many hours into this intense and sacred work, my Sisters and I, having begun our task at the precise moment the last light of dusk faded into star shine.

I could barely believe that two turns of the wheel had passed since I first came to the Island – and yet, I could hardly recall what it was like being anywhere else. The memory of my arrival was as crisp as late autumn; I had clung fearfully to my mother's gown even after Annick Velléda, who would later become my mentor, had called me forward. I knew, of course, the great honor of this calling; being chosen to serve Ker on the Blessed Isle brought stature to my family and was a blessing to my clan. Still, I could not help being afraid of this windswept island, swirling with legends like the sea around the prow of the boat that had brought me to these shores. And yet, I remembered, when I first set foot upon this sacred shoreline, a sense of homecoming had overtaken me in a way I could never put into words, chasing away any lingering doubt that this was, indeed, my destiny.

I struggled to recapture that feeling of center as the coiled serpent of my fear began to move in the pit my belly once more. As I had been taught in one of my earliest lessons, I slowed my breathing to match rhythm of the ocean tides that were the great guiding force in the lives of we Veiled Sisters. While it had taken some time to get used to the stinging winds that were a constant companion here on Enez Sun, called the Island of Sena by some, tonight I was glad for the lash of their icy censure for they helped me focus on the matter at hand, keeping my senses sharp and my intention clear.

Trained to look for the patterns in things and events, I followed the thread of the present – which saw me walking the length of this island and back through the darkness of the frigid night – back to the stitching that began this portion of the Great Tapestry. I traced the energies back to a fortnight ago, when the weaving that had brought me here first began....

****

I stood on the quay between the ocean and the two tall stone sentinels that guarded the main path running through the center of the Sacred Isle. The small priestess craft tied to the wooden platform was tossed gently by the waves that lapped up on the shore around it. Pulling the stopper from the mouth of the skin bag across my shoulder, I filled a low silver cup that lay hidden in a niche below the wooden planks. As I poured the libation of ale into the sea, I chanted a litany in the old tongue to appease the restless spirits of Ker-Is, the Sunken Lands.

My nightlong vigil had begun.

Each priestess took turns watching the mainland shore by night, immersed in prayer and ready to respond to a call for assistance from those we served in Her name. I wrapped my woolen cloak around me and settled in for the night, sitting in ritual pose with my back against one of the tall stone menhirs. Only twice before had I needed to make the journey across the choppy straits to the Breton mainland at night; both times, for those in need of healing. Most other requests could wait for the light of day – auguries and weather-workings were rarely so pressing as to come at night.

The moon had not yet moved a quarter of its arc against the sky when I saw it. Across the water, twisting in the night breeze, the signal fire had been lit. There was no mistaking the tongues of its urgency. I loosed the oak-hewn boat from its moorings and began to paddle across the waters to the other shore. The tide was with me, and it didn't take long to reach the far platform where I was met by a small group of worried faces, made ghostly in the firelight.

"Blessed Velléda," one of the men addressed me. "Thank you for responding to our call." He touched his hands to his forehead and bowed in my direction, making certain not to come in contact with an inviolate Sacred Virgin of the Isle.

A finely dressed woman pushed forward, her stance of need overriding her solicitousness towards one of the Veiled Sisters. "Honored one, I am Speaker for the Nemnetes Tribe in the south. There are many of us here concerned about the harvest. Mother Ker, bless Her name, sends too little rain and our ancestors can do nothing to assist us. We suffered many losses last season, and fear what this winter will bring. Will you beg Her mercy for Her children?"

[10]

"We will seek Her will on this," I replied, "for even the Sisters of the Isle can do nothing without Her blessing." With this reminder, the Speaker cast her eyes low, not wishing to dishonor her clan with her fears. Without meeting my gaze, she offered me two small bundles – one of earth from her tribal holdings, the other with a few heads of precious grain from the last harvest. The other petitioners did the same, and I filled my bag with the small homespun-wrapped packages.

I spread my hands in blessing over them, invoking Ker's abundance, before returning to my small vessel. It was not until I knew I had been swallowed into the darkness of the night that I allowed my shoulders to sag from the weight of my concern. The supplicants would return to their lands, I knew, reassured that we who had dedicated our lives to Her would petition the Mother on their behalf. But for us, I knew, the worry had just begun.

It must be very bad for them to have traveled so far and with such urgency, I mused to myself as I paddled back to the Isle. While every priestess knew it was the nature of the Mother to take just as She gave, to illuminate to the day just as She enshadowed the night, it was sometimes difficult for me to surrender to these tides when it came to suffering.

"That sentiment is what will make you a powerful healer," Annick Velléda once said to me during my training, not long after my arrival on Holy Sena, "but it is also what will hold you back from discerning Her will. Sometimes Mother Ker will swing Her sickle in a way that will seem unjust to us, but only She can know the full measure of the grain bin. Only She can weigh the potential of the tiniest seed against the bounty of a good harvest. Without death, there can be no life; all things exist in the rhythm of this balance. She who consumes will one day be consumed. She who holds the scythe will one day be felled by it. Look at us here on this island! We live a blessed life of abundance, serving the Mother and all of Her children. And one day, it will fall upon us to give our lives back to Her. As is Her will."

"As is Her will," I had whispered into the night air, so focused on my worries and lost in reminiscence that I did not notice that the sea around me had become as troubled as my mind until I realized how difficult it was to slice my paddle through the dark waters. The sudden surges became more and more violent and I felt as if someone were trying to pull the oar from my hands each time it dipped into the sea. I was halfway back to the Holy Isle when it happened. Watery fingers formed from the sea spray and grasped the bow of my vessel. Before I could react, a sea swell brought the creature into view. I knew it now – a watery wraith from the Sunken Lands!

Startled, it took me a moment to compose myself and deal with the creature as it tilted my small craft forward, seeking to topple me into the ocean. I dropped the oar into the boat and raised my arms out to either side as

I chanted the sea-rune to calm the waters. The creature reached towards me, wetting my face with its spittle-like spray as it opened its mouth to scream – a horrible, gurgling sound like someone drowning. As I pushed forward to complete the third repetition of the chant, it hissed as it bubbled back into sea foam and slipped into the waters. I poured the remaining contents of my ale-skin into the calming ocean, seeking to appease the disturbed spirits of the Sunken Lands. I passed my hands over the waters as if to smooth the wrinkles of the waves, and the sea grew calm once more – but what had troubled it to begin with?

Heart racing and lips moving in silent prayers of gratitude, I returned to the safety of Enez Sun's shore. The night sky had remained clear through the visitation of the sea wraith; clearly weather was not to blame for the phenomenon that had threatened to capsize my little vessel.

A very bad omen, indeed.

****

I arrived at the place of the twin bonfires, swirling hungrily in the wind's currents. I placed the precious bundle of rushes I had carried with me across the length of the island carefully into the fire's care, and watched it become devoured by the flames. I chanted a prayer to Holy Ker, committing it to Her care, then turned to walk a bit further down the stone-lined pathway to the covered roundhouse where the new rushes were stored.

I entered and gathered a new bundle from those laying on rugs woven especially for this specific use. Carefully, I selected the correct thickness for my bundle, and using the small bronze sickle which hung from my belt, I trimmed the rushes to a uniform size. I wrapped the bundle thrice in red twine, and hoisted it onto my shoulder – finding the right balance for the walk back across the island to the temple. I headed back up the stone avenue and walked with ritual purpose between the two blazing bonfires, purifying both the bundle of thatch and my own sacred purpose.

Once the fires were behind me, the night seemed colder and darker than before; I was grateful for the brooding presence of the standing stones on either side of me, keeping me on the path in the same way a river bank guides each drop of water along its inexorable journey to the sea. I chanted whispered prayers to Ker as I walked, as much to ask Her guidance as to drown out the pounding of my heart in my ears. The Velléda part of me was anchored in the sacredness of this work, while the part of me that was simply Rozenn was distracted by the underlying thread of menace that permeated every ritual action, every step taken. As I had been trained, I returned my thoughts to the bigger pattern, seeking Ker's will in the events that had led up to this moment.

****

When I had completed my shoreline vigil that night, I recounted my experiences to Maela Velléda, giving her the bag holding the bundles of earth and grain. Her lined face became shadowed when I described the Visitation of the sea-wraith, and she called an immediate council. Never in the time since I had earned the Veil had such an emergency meeting been called, and it deepened the sense of dread within me. Within the hour, the nine of us were gathered in the round council house, sitting on timbered benches around the central hearth fire. Our plain dark garments contrasted with the distinctive headdress and veil by which we had come to be known.

Although our clothing was the same, we nine were as different as women could be. Some of us were young women newly come to the isle within the last few years, others venerable elders with a lifetime of service. Several sisters had children who were fostered out to their clans, while some had stopped celebrating the Fires of Summer with the men of the mainland many years ago. A few hailed from noble families, while the rest were of common stock – all of us chosen because of our gifts.

As girls, we were called to the Isle and trained to use that with which Ker had blessed us in service of the Mother and Her people. Only we nine women were allowed on the shores of Enez Sun, returning to the mainland only when needed. Anyone else who set foot upon this sacred land would forfeit their lives, as Ker demanded. We remained in service to the Isle until our deaths, and when one of the Sisters dies, a novice is chosen from among the Breton tribes and trained to take her place.

We received our provisions from the peoples we served and were protected as much by the dangerous reefs around our island as by the awe and superstition that surrounded this sacred place. Feared and respected, we were consulted for our auguries, petitioned for our weather workings, and sought after for our healing arts. We were constantly working to protect the tribes in our care, to reinforce the wards that kept Enez Sun from slipping into the sea as Ker-Is had in ages past, and we sat in trance to divine the will of the Mother.

Today, however, something was different. The presiding Sister, Maela Velléda, stood and called council in Ker's name. When she had completed the ritual prayer, Maela Velléda turned towards me and asked that I recount my experiences from the night before. When I was done, I returned to my seat as a low murmur filled the roundhouse. "This is a grave matter," Oonez Velléda spoke loudly over the din, quieting the rest with her words. "We must perform the triple augury to ensure that Ker's will be known."

"Yes," agreed Maela Velléda, "the Moon wanes dark two days hence. It is then we shall begin." As we filed out of the council house, we set out to begin

[13]

our preparations for the rituals to come. Maela Velléda motioned for me to join her. "Come with me," she said.

We walked in silence for a while, as the autumn sun climbed slowly across the sky. The Sisters lived and worked on the eastern part of Sena, closest to the mainland. Leaving this behind, we approached the narrow land bridge – lined on either side by standing stones – that headed towards the western side of the island, jutting out into the open sea. Maela Velléda stopped at the mouth of the land bridge, turning to look at me rather than following the path to the temple and Ker's sacred precinct at the far end of the isle.

"There is a reason the water wraith revealed itself to you, Rozenn Velléda," she said. I swallowed hard, knowing that a Visitation from the Sunken Lands is an omen of death. "I want you to perform the third augury."

"Me?" I asked, incredulous. "But my gift is healing, Sister. Surely a situation such as this requires a more accomplished augur."

"Are we not trained in all of the arts? You can call the winds, I know, as surely as you are able to dress a wound. Perhaps the one comes easier for you, though this may change with time and practice. You would not be here if your skills were lacking."

"Of course, you are right, Sister," I conceded nervously.

"It is not I who has chosen you. It was Blessed Ker, herself. There is a rhythm to these happenings and you are part of the pattern. You have two days to prepare yourself, Sister."

"As is Her will." I replied.

****

How different the land bridge appears by day, I thought to myself, standing before it now in the night, carrying my holy bundle of thatch. I bowed my head to acknowledge this liminal space, a power place of transitions leading from the everyday world into the sacred. The Velléda of Enez Sun are many things, among them healers and seers, weather workers and mediums. But in truth, we have but one gift – the ability to straddle the Worlds; it is this that allows us to see future and past, and cultivate health through sickness. In the same way, the land bridge linked the two functions of the Sisters of the Isle – service to the community and service to Mother. Tonight, we will accomplish both at once.

Continuing along, I could feel the presence of the ancient stones as I passed more than I could see them in the darkness. The sea was close on either side, making it easy to immerse myself in her tidesong. Breathing along with the ocean's music, I could feel my anxiety begin to slip away and I became more connected with my holy task with each step I took. "This is the stance of a priestess!" I thought, giving myself over to the first tendrils of trance. I felt enveloped in a warm, comforting garment – pulsing with energy and united with the sea and land around me.

It was then I heard it.

My heart leaped within my chest, and for the first time – I stumbled, though I did not drop my sacred burden. Regaining my balance, I willed myself not to panic. I strained my ears to hear over the sounds of the ocean and the renewed swell of the winds.

Nothing.

Perhaps I had imagined it...?

But no! There it was again – the unmistakable sound of a tolling bell.

I clenched my jaw to keep my teeth from chattering and I wrapped my arms tighter still around my bundle of thatch. As the second tolling came to an end there was no doubt in my mind that I was hearing the bells of Ker-Is – the Sunken Land. Walking along this narrow piece of land, I did not need a reminder of how low the island was compared to the level of the sea. The Sisters dedicated a great deal of energy every day to setting and maintaining protective spells around the island. We gave libations to the restless souls of Ker-Is, and appealed to Ker to keep Her servants safe. The king of Ker-Is had turned his back on the Old Ones, and in return, their protection of his island nation was withdrawn, leading to its destruction.

Sending fervent prayers to Ker, I hurried along the path towards the temple. The tolling had stopped, making it easier for me not to dwell on its meaning. Instead, I turned my thoughts back once again....

****

The fabric-wrapped packets of earth had been separated from their grain-filled counterparts, and dumped together into a large bronze cauldron. Careful not to touch any of it with her bare hands, Oonez Velléda added three small measures of seawater and stirred it all together with a symbol-encrusted spoon.

The central hearth fire of the roundhouse had been permitted to die down, making the space especially dim. Oonez Velléda nodded and Annick Velléda placed a dried bunch of aromatic herbs on the smoldering embers. Soon, the air was choked with acrid smoke and my vision began to swim. Behind me, I became aware of Oonez Velléda softly beating a steady rhythm on her stretched-hide frame drum. More herbs were added to the fire and I behind to sway in sync with the drumbeat as the first stirrings of trance began to overtake me.

I closed my eyes and slipped into the Otherworld.

[15]

I tumbled down into the Realm of Sea; my arms stuck fast to my body and my unblinking eyes moving to rest on either side of my now-flat head, and with a flash of sliver scales, I flicked my powerful tail – born of transformation – and swam deeper into the waters. Oonez Velléda's drumming was drowned out by the sound of waves crashing on some distance shoreline, its source receding as my slim fishy body sliced further into the darkness.

Somehow, the wide circles of my eyes caught a faint glimmer of light in the ocean's depths and I swam towards it. Yet, no matter how hard I tried, my efforts brought me no closer to the source of the light. "Blessed Mother of the Depths," I prayed, "show me what I must see to help Your people." In an instant, a powerful current hurled me towards the ocean floor.

There, on the sandy bottom, stood a glowing bronze cauldron, not unlike the one I had left behind with my body in the Middle World. I peered into its round belly but could see nothing. I entered it then, and was immediately assailed by a patchwork of shadows, each screaming out to me with wordless voices. Buffeted about by so many energies coming at me, I hit the sides of the cauldron until it rocked over onto its side, spilling its contents into the water. As I swam out and the cauldron righted itself, a veil of darkness floated in the water above it, fanning out over the mouth of the vessel.

It hovered there serenely for a few moments and then suddenly the whole of the ocean shuddered at the peal of a deep, resonant bell. Twice it sounded, each time rocking me back and forth as I struggled to remain near the cauldron. When the last vibration ripped through the water, everything became still once more…but something had changed. Above the cauldron, the cloud of darkness had transformed; no longer black, it had become a deep, blood red.

The scarlet pool began to throb and shift, threatening to engulf me. It was sticky in my gills and I began to panic, bolting away towards the surface of the ocean. My mouth became human again and I screamed in terror as the red cloud tried to overtake me – and the sound of my own voice lurched me back into the Middle World. My eyes sprung open and as I tried to stand, the mud-filled cauldron that had been placed in my lap tumbled to the ground, spilling its contents over the hearthstones.

Annick Velléda gently guided me back to my seat as the last cobwebs of trance eased their snares upon my mind. "Easy," she soothed. "Here, take a sip of this, and tell us what you saw." The cup she offered contained a liquid that burned my throat as I swallowed, but I could not stop myself from gulping it all down. Finally somewhat settled, I recounted my experiences to the two Sisters, and as they exchanged meaning-laden glances, I began to worry once more.

I stopped reminiscing and tried to put all of my thoughts and fears out of my mind as the distinctive silhouette of the temple entered my line of sight at last. This was my fourth trip to and from the bonfire and with so many of us dedicated to this project, the re-thatching was near to completion. There was a very specific ritual order to it all.

We each carried a small sickle knife, and three long thatching hooks were leaned up against the outer stone wall of the temple for any of us to use. Several wooden ladders were spaced around the circular temple and we could move them to one of the gaps in the thatch where the ancient timbers below were naked to the star-splashed sky. Climbing the ladder, we would put the consecrated new bundle into an empty space, temporarily securing it to the wood below using the edge of the red twine that bound it. Then, we climbed back down the ladder to fetch one of the thatching hooks and a length of thick rope. Returning to our bundle, we used the hook to weave the rope in and out through the newly-set straw, effectively lashing it to the cone-shaped frame of the wooden beams below.

When the new bundle was firmly installed, we would remove an adjacent section of the old thatch, carefully wrapping it with some rope in preparation for the long walk back across the island to the ritual bonfires. It was meticulous, painstaking work. We needed to be fast but efficient. The entire process needed to be completed before the sun rose, for not even the faintest ray of sunlight was permitted to fall into the sacred confines of Ker's temple.

And not one piece of straw was permitted to touch the ground.

Taking a deep breath, I began to climb a ladder, preparing for the work ahead.

****

We gathered around as Morez Velléda emerged from the sheepskin flap at the mouth of the augury roundhouse, shielding her still-dilated eyes from the midday sun. Three days she had remained within its stacked stone walls, a perimeter of silence maintained around it. The central hearth fire had been extinguished and piles of rugs and cloaks had covered the thatched timber roof, ensuring that no light could enter. There, in the silent darkness, Morez Velléda lay suspended in the womb of Holy Ker. Then, when her time there had expired, two elder sisters abruptly pulled back the curtains at the windows and ignited the central fire without warning. Jolted back from her trance journey, verses of poetry tumbled wildly from Morez Velléda's entranced mouth, and the other women within committed them to memory.

Maela Velléda was given the information, and along with my trance augury and the results of the divination performed on the grain I had brought back from the mainland, she synthesized the three strains of information to reveal Ker's will.

"My Sisters, at the half waning moon, we will re-thatch the temple," she announced.

Nothing more needed to be said.

Later that night, when we were alone in our sleep space, Enora Velléda leaned in close and whispered, "This is a horror. How can they ask this of us?"

"It is the way of all things, "I tried to sound serene as I sought to reassure her, but my own doubts weighed heavily in my heart. "Ker gives, Ker receives. It is how it has always been.

"I thought you of all people would understand me, Healer," Enora Velléda hissed angrily. "When the time comes, will you be able to do what is asked?

I pulled the covers over my head without answering because I had none to give. I still do not know how to respond. Will I able to do what is required of me?

****

Descending the ladder with the bundle on my shoulder was a tricky feat, but I was soon steady on the ground and ready for the walk back across the island after successfully adding my thatch to the roof. Judging by the sky, there would be time enough for me to complete one more trip before the sun rose. I headed back across the temple precinct, aware of a sister not far behind me, embarking once more in the same leg of the journey as I. Ahead of me, I saw that in the time it took for me to work on my section of the roof, Enora Velléda had made it to the bonfires and back. Her distinctively tall frame passed me once more, but I could not glimpse her face in the darkness as she hurried by.

As the night wore on and I concentrated on my tasks, the fear threatening to bubble up from within me began to subside. We were almost done, I reasoned, perhaps the worst would not be asked of us. I renewed the recitation of the litany to Ker in my head, willing myself to stay focused and present, even as fatigue from the night's work began to set in.

And then it happened.

I stumbled and fell, scattering my bundle of old straw all over the flagstone path.

I lay there in shock, feeling as if I had been doused with icy water – waiting. I heard the screeching of the other Sisters and the sounds of running. I squeezed my eyes shut and prayed for Ker to receive me in the Otherworld.

"At least," I thought over my rapid breath, "whatever may come, I will not be forced to take a life."

Moments passed. Then minutes, and I was still alone and lying on the ground. The sounds behind me drew no closer and my eyes flew open at the terrified wail of a high-pitched scream.

I sat up and turned towards the horrible sound, and saw a group of dark clothed women descend upon one of their own like ravens at a carcass. I struggled to my feet and stumbled over to the milieu. Sickles flashed dimly and made sickening sounds as they fell and were raised again, biting into all-too-yielding flesh and hitting upon much too brittle bone. The screaming continued, but somehow it did not originate from the sister at the center of the carnage.

I looked towards a lone figure, screeching in the darkness. She saw me and ran to grab me by my shoulders. "They…they, pushed her!" Elora Velléda sobbed uncontrollably. "Ker help us! They pushed her down!" She dissolved into hysteria but I could no longer hear her over the rush of blood in my ears.

I pushed her away from me and fought my way through the writhing mass of women. It was then I saw her – my beloved mentor, Annick Velléda – her robes in tatters and her flesh torn; everything was covered in blood. "Stop it! Stop it!" I screamed. "I dropped the bundle – me!"

"How dare you interfere…!" began Oonez Velléda, but Annick Velléda gestured weakly, quieting her.

"Come closer, dear Rozenn," whispered Annick. "We knew this would be hard for you…but you m-must see and understand…look – look into my eyes…."

I took her mangled hand in mine and leaned closer to her face – it was difficult to see in the darkness, but her eyes were shining with an inner glow.

"Look," Annick bade me, "… mind what you see."

I met her unflinching gaze and beyond her fading eyes there was something…a presence I recognized from trance vision and high ritual…it was the essence of Mother Ker, Herself. I blinked in disbelief, and looked once more upon Annick's face. It was strong and placid, not wracked with the agony that should have accompanied her wounds. The healer in me struggled to reconcile how this could be so – but then Annick touched my forehead tenderly and understanding rushed over me.

"This is done w-with…with love, not cruelty. Don't you see? It is through this that…that the Mother can give all for Her children. Through us…She is the sacrifice. We are but the vessel of Her gift…Let go…so you can witness the bottomless cauldron of…of Her love…"

She turned away from me then, her vision focused on something I could not see – her bloodied lips smiling. I stepped back, weeping – yet through my prismed eyes I saw a great mystery unfold before me. The Sisters resumed the winnowing of Annick Velléda's flesh from her bones, and I watched as her mortal essence fell away, revealing a blinding light that was absorbed into the ground in gossamer tendrils with Annick's blood.

The earth below us began to glow, and a line of illumination shot forward from this place of sacrifice, hurtling along the avenue of standing stones that crossed Enez Sun and rushing over the waters to explode upon the mainland. Although I could no longer follow its progress with my physical eyes, I was granted the vision of the journey of this arc of light as it traveled across the landscape – directed by stone alignments and cycling through stone circles, splaying out into the body of the Earth. Every dolmen was set alight, awakening the ancestral powers of the land. I watched as the blessings of Holy Ker traveled to the far ends of our country, revitalizing every growing thing with Her abundance.

As the energy flowed out from the island, a powerful wind rushed in bringing dark clouds, heavy with rain. The sudden gale whipped at our cloaks, and lightening illuminated the temple as Annick Velléda gasped her last breath. A clap of thunder heralded the rain, and the sky over all of Ker's lands opened with Her tears.

Streaked with mud and blood, we danced in the deluge, our arms lifted to the skies as we chanted thanks to Ker in our frenzy. Our feet beat the lifeblood of our fallen sister into the earth as tears of joy and sorrow mingled with the rain.

The Great Work was complete.

****

We found her body three days later when the rain finally stopped. Our small oaken craft had been unloosed from the quay and we guessed that Enora Velléda had tried to reach the mainland when she had been caught in the storm. I shivered with the certainty that in the crashing of the waves that night, a sea wraith had claimed her and brought her down to the Sunken Lands.

I wept for Enora, understanding why she had run, yet wishing I could have shared what I had seen with her. As if reading my mind, Maela Velléda put her arm around my shoulders. "There was nothing you could have done to change her mind. This part of the weaving was meant to be. The augury foretold that two of our sisters would be called, one unexpectedly."

I looked up at her in surprise. "I didn't know," I said simply. "That must be why I heard the bells of Ker-Is ring twice."

It was her turn to be surprised, looking me over as if for the first time.

[20]

Then she smiled at me gently. "To be honest, we thought you were going to be called. But we see now that Ker needs something different from you."

"If this is so, why was Annick Velléda pushed? Had she not been, it would have been me."

"The second augury said that an elder was needed, someone who could allow the energies to pass through them without resistance. There was great need, Rozenn Velléda. This demanded great sacrifice."

"I think I am beginning to understand, Maela Velléda. I see that which was closed to me before."

"That is good to hear, dear sister. There is much now for you to learn."

She turned and walked to the temple to offer the daily libation; the new roof had withstood the violence of the storm. I went alone to the westernmost end of the island, where the Dolmen of the Veiled Ones stood silhouetted against the sea. The bodies of Annick Velléda and Enora Velléda were laid in the long chamber, and three days of funerary rites would begin at sunset. The bones of generations of Priestesses were piled together in the shelter of the dolmen, and while I had brought many offerings of food and milk here to our foremothers, I felt my connection with them had deepened from the events of this past moon.

One day, I too would lay here. Whether I pass into the Otherworld from illness or old age, or I am called to restore life to many by laying down my own, it is my honor to be counted among these women, these Sisters. The Gallisenae.

"As is Her will," I said aloud, and turned to take my place in life with the others.

Balbilla's Reply
by Michael Routery

I thought again of those lips, that forehead, that some think stern, stamped by tiny lines of worry, even neglect (even though you might ask how such a thing is even possible). The soft sweet limbs, anointed with aromatic oils....O empress, O Sabina, you are the most beautiful; your eidolon plays upon my lyre, and so my heart stirs, in these long nights so far adrift from home, as we continue day after day ever southward, away from civilization. Despair stains my lips with the feeling that we are sinking into the world of the shades, where the hollow rustling sounds jar and unnerve. But then I am back in this howling gloom he has created, ever since Antinous drowned in the river water.

On the observation deck of the empress' barge, the gentle breeze of the night blushes my cheeks. Diana sails high above us, but we cannot see her reflection in the river's silted mirror. Much has been occluded on the never ending voyage; why can we not return to Alexandria and depart for home? I whisper to the goddess, "Do you still long for Endymion? Is such grief eternal?"

I look out onto Thebes: a few lights glow in the panoply of shadows and silhouettes of the ancient city that had grown up on the bank of the annually flooding river even before the heroes of Hellas fought at Troy. Somewhere a dog barks. The water laps against wood far below.

The small boat is ready to transport me to the emperor's dinner. Vibia is waiting. She will accompany me: quiet Vibia, the empress' sister. Sabina lies in her bed, the noon heat having overcome her, her delicate skin assaulted by the weapons of the sun; within the storm clouds of her heart she yearns deeply for return to Roma. This long journey has taken so much out of her. I remember the storm, when crossing to Egypt, a day when we could hardly venture from our bed, the very floors lurching from beneath our feet, as if we were drunken revelers in the train of Bacchus.

Today, we had ventured out in the hours when the desert to the west was still a blackness, a shade the color of most ancient night. And in the dawn light the stone, the stone of the great colossus remained mute — Memnon,* standing high, but mutilated, tongue cut out by an angry and impious king, jealous of his enduring sculpted glory. Later we saw the sights, the guides showing us walls covered with the odd picture writing of this ancient country, beetles and suns and wings; animals — vultures, crocodiles, and baboons. Sometimes they argue over the meanings. How much have they forgotten?

[22]

Later within the monumental temple with its beautiful papyrus-crowned pool we conversed with the priests. The god they honor is the serpent Phanes who encircled the cosmic egg, told of by the Orphics, in times primordial. In this place with its lotuses, huge snakes were shown us and the dog face monkeys; we felt near to beginnings.

The water so close to hand in the small skiff smelled rank, its depths as unyielding as the Styx. Surely for the emperor it was the Styx and would be for the rest of us as well, as it seemed nothing could shake him out of his Stygian course.

With relief we boarded the imperial barge. Lamps twinkled merrily in denial of the enveloping darkness. Delectable foods and wines were at hand, but the throng was subdued, the emperor half-concealed in night's shadow and half within his own gloom, a gloom copious like the ink expelled by a great cephalopod. Zenia, my slave girl, took out my lyre, as I nibbled on a bite of succulent pheasant stuffed with fig, wrapped in the lightest pastry.

My fingers caressed my lyre, plucked taut strings, the imperial party rapt.

> Hector, loved by Alexander, lion slayer,
> Beauty burnished, arms strong, his waist slim, smile of
> Shining ivory; godly, the gaze of sea and
> Sky that caught in his mirror leonine. He,
> Bright as rising sun, and yet lost in night's shade,
> Sank so deeply, drowned in the Egyptian night.
> Raised in praise and memory, may he keep bright.**

Lucius Verus pranced about, his eyes heavy-lidded with paint, as spoiled as a pampered courtesan. Something of the serpent in his pupils, or maybe I imputed too much to he whom the Alexandrian gossips now called the western favorite. But he certainly was over ready to fill and perform in the vacancies left by the Bithynian youth, Antinous.

"Don't you presume too much, daughter of Pergamon? Do you speak for the philosophers?" he asked, resentment clouding his brows.

"Like Sappho of Mytilene, so long ago in the rosy dawn, I thread the love of wisdom, the eye of inquiry into the words that play over my lyre," I replied. "But I know that you too grace the night with the tickle of the nymphs in poeisis."

Lucius' furious eyes and spoiled mouth fought as if at battle, a languorous python full of contradictions, his once trained body now with just a film of softness upon its muscles.

A voice from the shadows said hollowly, "Yes, Lucius, let's have a poem from you tonight." A voice tinged with charcoal.

Lucius' own minions hovered about him expectantly, pretty girls and ephebes, as he rose, the peacock spreading his tail feathers. So much color artificed above his nether. One plucked a honeyed dormouse from a platter. Lucius moved to the fore, his body languid, and declaimed:

A nymph of a chaste goddess appears before
Us. Blessed are we to receive the emissary
Of a pale huntress, who like the Lady
In the woods reclines unseen by men in
Her golden cave, yet in her beneficence
She sends us Julia Balbilla, daughter of Commogene!

The acrid tone of his praise was like bitter herbs burning. I felt many eyes brushing my face. I rose, my backbone erect. "Julia Balbilla I am. Granddaughter of Antiochus IV, brother of Philopappos the benefactor of Athens and once Prefect of this very land of Upper and Lower Egypt, scion of the ancient throne of Commagene, but no nymph am I." I laughed, and it sounded like the shattering of glass from an expensive vial shivering the scented air. I do know how to command attention. "The Augusta is overcome with the torrid air of her midday excursion and the rank vapors of the river and has been advised to take to her bed early," I said, my eyes falling on the sorrow-ravaged face of the emperor.

Lucius practically danced before him, always seeking praise, attention. His beard trailed like a ram's. Unsmiling, Hadrian, replied, "Julia is invigorated with the blood of philosophers."

I wondered if he were thinking of Balbillus, my Roman grandfather so knowledgeable in the pathways of the stars and the wandering planets. Although the barge is many-storied, I felt the slight sway of water beneath us, the river who gives life to Egypt, but who also takes so many lives away. The Egyptians say it is an androgyne, of the name Hapy, and shaped like that strange animal the river horse, which in truth looks more like a giant and naked pig. We saw one in the menagerie in Alexandria. We also visited many soothsayers, diviners, and prophets there. I prayed Hadrian would soon see the omens that would make him turn for home, although word was we would be continuing upriver in a few days.

Suddenly, one of Lucius' boys tottered forward. Had he been given a gentle shove? The poor thing looked half-starved, but that was the way Lucious liked them. "So tell us noble Commogene, imbued with philosophy, what is beauty?"

I offered my glass to a passing steward; a beautiful cup, its stones glinted in the light of the torches all about. I took a sip and tasted fine vintage. "That is a question pondered well by the tenth muse, Sappho of Mytilene. For some she said beauty is the sparkle of fine armor on the men of the battlefield, the heroes arrayed before Troy's walls, or upon its parapets." I paused. The Ceaserni brothers were watching me closely, those most handsome men. Lucius imbibed freely from his glass. I continued, "For others it is the treasure boats being loaded with cedar and incense, the jewels of India, the pearls and dragon blood of Arabia, these being the greatest desires of some. However, for Sappho it was that which shines through the ardor of love. I drink to her philosophy!"

Again I felt the august eyes burning like coals from the shadows where he sat with his Theban priest before him.

Lucius now more inebriated pressed on — "Yes, Balbilla, you are a poet of Sappho's school, but what is your answer?"

This was bordering on impertinence; all glanced my way. I plucked a spiced date from a great basket held nearby. I could hear Lucius' breathing overly loud. "I praise the beauty of the Augusta, her imposing calm, a coolness in hot lands, her feats of endurance, the marmoreal sheen of her skin, those eyes of Athenian intelligence, those blue pools of Capri's grace."

The boy with the gold-powdered eyes was whispering in Lucius' ear. Lucius interrupted — "Surely, there is a time for beauty and a time when it passes on." His voice was thick, he seemed choking on something, coughing, barely suppressing a giggle.

"Lucius, that is sufficient." Hadrian lay there with the poise of a reclining lion.

"But," he was sputtering, his cheeks inflamed.

"Enough." This time the voice asserted itself, crackling with power, with the purple, to put it bluntly. Hadrian had risen; he came toward us. I saw a tear in the corner of his right eye. I saw the mask of rule cracked. I saw the man beneath, vulnerable and frayed as a child in a ransacked village. My soul fluttered her feathers, and something stirred deep in him and fluttered as well. I, a descendant of queens and kings, would exchange gifts with him.

I pulled my palla about my hair and prayed to Aphrodite:

O daughter of sea,
Your chariot resplendent
Pulled by sweetest sparrows,
I hear your whir and thrum
On your countless errands.
I will offer you doves upon
our return to Roma.

[25]

****

We settled down for dinner; it was a simple one. A harpist played and softly sang the melancholy songs of that land, and Hadrian and the Egyptian discoursed upon the name of the city, the same that Homer so long ago had called The Hundred Gated — it seemed it had fallen much. It is called City of Zeus, for the Egyptians call Zeus Amon and therefore the city, Amonophis. And so we reclined, sampling the fragrant dishes in the warm air of that Nile evening, the Augustus couchant across from me. Lucius, of course, in his shade, but sated and declaiming upon this or that morsel, for he fancies himself a gourmand of the first rank, sharing one or two with his golden-eyed favorite, at times the faintest shadow of a smile upon his lips.

I rose up, a sphinx upon my scented cushions; Vibia, shy and modest by my side, her gold curls trembling slightly. "It is such a wonder to see that son of Aurora up close, that dawn-smoldering statue, that colossus raised up long ago, and even if he be sadly mutilated, as no king should be, no son of a goddess, and one that is always greeted with the garlands of joy, still this hoary ambassador suffers from your absence. Surely, it would delight him for your attendance tomorrow at dawn, and with your presence, in gratitude he would sing!" I raised my voice to a high note, and everyone looked upon me. The emperor's eyes seemed to spark. Even Lucius looked attentively without his usual smirk. I am sure Vibia was blushing; I could feel her warmth. "Already a visit from the Augusta, and as magnificent the sight, the ears are unrewarded, but I am sure he will be musical if you, Augustus, do greet him. And furthermore, the ephemeris promises beneficent outcomes for the meeting of two rulers in tomorrow's solar court."

The Ceaserni brothers were attentive, smiles on their lips. "You have been busy, Julia. It is well," said Macedo, his voice deep and resinous as Greek wine. "It would be excellent, would it not?" said the younger, Statianus, looking at Hadrian.

Lucius muttered, "And it will make the Augusta happy, and surely that is your aim, Commagene."

I never said he was unintelligent; far from it. The canopy rustled a bit in a wind that struck the river from the western desert.

Lucius' favorite exclaimed, "Zephyrus blows!"

"And he can blow hard and jealous," Lucius replied.

Hadrian roused from mournful torpor, an eagle rising above dusky clouds, and said, "Prepare for disembarkation before dawn. We will see the Colossus and find out whether he still has his voice, even if he be without tongue." Turning to me, "Will the Augusta be able to rouse herself from her sickbed?"

[26]

I felt fetters I had hardly known were binding my heart loosen and fall. "I am sure she could cross the desert to the oasis of the red lotus for this," I replied, and plucked a sweetly confected nut from the table. Hadrian smiled. I felt things shifting, tides, river currents, as something great dislodged, and the huge barge swayed in the current. I mused on how one small motion can nudge further greater ones into motion.

****

If you have not read my poems, I assure you they are carved upon the foot of the Colossus, opposite the city of Thebes in Upper Egypt, for how he did sing that following morning in the rose-petaled dawn, that son of Aurora!

*There were two Colossi Of Memnon, enormous statues which were believed by Greco-Roman tourists to be representations of an Ethiopian king (and son of the goddess of the dawn) who fought in the Trojan war on the Trojan side and was slain by Achilles. One of the Colossi emitted a striking sound around dawn, probably caused by the porous stone reacting to rising temperature and evaporation of moisture. The Colossi are actually statues of Pharaoh Amenhotep III of the New Kingdom's Eighteenth Dynasty, c. 1350 BCE.

**This Hector was a beloved of Alexander the Great who, like Antinous, drowned in the Nile.

Sinikka Journeys North
by KA Laity

Sinikka paused at the edge of the clearing. A wind whispered through the birch trees that huddled protectively around the glade. At the center lay a rocky outcropping, flat enough for the pitcher of water the young woman had carried with her. She set the jug down carefully and seated herself before it. She lay her hands upon the soft earth, fingers spread. Sinikka wasn't sure this would work, but she was desperate.

"Oh Maaemo, hear me, your poor child. My people starve without your help. Some envious noita has cast a curse upon us — our crops die, the forest creatures have fled. Even the spring has slowed to a trickle. Mother beneath our feet, Mother of grass, trees, rocks and clay — hear me, heed me. Take pity on us and share your abundance!" Sinikka tried to feel the heart of the ground with her fingertips. Maaemo must answer. Please, please, please.

A sudden breeze lifted the hair from the young woman's forehead and she raised her eyes to see a sudden swirl of leaves rise from beyond the rocks. The wild motion did not dissipate, but rather grew stronger, faster, until Sinikka could see the vague outline of woman in the leaves. She felt a thrill of excitement — and fear. Now sticks and dust joined the leaves and the form became clearer, though the movement never ceased. It was hypnotic.

"What is your name, child?" The voice had the quiet resonance of an owl's, but the light touch of the cuckoo, too. It was both beautiful and fearsome.

"I am Sinikka, daughter of Laina, and I — "

"Why did you not send your tietäjä?"

Sinikka bowed her head. "We no longer have a shaman. Old Matti and his boy were killed by a great mother bear. No one else had been brought up in the traditions. Forgive me, Mother, for being so bold, but my people are desperate."

Maaemo's form swirled more slowly now, rustling softly. "What is it you want, child?" she said at last. "Why do you beseech me?"

"Help us," Sinikka begged, willing the tears to remain in her eyes and not pour forth. "Onni works against us. Return his favor to us so we may share in your many blessings."

Maaemo's leafy shape seemed to laugh. "I do not control Fortune — Onni is free to travel as he wishes, as may all creatures who walk upon me. My bounty is free to all who wish to partake of it. I neither help nor harm anyone. I do not tell Tapio how to grow trees, nor Ahti how to wield the tides. I do not tell the rocks what they may do, nor the birds where they may fly, and I do not tell Onni whom to favor."

"But, Maaemo!" Sinikka caught herself. Not wise to use her true name before the goddess herself — especially when one is a foolish young woman with no experience in such things. Biting her lip, she began again. "Dear Mother of us all, I ask pity. Pity for my people, starving and hopeless. We have no one to guide us or to speak to our wise ancestors. No one to charm the swift elk, to sing the fish into our nets, or to enchant our corn crops. We will perish, Great Mother!" Sinikka could not halt her tears now. Bitter and swift they poured forth through her fingers and splashed in small drops on the rock before her.

Maaemo sighed. "What you need is a new tietäjä. Onni comes and goes — one can never rely on Fortune." The goddess sighed again, and her ephemeral body twisted snake-like in the air, coiling and uncoiling, round and round.

It was mesmerizing, Sinikka realized, when at last she looked up. Wondrous, too, but now the emptiness of despair outweighed her awe. Without Onni her people would starve. This was her last hope. She did not want to leave the beautiful valley that had been her only home, but that was the plan her father and mother had argued with the elders. It would be an onerous journey to fight through the wilds, to risk crossing other people's hunting grounds. How far would they have to go? If Onni abandoned them, would any new homeland be any better? Sinikka could not rid herself of the image that had frightened her for weeks — herself, alone, dying in the frozen North, the icy blasts mocking her. She shivered.

But she had a final tribute to offer. Though it would not alter the goddess's words, Sinikka must honor their meeting. "I have brought water to cool your dry earth, Great Mother. Let me offer this sacrifice to you." She poured the water from the pitcher upon the rock and watched the precious liquid run over the surface and seep into the grass surrounding it. She tried not to think of the dry fields around the village, the dust curls that followed everyone's footsteps, the brown husks of vegetation. One jug of water would not do much anyway.

The whorl of leaves fell to the ground, and at once a rippling track, like a lemming's trail, arose on the earth and made a bee-line for the water. The goddess's immense power drove up the rock shelf, effortlessly lifting the boulders and juggling them one atop another. Sinikka's amazement, however, did not keep her from jumping back, away from the grinding stones. She did not want to end up like meal between them. Maaemo laughed at her fear, but her words were kindly.

"It is kind of you to offer something so precious to me, child. I remember kindnesses. I cannot help you to capture Onni, but I know someone who might be willing to undertake such an inadvisable pursuit. Seek Louhi, in the North, in Pohjola. She is crafty but wise. Be very careful — and be kind. She has suffered much at the hands of mortals."

Louhi! "They say she is an evil sorceress," Sinikka stuttered. "Why would she help me?"

"Why indeed? It is a question you must ask of her." Maaemo laughed. The stones wobbled, ready to fall.

Sinikka wailed. "But how will I find her? I have never been out of this valley."

"Keep your shadow to your left. At night follow the Great Bear. Do not stop until you reach her. Leave at once." The rocks tumbled to earth like giant hail, crashing and rumbling across the ground.

Sinikka stood there with her mouth open. Leave now? Find Louhi? Follow the Great Bear? Don't stop until you reach her — who? The Great Bear? Or Louhi? She trembled to think of meeting with either one. I could just go back to the village and say nothing, Sinikka told herself. And watch my mother starve, and my father burn with anger and disappointment—and feel my shame. She sighed. It would be so far, so cold. And only her pretty shawl covered the thin shift and three skirts — hardly enough to keep her warm. I will probably die before I have to worry about facing the powerful noitakka, Sinikka told herself glumly.

But she set off at once as Maaemo had instructed her. She kept her shadow always on her left and ate berries that she spied in the woods. When night fell Sinikka found where the Great Bear hung in the sky and kept her feet moving, though they had already grown more tired than she could ever remember them being, even last year dancing at Vappu to welcome the new green leaves. Then she had danced until the last embers died out and the next day paid the price as she carried out her chores. The village spring had seemed far indeed that day, and each step agony. At least then the spring still ran freely, bubbling up over the rocks. Remembering their despair as each day the trickle grew less, Sinikka lifted her tired feet more quickly, hurrying on to whatever lay ahead.

On the third day, toward sunset, she finally fell. Long before, the ground had become hard and cold, and this morning Sinikka had been dismayed to find herself trudging through snow. She sought to ignore the protesting of her feet and the numbness that was creeping along her legs. Just keep on, she told herself, you must, you must. Every step was higher than the last, as the hill grew sharply steeper. When at last it happened, Sinikka was on the ground before she knew she had fallen. Well, here is my dream, dying , alone in the frozen lands. My parents do not even know where I am, she thought dully. I cannot even cry, I am too tired, too thirsty. At least it is quicker than starving, Sinikka comforted herself. Let the snow come down and cover me. I am going to finally sleep.

But even as she resigned herself to her ill-luck, Sinikka heard a strange noise. Something was coming through the drifts, down the mountain, with a shambling gait and labored breath. An undeniable curiosity raised the young woman's eyes to see the approaching creature. Oh dear, thought Sinikka, my death is going to be even more horrible than I thought.

It was a bear.

It was an enormous she-bear who ambled slowly down the path, muttering to herself as if she had forgotten some important chore. Just kill me, Sinikka thought. One way or another I will end up in Tuonela. Let the black waters of Death close over my head now and bring me peace. She closed her eyes once more, laid her head down, and began trembling violently. It is only the cold, Sinikka assured her swiftly beating heart, even as the back of her neck grew hot.

After a time, when nothing happened, Sinikka opened her eyes again. She realized too that a strange sound filled her ears. With enormous effort, she lifted her head and turned it the other way. The bear had stopped to scratch herself on the rough outcropping of rock that hung over the path and was evidently enjoying the biting surface, as her whuffling grunts attested. When at last her wriggling stopped, the bear dropped back down to her four footed-stance and sniffed at Sinikka. Her breath was warm and meaty.

"You come ill-prepared for the cold, skinless creature," the bear said at last, rubbing her nose. "You will perish. Soon."

"I suppose so," Sinikka agreed. Her fear had evaporated with the last of her body's warmth. She had become indifferent to the bear's hunger. It was rather peaceful.

"I know what you are. Your kind work in packs. Steal my sisters' and brothers' skins. Never ask. If you stayed where it was warm, you would not need them." Sinikka could not even work up the energy to respond. She stared up at the bear and watched how the wind made patterns in her fur. The great bear stuck her nose right up to Sinikka's face and sniffed noisily. "Why do you come here?"

Sinikka tried hard to remember. What did it matter anyway, her tired thoughts scolded, you are almost dead. I could not do it anyway, Maaemo was wrong. "Maaemo." The memories of the green forest, the warmth of it, flooded back. Sinikka smiled at the memory. My last visions will be warm.

"Maaemo sent you here?" The bear grumbled to herself for a few moments. "What for?"

Sinikka strained to recall the reason, the name. In Maaemo's voice, it came to her: "Louhi." And it all returned: the meeting in the woods, the appeal, the disappointment — the fate of her village. "Louhi, I need to find Louhi."

The she-bear grumbled further irritation. "I suppose Maaemo told you I would help you find her?"

With difficulty Sinikka answered, "She just told me to go north, not stop, until I find...her." Now maybe I can sleep, Sinikka thought warmly, closing her eyes again and laying her head back on the snow. Soon, soon, it will all be over. So she was quite unprepared for the sudden jerk at her neck, the choking sputtering of her throat rebelling as her body was dragged across the icy surface. "What...?" But of course the bear's mouth was full and she could not respond to Sinikka's query. At last the cold cruel sensation stopped.

"Well, you'll have to get up on your own."

Sinikka raised her head, fighting its urge to tremble with weakness. The bear was sitting upright, back against the rocks, paws on her hairy knees. Just like one of us, Sinikka thought.

"You'll die soon if I don't keep you warm. If Maaemo sent you, I suppose I must show kindness to one of her kin. But you have to come to me." She opened her paws wide, like a welcoming mother — a mother with long black claws. "Come, child. Before I lose all patience."

Sinikka rolled onto her side, then pushed with one arm. She was not surprised to see that her fingers looked blue and pale. Her whole body shuddered as she tried to regain her feet, but somehow she stumbled — half walking, half falling — toward the great mother bear. At once Sinikka was enveloped in the earthy warmth, her head lolling with relief. She was asleep before the great head rested upon her own.

Sinikka awoke to the sensation of falling. She had no idea how long, how far, and feared that it would hurt a great deal when she hit the bottom at last. If she hit the bottom, Sinikka thought moments later when her fall seemed no closer to its end. Perhaps the bear has thrown me down a crevice between mountains, she wondered with very little fear. How did I get here? The question did not concern her greatly. But she was looking for something...someone? Louhi.

And as the word entered her head, Sinikka found she was no longer falling but standing in a dark cave, its roof arching high over her head and several torches whipping their light around its broad expanse. And just as suddenly a figure was there before her — Louhi.

She had no claws, no sparks flew from her eyes, her skin was not scaly and green, yet at the sight of this old woman Sinikka felt terror flash through her body like the cold of the first swim in spring. Old woman! Was she even that? Human?

"I was human," Louhi growled. "But humans showed me only hatred, crossed my magic, stole my daughter, my only treasure. Humans — and that damned rune singer." She turned away from Sinikka, fussing with some pots and grains as if the matter were already settled.

I must be wise, Sinikka, scolded herself. No time for anger. I need her help if I am to get back, get out, help my people. Again the urge to think about how she got here rose up, but Sinikka turned her jumbled thoughts to Louhi. She clasped her hands together (blue, blue hands, but no longer cold) and fell to her knees. "Wise woman of the North, on my knees I beg you, please help me to save my village!"

Louhi turned, knife in one hand, pot in the other. "And why should I do such a thing for some little wen like you? I have enough to keep me busy. Why should I take such a little bird under my wing?"

Sinikka thought hard. "Your knowledge is so great. What a waste not to share it — "

"Ha!" The old woman's eyes flashed in the murky light. "Always your people come, stealing my fire, stealing my gold, stealing my daughter. And what do I get in return? Hatred, tricks, lies!"

"I am but a poor young woman, great mother, trying to help my village keep from starving. I will offer you anything you want, if only you will share your great knowledge and teach me how to entice Onni. Our fate must change. Anything, anything I can give you."

Louhi squinted at Sinikka shivering in the flickering darkness. "Hmph. You come here in most unsuitable clothes — not a gold thread upon your hair, no silver strands upon your chest. No treasures, no staples even, no gifts. What do you have to give?"

Sinikka's head dropped. "I have nothing. I came here because I have nothing, my people have nothing, and we are desperate. I asked Maaemo for help but she refused to help me catch Onni. But she did send me north to seek you. She said if anyone can capture Onni, it is you. You are so clever and learned — "

"Bah! Learned! I am simply old. Living long has been my learning, keeping my eyes open. I am no foolish wizard or rune singer. I just know a thing or two." She smiled at that and seemed to lose herself in thought. Sinikka thought it best not to interrupt her reverie. In time she continued. "So you have nothing, and you come to me empty-handed, unskilled, unschooled, and unwanted. Ha! You are worse off than you know."

Sinikka felt the sting of her words and her cheeks grew red as berries. But a spark of inspiration glimmered in her thoughts. Would it work? Oh, may my foremothers preserve me and give me courage! She took a deep breath. "It is true I have nothing. I can offer only myself. You have lost a daughter. Let me be a daughter to you."

The old wisewoman's hands froze in mid-air. In the sudden silence, Sinkka realized just how much noise the two of them made. There was only the whispering sputter of one of the candles as it went out. Time hung in the quiet. Louhi turned at last to stare at Sinikka, her hands on her hips now. Though it made her tremble, Sinikka looked into the eyes of the old sorceress, eyes the blue of a glacial river — just as cold, just as fierce. I am the cold, I am the snow, I am the ice, Sinikka told herself. I can face her fury.

Just then the old woman threw her head back — and laughed. She roared and shook with it, until she had to hold her stomach in pain. At first Sinikka could only gape at her in surprise, astonished by this unexpected outburst, but gradually she blushed red once more and became angry herself. "You laugh at my offer. I know I am not much. I am not worthy. You might as well kill me now, before I become so angry I try to kill you!"

But her speech had only the effect of increasing Louhi's merriment. The old wisewoman finally sat down upon the floor and dried her tears with her apron, chuckling to herself all the while and rocking back and forth. "Come, sit down beside me, daughter!" She beckoned to Sinikka, who reluctantly got up from her knees and walked over to Louhi and, after peering carefully at her face, sat down.

To her surprise, the old woman clasped Sinikka's hands in her own, forcing the girl to meet her eyes. But the blue that had been the color of stormy rivers now crinkled like waving cornflowers, and a smile lit the ancient face. "You made me laugh, now there's a thing. I can't remember the last time. Now, now. Don't feel embarrassed again. You cannot know what a terrible life you offered yourself up for — your simple gift. Your immense sacrifice." The smile had faded away, but her voice was gentle. "What is your name, girl?"

"Sinikka."

"Sinikka, you must be very, very careful to whom you offer the only thing you humans truly possess. Your spirit is not only the greatest gift, it is your only true value. All else fades."

"But I only wanted — "

"Yes, yes, I know. To help your village, to save your people. Your generosity is admirable — but misplaced. You cannot deliver the ones you love from harm by giving up the only thing that will protect them: You."

"Me?"

"Girl, your spirit is bold and fearless and will continue to grow. You are the source of power for your village. You need not look here for my aid. Trust your own strength. Trust your own thoughts. Don't wait for anyone to save you. You have the source within you."

"But I know nothing," Sinikka cried. "I have never been out of our village, I can't ever weave cloth straight, and I've never even caught one fish that didn't slip away. I drop things all the time too," she added, eyes downcast.

Louhi barked with quick laughter. "You have spoken with Maaemo, traveled alone to the frozen north, survived a bear and," she slapped her chest, "the terrifying Louhi. Have you ever thought that you were not meant to weave cloth and catch fish and sow barley in the fields?"

Sinikka let an awkward smile creep across her mouth until it became a grin. Louhi let go her hands and clasped her shoulders warmly. "Come! I have something to show you, a simple charm, but it will attract our friend Onni."

"You mean it?!"

"It may attract him," Louhi said, her face again stern, "But you will need to persuade him to stay. He is greedy and fickle, he must be wooed. Now help me up, dear, my bones ache so today."

Sinikka leaped up, pulled the old crone to her feet, and they turned to the table filled with pots and jars. The candles seemed to burn more brightly now, or perhaps her eyes had adjusted to the darkness. Sinikka watched carefully as the wisewoman concocted a pleasing variety of scents and textures: berries and herbs and nuts and roots and even some kinds of dried fruits. She sang a runo that told the origin of the charm, detailing the ingredients. "Remember them!" she admonished Sinikka with a wagging finger.

When Louhi was satisfied with the blend, she poured the contents into a small bag of soft leather. Tooled into the skin were ancient symbols which Louhi patiently explained one by one. "This for the sun, and this one for the moon. Here is Maaemo, here Tapio. And here, this you can see is Ahti's river, there Ukko's thunder. And here, under all of them, me. I lie at the depths. Our names summon power. Use them carefully." She handed the bag to Sinikka. It felt warm to her skin.

"Thank you, thank you so much, Louhi." Sinikka felt the tears ready and blinked them away. She knew this small bag held the salvation of her people.

But the old woman waved her gratitude away. "You should be going. You still have a long way back."

Another inspiration seized the young woman. "Come back with me. My people will sing your praises, we will honor you, we will celebrate your wisdom."

Louhi laughed. "They will run from me, they will cower in fear, they will curse my name. I am not fit to be seen by just anyone, girl. But you are kind. No, I will ask though, that you come back and see me from time to time, to share my dark world for a time. But now, you must go. Stand here, upon this rock, here. Arms crossed, there. Now, close your eyes. Take care. Good-bye!"

And before Sinikka could echo the farewell, she felt herself hurtling upward, faster and faster, as the world outside her closed eyes became brighter and brighter. The wind whistled in her ears like shrill winter until it seemed almost too much and suddenly she stopped. Sinikka opened her eyes and she was back in the snow by the rock, but this time she felt warm and awake and alive.

Sinikka sensed a weight upon her body and turning her head, she saw a great bear cloak wrapped around her shoulders. Her mouth flew open. She jumped to her feet and held the huge paws out. It was huge. For a time Sinikka could only marvel at the beauty of it. Then she wrapped herself once more in its warmth, threw back her head and cried out, "Thank you, Great Mother Bear! This gift I will honor for the rest of my life. I will remember how you protected me on my journey and kept me warm. Your kindness will be praised for ever."

And Sinikka turned back the way she had come, her shadow on her right this time, and ran through the snow down the mountain side. The runo for the Onni charm came to her mind, and Sinikka sang the secret words aloud as she hopped from one frozen rock to the next.

Sinikka had nearly reached the valley again when a swirl of leaves rose up before her. The young woman was tired but still oddly joyful, and the sudden appearance of Maaemo was a welcome one. She knelt to touch the earth, calling out, "Greetings, Mother! All blessings upon you and your abundance."

"You look happy, child. I take it your journey has been fruitful — and that you found the Great Bear as well," Maaemo said, as the winds lifted an eddy of leaves, twigs and stones.

Sinikka smiled and patted the cloak slung over her shoulder. "Thank you for sending me forth. I have learned much and," she added, holding up the small leather bag, "Louhi has shared her knowledge with me. This will return fortune to my village, she has promised."

A chuckle swelled from within the debris. "Louhi's help often has costs. Be prepared. Still, I am glad you found what you were seeking."

"Louhi was frightening — at first. She is a difficult teacher, but a wise one. It is a beginning. But Louhi told me that we must woo Onni if he is to remain with us. I am not entirely sure how we will do so. My people still have no tietäjä."

"Oh, yes. Yes, they do." The laughter this time was full and echoed all around the young woman where she knelt. When at last it died away, Sinikka stood, smiled, and walked back to her village, her spirits soaring higher with each swinging step.

[Author's Note: Originally published in the short story collection Unikirja (Aino Press, 2009). ISBN 978-0982172506]

Power of the Gods

by Steven Gepp

Kokus stayed right where he had landed, staring through tear-filled eyes up at the three bigger boys. The largest, Tarvor, started laughing and the other two joined in immediately, all prodding at him with the tips of their wooden practice swords. The three standing were all two years younger than Kokus, but a problem with the older youth's birth and diseases as a child had left Kokus with a withered leg and a body more like a nine year old than some-one four years older than that. He did not have the body or strength to be a warrior of any sort, nor the family history to be a merchant. And Sage Honiror would not take him on to learn of the mysteries of life and death until he had reached his sixteenth year, and even then only if another had not been taken on as an apprentice. Even the priesthood was only open to those who could wield a sword in defence of the gods. His life, it seemed, was lost.

One of the boys smashed the side of the sword into Kokus' hip, bringing out a whimper of pain from his throat and a further tear sliding down the cheek. How he wished he could fight back! What he would do to these boys if he had the ability, the power. But it was not the case. His mother had often said that she wished men were like the deer which roamed their world, to have the freedom to roam and the lack of worry that deer have. But Kokus knew what she really meant. In the deer herds the old, the sick and the infirm were left behind by the traveling groups, to be taken by wolves so as not to be a burden to the majority. The inference was clear to him – even his mother thought that he was better off dead, for the sake of everyone.

She never said so to him, of course. She was always there for him, cooking his meals, making sure he was safe and warm, helping him walk when the snows were too deep, watching out for him. But he knew the truth. Her shows of affection were to ease her own guilt. He knew that she cared little about him.

"Hold!" boomed a sudden, loud voice and the three bigger boys stopped their mocking and gazed in fear at the newcomer. Like themselves, he wore thick furs against the cold of their northern homeland, but he also had a metal helm upon his head and the long sword in his hand was made of iron.

"Neton!" called Kokus, tears now flowing freely down his face.

"Quiet, rodent!" growled the newcomer as he strode forward. He stopped in front of the other three, now quivering with fear. "What do you do to my brother?" he demanded.

"Just games...." stammered Tarvor meekly.

"Well, play your 'just games' with others," Neton rumbled, lifting his sword slightly, threateningly. Without another word they ran for the safety of the nearby trees.

"Thank you, Ne...." Kokus began, but was cut short by a sharp slap to his cheek by the back of a gloved hand.

"What are you?" Neton hissed. Kokus could not answer. "Even now our mother cries over you, asking the great goddess Frigga why she was burdened with you, a selfish rodent! That she loves you is a wonder to me. You are a disgrace to our father, dead but living in Valhalla in the host of Odin. None of our offerings to him have been taken in over a year and Wise Enier the priest says 'tis you. Mother refuses to believe it, but I do. Have you ever wondered why our mother cries around you so often? You have brought disgrace to our family, more than anyone can remember in the epics of our village. Even Atheor, founder of our town, was not as disgraced by his son who fought with the barbarians against the Viking host.

"And now I come here and find boys barely in their eleventh year fighting you and winning with wooden swords. Even Ingrid, Svarson's youngest daughter, has been awarded her iron sword for her skill, and has even made her first kill of wild boar. She is but twelve! You are my brother and I must treat you as such, as even the gods treat the evil Loki as a brother, but you are a disgrace, an embarrassment to the family. In your selfishness to keep on living you have cursed us all!

"Why the gods have cursed us, I do not know. Our only consolation is that our father sits in the halls of Valhalla and that, by the will of the gods, I may join him there and never have to put up with you again once this life is over!" He paused a brief second to glare into Kokus's red eyes before striding away from the young man still sitting in the mud. The water had seeped through all the layers of his clothing and his face was awash with tears. If he had Neton's strength, he would show them all, would defeat them one by one. But he was in this useless husk of a body. He now wished people were like deer, then maybe none of this would ever have happened to him. Or maybe he should have been stolen at birth by the evil goblins. Or maybe the gods should have sent a disease strong enough to kill him. Or maybe he should...maybe he should just leave...Maybe....

****

The dark clouds at sunset told of an impending snow storm. They completely blocked the stars and moon, plunging the world into the blackness of Hela's realm. The winds rose and howled, the hungry Fenris Wolf crying to all the world from where it was bound until the time of Ragnarok, summoning

[38]

storms and snow in his rage. But for Kokus there was no turning back. He would be like the deer who knew they were a burden to the herd. He would go out and let the gods, the elements, the animals or whatever take him. No more could anybody say that he was a disgrace or selfish. He was doing this for everyone, sacrificing himself for all of them. However there was a part of him that still wished to have some sort of revenge upon them all first....

Maybe his death would be the revenge he desired. They had to know he was more than the person who had been tormented his whole life.

A small pack carried but a few provisions – a flint to make fire, cured fish and deer and boar meat. Strapped about his waist was a small, metal dagger taken from Neton's belongings. He had many and could not possibly miss one as insignificant as this. Water he could get from melting snow, other food from trapping small animals – surely even he could do that without failing! He might even survive out here, a lone hermit, if he were good enough; Sage Honiror had told him of such men many times in the past. Thus it was that Kokus left his home town, probably, he knew, forever....

Kokus knew not how much time had passed but he was exhausted and even the faint glow of the village Bryatheor's bonfire had not been visible for a long time. Only the vaguest outlines of the things about him could be seen. He had followed as well as he could the road to the neighbouring village of Johthyn, a day's horse ride away, walking in the trees alongside it to minimize the chances of his being discovered. And when the morning came and there was light, he would leave the road and travel through the forest and keep going for ten days, finding places to sleep each night. And after this time he would stay in the one place and try to survive. There were many caves he could settle in and be shielded by; there were plenty of trees for him to make whatever he needed. He knew how to do all these things although he was not very good at it; but maybe having to do it would improve his skill. His brother often said that "practice makes perfect" and he trusted that advice. He had no choice now.

As he walked on he felt himself grow colder and colder. Despite more layers of clothing than he had ever worn before, he could not feel his numb toes nor his frost-bitten fingers and nose. Maybe he should find a place to shelter on this night instead of following his original plan of walking all night and all the next day before resting. A crack of lightning briefly lit his way, revealing only snow and trees and rocky hills. This was followed almost immediately by a resounding crash of thunder and Kokus winced. He knew from experience that that meant a storm was almost overhead and that he would clearly be caught in it.

He looked wildly about in the darkness. No matter self-sacrificing intentions were, he did not want to die frozen to dea

[39]

he had heard described as horrific and one of the worst a man can suffer. They said it was better even to drown; drowned men often had smiles on their faces, while those frozen had the most pained expressions ever described. And so Kokus looked all about for protection.

A rocky hillock. Maybe there would be a small cave beneath it. He jogged as well as he could on his withered leg across to it and started up its snow-covered side. Suddenly his foot slipped and he lost his balance. He fell and rolled, bouncing off the rocks until landing in a muddy ditch. He waited a few moments, feeling the pain in his every muscle, before opening his weary eyes. A flash of lightning lit the scene and a slight smile managed to cross Kokus' blue lips. He struggled to his knees and crawled urgently forward. And sure enough he found what he had seen so briefly moments before. A small opening under a rocky ledge. He squeezed himself into it, finding to his delight that it was large enough to house him comfortably. No snow was in here and the dirt on the rocky floor was still dirt, not mud, which meant no water seeped in either. He thanked the gods and his father in Valhalla before making himself as comfortable as he could and settling down into a disturbed sleep, feeling that maybe even his father looking down from Valhalla was proud of him right now.

Kokus resumed his journey after resting until the sun was high overhead. He knew that that did not give him much traveling time on this day, but he no longer cared. He was confident in himself. All of his childhood fantasies of being a great warrior were coming to a type of fruition. After the previous night's storm, he knew that the people of Bryatheor would believe him to be dead. They probably would not even consider sending out men to search for him. They may even grieve for him, but he doubted it. This was almost as good as exacting physical revenge on those people who had treated him so badly for all of his life. But that thought did not depress him. He believed now that he could survive anything.

****

As the sun rose the following morning the last of Kokus's self-belief had all but disappeared. Huddled in the smallest possible space in the hollowed trunk of a tall and ancient tree, he could barely move his stiff muscles as the sun woke him from his light sleep. He did not even want to risk trying to stand on his withered leg, after this tree, the only shelter he could find, still left him exposed to the bitter cold of the night. He did not want to look at his numb toes if his blistered and sore fingers were any indication. He had seen frost bitten limbs before and did not want to see his own body in that predicament...although he could feel it coming too quickly for his liking.

Kokus started to cry. His mother should have been like a deer; if she had left him out when he was but an infant, then he would not be going through any of this now. "Why me?" he screamed to the heavens.

The response he received was unexpected. "Help me! Please, somebody help me!" It was a soft cry, but obviously male and obviously full of intense pain. It grew quickly louder and more pained. Then there came a scream, a scream of such violence and terror that Kokus shuddered to hear it. It was an unworldly scream. His years of upbringing in a strict Viking world made refusing this seem unnatural. What if it was a fellow countryman being tortured by the barbarian hordes?

What if? his mind countered. What good could Kokus, the reject, possibly do for anyone? He could die an actual hero and enter Valhalla, to sit by his father's side, that was what he could do. And all other mental resistance disappeared with that thought. He struggled to his feet and, using a fallen branch as a crutch, hobbled in the direction of that cry. Then the scream sounded again, even more pained than before and, despite himself, his own pain and all of his self-doubt, Kokus sped up.

He soon came across a small track cutting its way through the forest; probably a hunter's trail, he decided. And the sound was coming from a pile of rocks to his left. The scream came again, this time chilling Kokus to his very bones. It echoed in the quiet of this early morning, sending birds flying into the air and smaller creatures running for cover deep in the white-blanketed underbrush. Kokus managed to increase his speed once more.

He saw the source and managed to break into a sprint, ignoring the pain searing up his leg. Wielding his crutch like a sword, he limped forward and beat at the rear end of the nearest wolf. The animal yelped and faced him. Kokus reached down and pulled out the dagger from his hip. He struck forward, scratching the nose of the creature. The beast yelped again and ran off immediately. The second wolf, its bloodied snout clutching the arm of the man who was screaming, stopped what it was doing and gazed at the new arrival. Without thinking Kokus jabbed the crutch he leant on at the wild beast, stabbing it in the eye. A fountain of blood squirted out and the creature howled pitifully as it ran off with its tail between its legs, following its companion. The young man watched the animal go, then turned his attention to the man before him.

He was a large man, dressed in the fine furs of a merchant or maybe of nobility. Pinning him to the ground was a fallen tree, laying across the man's broad chest, and his arm showed where the two wolves had started to feast upon him. His hand was barely attached to the rest of the mangled forearm and the white snow was stained crimson. His face was pale from loss of blood and his eyes were slightly glazed. Kokus did not know if he would survive.

[41]

Kokus looked all about and saw a smaller tree lying on the ground. He grabbed it and rammed it beneath the trunk of the tree crushing the older man, leaning against one of the many stones buried under the snow. With the greatest effort he could muster he leaned down on the end of the tree. It started to creak and crack, then finally broke. But as it did so it pushed the larger tree off the merchant type and sent it rolling over his legs and to the snow at his feet. Almost immediately there was a sigh of relief from the man and his body relaxed.

"Are you all right?" Kokus asked urgently.

The man smiled. "My friend, you may have done yourself quite a favour," he grinned as he pushed himself to a sitting position. The colour had already started to return to his pale face and his eyes sparkled with renewed vigour.

"How so?" the younger man asked in confusion, unable to take his eyes from the mess that was this man's arm.

"Ash tree," the man said, indicating the plant which had fallen onto him.

"So?" Kokus could not tell where this conversation was leading.

The man was now clutching his injured arm. "Ash trees negate the magic of males," the man explained. "Because of the creation of man and woman from ash and elm. You know the tales."

"Magic?" muttered Kokus. "I still don't understand...."

"Then watch." And the man's smile widened. As Kokus looked on, the wound on the man's arm started to shrink, to heal and close. The blood stopped flowing and the skin closed without scar or mark. Finally it was as though the two wolves had never even been present. "Magic," he whispered with a sly grin.

Kokus was speechless. Finally: "So why didn't you use that to save yourself?" he asked.

"As I explained, 'tis the ash tree. It stops male magic. And I, as you can see, am a male." He smiled again and stood up. "A male with magic. Strong magic," he reiterated, then stared deep into Kokus' eyes. "So, what is your heart's desire?" he asked casually. Kokus felt his mind start to drift. His will was not his own. And the words that came out were the truth, but not what he wanted to say:

"I wish to be raised to the heights of Valhalla, to be with the host of Odin," he muttered softly, then slowly he shook his head. "No," he whispered, feeling his head go even more misty. "I wish to be of the gods, one of them, more powerful than any mortal."

The man nodded sagely. "Do you know what you ask?" he queried.

Kokus nodded. "I wish to be a god."

"Do you really know what that means?" the magic-user asked, then continued before Kokus could answer. "You have power, almost unlimited power, but only so long as there are living people who know you and believe in you. When there are none living left to worship or believe in you, then you shall just disappear. Not to the halls of the goddess Hela, nor to the fields and feasts of Valhalla. You just disappear. Gone. Forever." He paused to let this sink in. "Do you still wish to be like the gods?"

Kokus nodded without hesitation. "Yes," he hissed, the thoughts rushing through his mind too many and complex to be controlled and seen clearly. "Yes," he repeated and smiled. The man also grinned and nodded slightly.

"So be it," he whispered and held his hands to the sky....

****

It all happened so fast. One moment Kokus was standing in a forest of rock and snow, his body a mess of aches and pains, the next he was in the midst of Bryatheor, his home-town, standing atop the burning wood of the bonfire in the centre of the village, as fit and as healthy as he had ever been before in his life. The flames licked at him, but did not even singe him or his clothing. And standing about were several of the town's warriors, just staring in awe. "Kokus!" hissed one. "What goes on here? Where did you come from? What do you do?"

As the man said his name Kokus felt a surge of power run through him. And Kokus understood what was happening immediately. The old thoughts of revenge filled his mind. "What do I do?" he returned evenly. "Whatever I want."

"What magic is this?" another asked in fear.

"My magic," Kokus replied. And he held his hands up high in the air. Immediately a flash arched across the sky and a bolt of lightning struck the ground at the feet of the men. "I am your god," he growled. "Worship me."

"Never," replied the one who had spoken first. "The disgraceful son of a dead hero. You are no god. Some magic is afoot here and I wish no part of it."

Kokus's face grew angry and he pointed at the man. At that, the warrior's face screwed into a mask of pain and he clutched his chest in agony. He fell to his knees, then his face, and finally was still, the expression of shock still etched onto that horrified visage. The man beside him dropped to his knees and examined his dead comrade. "Death," he hissed. "An evil spirit. No god would do this in his own town!" And Kokus pointed at him, with a similar, sudden effect.

Now the young man with the new-found power looked all about. The streets of this village had quickly become deserted, the shutters pulled across the windows, the doors firmly shut and barred. "People of Bryatheor!" he boomed, his voice echoing like thunder, making the very walls of the buildings shake with the force of the words. "Come and worship me! I am your new god!"

The only movement was of the fire crackling beneath his feet, but all the time he felt his power grow and grow and he knew that the people were saying his name. It did not matter how or why, the fact that they were speaking of him out loud gave him more and more energy. "Come! Now!" commanded the new god.

And a lone figure stood at the end of the street. It paused before starting to stride forward with slow, deliberate steps. It was his brother, Neton, yet Kokus said nothing. "What do you do, Kokus?" he eventually called.

"I am a god," Kokus stated firmly. "Your god."

"Our mother died when you left two nights ago. Grief killed her. You killed her. If you are a god, then bring back our mother." Neton's face was etched in stone.

"Dead?" Kokus asked, feeling his confidence falter slightly. Then: "I do not believe you. She hated me. I hated her...."

"You ungrateful swine!" Neton screamed and rushed forward, sword drawn. The cold metal slammed into Kokus' leg, but bounced off as if striking stone and the young man kicked out as hard as he could. The foot connected with Neton's jaw and, in a fountain of blood, the head of the Viking warrior sailed from the body, killing him instantly.

Kokus stared at the carnage suddenly before him. "What have I done?" he whispered, staring at the decapitated body. He did not understand. Why had he done that? He had let his power get the better of him. What punishments were there for gods who killed their siblings? Mortals were given a special torture by Hela, but gods did not die, they lived forever. Surely it was not just the guilt of having done the act...but did gods ever do this sort of thing? He could not remember hearing any stories of such a thing...and then he hid his face in his hands. No other god had a mortal sibling to kill. He was the first. Would the other gods punish him? What would be his fate?

"Why?" he cried. Again all the buildings shook with the power in his voice. Strong negative feelings towards him started to enter his mind, but he could feel his power grow inside as his name was mentioned more and more by the people of Bryatheor. A killer of a brother; would anybody worship him and give him the power of a god? The guilt he felt at Neton's death started to fade from his mind as he worried about his own survival. For maybe, just maybe, that was what Neton deserved. He had given Kokus no help in his struggles in life and now he was where he wanted to be, in Valhalla, feasting with their father.

But that did not help him in this new problem. If these people did not trust or respect him, would they worship him, give him their power? Three deaths already, all at his hand, all because of his power as a god and his anger. They had seen that; then surely fear would make them worship him. They must know the sort of revenge he could wreak upon them. His confidence started to grow, and once more he felt his anger also rise.

"Come worship me!" he screamed, and the earth rumbled with his words; cracks appeared in the walls of some buildings and the roofs of many started to collapse. A woman wailed somewhere and somewhere children were crying. "Now!" he demanded. And two of the closest houses collapsed in on themselves. But still no-one emerged.

Kokus's anger reached boiling point. He leapt from the top of the fire and looked all around. Not even a face peered at him from behind cracks in shutters or walls, not a movement came from out of the piles of rubble. Very well then, if they were not prepared to do things on his terms, then the revenge he had dreamed of so often would come down upon them.

"So be it," he growled and raised his fist high. With a sound like a rushing gale he struck down as hard and as fast as he could at the ground. His blow left a dent in the hard earth, and almost immediately the world rumbled. He had disturbed the Midgard Serpent, the beast that circled the world with its tail in its mouth. The ground moved and rumbled and then split open beneath Kokus' feet.

The youth yelped before he realised that he was not falling, but floating in the air above a huge crevasse. Yet all about him Bryatheor was disappearing, each and every building tumbling into the huge hole in the ground, bodies of the people he had known all of his life lying amongst the debris like discarded dolls. And then the earth was still. Kokus locked down at the death and destruction beneath him. Death and destruction he himself had created, all in his revenge against a village which he believed had wronged him. He had destroyed everyone he had ever known. Then the earth rumbled again and the hole filled itself with dirt, burying all traces of Bryatheor forever. If anyone had survived, there was no way they still lived after the tons of soil and rock fell atop of them.

He felt his body grow suddenly light, his head dizzy.

Kokus found it hard to think and he fell to his knees. "Wh...what's happening?" he muttered out loud.

"You foolish child," said a voice he knew. He looked up and saw the merchant he had rescued earlier that day. "You have destroyed yourself."

"Wha...what do...do you me...mean?" Kokus was finding it increasingly hard to even talk.

"The only people who knew of you were those in Bryatheor," explained the man. "You were their disgraceful secret. They told no-one of you. And now you've killed all of your worshippers. They sit in Valhalla or the feasting halls of Hela's lands. And you are condemned to nothingness."

By the time he had finished speaking the only sign that Kokus had ever been there was a small foot-print from a withered leg in the fresh snow....

Corrupting Influence

by Brandon Cracraft

The good people of France beheaded my younger brother after they bludgeoned my parents and grandparents to death. The filthy, toothless peasants cheered and threw tomatoes at the frail boy as he limped his way to the guillotine, poking and beating Ramon with his own cane. My hand shook as I continued to read the account from the French diocese. I crumpled the parchment up, unable to read any more.

I stared at my reflection from behind a squall of tears, scratching at the priestly habit and resisting the urge to tear it off. Young men spent most of their lives preparing for the priesthood, but my mother's money and title bought me the white collar in just under a year. The Franciscan Order seemed the perfect place for Lyonesse de Soule to hide her wayward son.

"I can't be the only one left," I slammed my fists on the altar and barely resisted the urge to spill the holy water. "Do not tell me that Ramon deserved to die. He wasn't even seventeen. My brother was a pure spirit. He never complained about his infirmity, and he was always rescuing birds from cats." I thought about the last time I had seen Ramon, six years ago. I put the skinny boy on my shoulder and he stretched out his arms so that he could pretend to fly. I had joked about him being an angel.

"Be thankful that the Blessed Virgin brought you to New World, Father Atxular," Father Ximenes said. "Your mother wanted you hidden away in a monastery in Navarre until all the rumors began to die down. If not for the Lord's providence bringing you across the ocean on missionary work, you would have died with your brother." The older priest offered me his hand, but I pushed it away.

I laughed cruelly. "The Holy Mother had nothing to do with it. My desire for men saved my life." I trapped the elderly priest in my amber eyes. I wanted to shock him, make him hate me for living when dutiful little Ramon didn't even get the dignity of a decent burial. "If I hadn't been a lover of men, my parents never would have shipped me off to the church."

Father Ximenes did not flinch nor argue. "I brought you to New Spain with me, because I felt the only way for you to resist temptation was to stare the serpent in the eyes. I knew this place was filled with half naked savage boys. Your resolve impressed me. Weaker men would have snuck out in the middle of the night to lay with the savages."

"I took a vow of chastity," I said with a shrug.

"Few boys have the strength of will to keep those vows, Father Atxular," he said, giving me a reassuring hand on the shoulder. "Must be that stubborn, passionate Basque blood I kept hearing about."

"What am I supposed to do now?" I asked, not certain if I was addressing Father Ximenes, the Holy Virgin, or myself. "Maybe I can go back to France. I still know how to fight. Maybe I could – "

Father Ximenes moved closer and shook his head. "I need someone to investigate some accusations of witchcraft," he said, whispering the last word and looking around to make sure none of the demons were listening.

"Witchcraft?" I said with a laugh. "This whole territory is pagan."

Father Ximenes narrowed his eyebrows, and I swallowed my laughter. "There are some members of the church that would rather we burn down every single Indian village rather than educate them in the ways of God."

"Could it just be the Indians?" I asked. "If we do not respect their ways, they will never be open to hearing the Word."

"The village is close to the Indians known as the Navajo. According to the governor and his wife, all the accused witches are either Spaniards, Portuguese, Italians, or Mexicans. Any Indians that might have been amongst the accused are probably long dead." He crossed himself.

"What do you need me to do, Father," I said. "You need me to make a report and take it to the diocese?"

Father Ximenes shook his head. "All of these accused witches are boys ages eight to seventeen. Most of them speak French as a first language, so they might not even fully know what they are accused of. I need someone to be their advocate."

"You want me to defend witches?" I looked at the Holy Virgin and crossed myself quickly.

"They locked the boys in their school. I doubt anyone is even giving them proper food and water. They are probably half crazed from the heat. I remember what happened when we accused this poor old woman of witchcraft back in Spain. She would have admitted being the Devil if it meant getting a crust of bread and the end of torture."

I thought a moment and shook my head decisively. "They will burn me with the rest of them."

"The Frenchman who taught at the school should have been behind a desk rather than a podium," he continued, ignoring my shock. "Have you ever heard of a seventeen year old schoolmaster?"

"Ramon was a school master," I argued before I realized where the conversation was going. "He had my father's gift for mathematics and physics."

"Sebastian Marquette was from Basque Navarre," Father Ximenes continued. "He had a lot in common with your younger brother." He sighed. "Just like Ramon Atxular, he will probably be brutally executed by rabble."

"Are you trying to use my brother's death to manipulate me?" I asked.

"The Lord works in mysterious ways, Father Atxular."

****

The heat of the ride strangled me, and I rode bare-chested whenever I was certain that no one but the cactus and snakes would see my flesh. Father Ximenes told me that it would be a month's ride, but I managed to travel most of the distance in a week. I looked at my pack and realized that I had never touched the dried fruits and meat. I chewed into the leathery snack and quickly spat it out like it was poison. Bile burned its way out of my stomach, and I clutched the pommel of my saddle as my head spun. I tried to sip at wine and then water, but they both tasted like mud.

I climbed off my horse and laid down in the sand, preparing to die just a few mesas away from the village of Magdalen. "Waste of a miracle," I told the burning sun. "You carried me most of the way across the desert only to die within sight of my destination."

When I felt a hand on my forehead, I expected to get stabbed by the devil's forked tail and dragged down to Hell to be burned on a spit for all eternity. My body ached, and I reached for my sweat-soaked shirt. My vanity refused to let me face my damnation half dressed.

Instead of the image of Lucifer, I saw Ramon's gentle smile. "I guess you really are an angel now, Ramon," I said, speaking in Basque instead of Spanish. He had grown a head taller, but still fit under my chin, and he still wore that faded, periwinkle cloak that used to be his childhood blanket.

"I love you," I told him, "but I am not ready to die."

Ramon nodded and pointed toward my destination. He lifted me to my feet. I looked for my horse, but the old nag had vanished. "The Lord expects me to walk with all this acid in my belly?" I asked the apparition. "Is this some lesson in humility?" Ramon did not answer, merely smiled and pointed. "I guess I should count myself lucky that he did not send a giant fish to swallow me whole."

My hands shook as I buttoned the shirt unevenly, thankful that the collar was not hanging off my neck. My bladder rattled my manhood, and I almost did not open my trousers quick enough. My entire body rebelled against me.

I looked back and saw the ghost of my younger brother standing there. Instead of pointing, he was waving. His grin widened, and he looked more like the giddy little boy that I grew up with than the young man he grew into while I was gone.

A shadow began to pool around where the ghost stood, slowly oozing out of the ground. My brother's face twisted into a scream before he suddenly vanished. I heard a howl on the wind as the figure of a gigantic wolf appeared in front of me. The monster was larger than my horse, bigger than a wagon even. Its black eyes burned into me and its lips curled into a human smile. Night fell in a matter of seconds, possibly at the monster's command.

"Run," the beast commanded in Basque. "I need sport."

I started to stumble toward the village, but the wolf forced me to run into the desert. I tried not the think about anything, especially not my pain or the fact that I was running to nothingness. If I stopped running for an instant, the monster would kill me. When I was a little boy, I never traveled at night. I knew a monster was out there hunting me. This monster.

My legs burned, but I continued to push. The beast toyed with me, staying just far enough behind that I could feel its jaws snapping on the air. Dust and desert air made my lungs itch and fatigue cracked and pulled at my ribs.

I never noticed the rock that tripped me. My face tumbled into the sand, and I let out a quick prayer of thanks that I didn't swallow a scorpion. When I turned suddenly, terror clamped down on my spine. The wolf stood on its hind legs, rows of teeth revealed as it began to look more demon than animal.

"Gaueko," I said, remembering the boogeyman that Mother assured me waited for any child attempting to travel at night.

"It feels good to be recognized," Gaueko replied, his voice more of a slither than a growl. He leaned back and let out a mockery of a howl.

"King of witches. Father of nightfall. The Trickster. The Nightwalker. The Master of Shadow." I kept reciting his various titles, hoping the flattery would buy me time to think.

Grandmother told me that the Catholics drove Gaueko out of the Basque territory. I stood up, trying to look defiant and fearless. I held my crucifix out in front of me, rebuking the monster in Latin. I used every prayer of protection Father Ximenes ever taught me.

"Oceans of Christians burn in Hell, priest." He opened his mouth, dislocating his jaw so that he could swallow me whole. "You shall soon see for yourself."

Before my crimes forced me into the priesthood, I planned to be a soldier. I spent most of my youth training with one weapons master after another. Clearing my mind, I pulled my knife from my belt and focused on the wolf's dark head. The knife sank deep within the monster's right eye as I forced my tired legs to move me far away from its jaws.

"I hate priests," Gaueko said with a snarl. "You even taste bitter."

Gaueko started to pounce again, but I grabbed my short blade. When I was boy, I won a fencing tourney. I hoped that I could adapt some of those skills to wound rather than score points. I shoved the blade into the monster's mouth and wrenched out a tooth. He knocked me to the ground, so I shoved both of my legs into his stomach. Blackened blood erupted on me. I felt sick, like I was drowning in a sea of filth.

"Not a bad fighter," Gaueko said. "But you forgot that I am the lord of witches. I have no need to fight you." His claws drew circles in the air as he formed arcane symbols and spoke in the darkest of languages.

"Hunting in our territory is forbidden, Nightwalker," a loud masculine voice boomed in Basque. Gaueko's night ended, and the world was engulfed in deep twilight.

Gaueko choked down his spell, backing away from the shadows that suddenly surrounded us. A boulder landed inches away from his enormous skull.

"That was your final warning," the booming voice demanded. Gaueko licked his bloody lip with a purple tongue. The lord of black magic disappeared in a cloud of toxic smoke and cold fire.

"Thank you, sir," I said. "My name is – "

"Francisco Atxular or Francois de Soule depending on which side of your estate you are walking," a voice with the tenor of youth said. "I remember you from our boyhood – "

"Silence, Mairu," the booming voice demanded. "Do not get too comfortable, Christian. You are a trespasser as well."

"What is your business here, boy?" a feminine voice asked. I heard a jumble of voices speaking an ancient language that died before there was a France or Spain.

"I was sent by the church to investigate a claim of witchcraft," I started. "Gaueko drove me here by accident. He was trying to keep me away from the village of Magdalen."

"I doubt he could find his way back even unless we gave him a map," the booming voice sounded old and tired. "Mairu, lead the Christian back to the human territory."

"Yes, father," Mairu responded proudly.

"Are you sure that is wise, my king?" the female asked.

"Atxular could tell the world about giants, but no one would believe him. Civilized people want to believe that we are nothing but myth."

My mouth dropped open. "The Jentilak. I thought you all were extinct, well, mostly extinct, except for –"

"Old Father Christmas?" Mairu said. "I bet you believed that we all drowned ourselves when your Christ child was born. Did it ever occur to you that we simply left when we realized that we were not wanted?"

[51]

Mairu stepped forward out of the shadows. He stood just over nine feet tall with skin the color of desert sand and bright yellow eyes. He wore the clothes of a fashionable young man but made from hide and fur rather than leather and lace. His long black hair was tied back with a piece of intestine. His dark eyes and gigantic powerful hand greeted me like an old friend. "Mairu, son of Basaljaun and Basendere."

"Do you know anything about the witches?" I asked Mairu.

"You can walk with him, son," the booming voice warned, "but don't give him any information if you value the skin on your backside."

Mairu let out a sigh and shrugged. "Yes, father."

I started to walk with him but my body finally collapsed. "We have to do something," Mairu said. "Gaueko poisoned him." He held me in the nook of his arms, ripping off my clothes. Fever kept me from worrying about shame. Whenever I tried to cough, I thought I was going to choke to death on my own ichors.

The woman who stepped out of the shadows stood over twice the size of her son. To her people, she would have beautiful. Humans saw only the massive amounts of hair that sprouted from her legs and chest. I remembered that, in the tales, the Jentilak never stopped growing. Basendere was over a thousand years old according to legend.

"I forbid you," she said. "Let this Christian die. You are being nostalgic, Mairu." She turned toward her husband, who remained nothing but a shadow. "Stop him."

"He is not a child," the Jentil king said. "He is free to make the same mistake his mother once did." The tone of his voice said that Mairu would always be a little boy to his father.

I thought that Mairu was reaching down to kiss me, and I almost protested and told him of my vice. The Jentil boy shared a sliver of his life to me, passed from his lips to mine. I felt the heat of electricity. It was not a kiss, at least not as a human would understand it. Mairu let a small thread of his soul touch mine.

Mairu let me go as I felt something burn its way out of my body. I hacked until a sliver of Gaueko's claw worked its way out of my system. I wiped an acidic substance that leaked out of my nose from my face and nodded thanks to Mairu. When I finally made my way to my feet, I felt strong again.

Basendere gave us both a disapproving look. "That was a foolhardy thing you did. My son believes he knows you, because our old kingdom used to touch your property."

I covered my groin, realizing that I was naked. "I appreciate – "

The queen cared little about my nudity. "You had better appreciate it. For the rest of your life, the two of you are connected. If you ever use this gift to

[52]

harm my son, I shall destroy every human village on this continent…maybe even the planet."

"I do not —"

"You have come to this territory to protect the Sorignak," she said. "I wish you nothing but success. I truly hope that my son is right about you." She walked into the shadows and vanished.

Mairu handed me the remains of my clothes, my knife, and my short sword. He nervously played with the cameo that kept his deerskin cravat knotted while I dressed. He stood close to me, opening his mouth to talk than shutting it, only adding silence to the conversation.

I blinked when I realized that the cameo was actually a medallion of St. Laurent. "So you don't fear Christ," I asked.

Mairu started to say something then remembered his father's warning and shifted his fur breeches. "The only thing I can tell you, Brother, is that we never feared Jesus or the Virgin. We were scared of what your religion brought with them."

****

The good people of the village of Magdalen had denied the children of St. Abanoub School for Young Gentlemen food, water, and sunlight. They had turned the school into a tomb. I said a silent prayer for the poor souls inside, expecting nothing but madness and dead bodies when I finally found a way in.

"Sister," I heard a parched voice several seasons from manhood call out from inside the school. "Sister, is that you?" He waited a few moments. "Sister, it's Etienne. Please, Sister, I think teacher is sick."

"Where are you, lad?" I asked in French. "My name is Father Francisco Atxular. The church sent me to help. Tell me how to find you."

"A nun comes by to feed us when she can," Etienne said. The boy was suspicious, panicked. "She took a hatchet and smashed up one of the boards near the floor."

"What if he is one of the bad priests, Etienne?" another boy asked in French.

Etienne breathed hard. "Do you want teacher to die?" he said defensively. "Someone has to help him."

I searched around until I found a tiny hole that could be used to pass food through. It must have been the only way these prisoners ever saw the stars. "What is wrong with Monsieur Marquette?" I asked. I saw the older boy sitting by himself in soiled clothes. Despite his confinement without a razor, whiskers barely brushed his face. The teenage boy looked at me and I saw the stare of an old man ready to die.

Etienne ran up wearing nothing but his shirt, his trousers and stockings long ago discarded from the heat. He looked to be around ten years old, his blond hair cemented to his forehead from sweat. A Tohono boy stood behind him, clinging to his leg. I guessed that twelve children were locked up inside.

I let out a string of curses in Spanish that I hoped the boys would not recognize as I sliced at the boards with my knife. "Monsieur Marquette!" I called over and over until the seventeen year old finally met my gaze. "I need you to pull it together, lad. I am getting you out of here."

The sound of a pistol's hammer froze me in place. "What do you think you are doing?" a woman with perfect Spanish diction said. "I am arresting you in the name of my husband and the Holy Catholic Church."

I turned and saw three soldiers being led by a woman wearing black and aiming a pistol at my chest. She aged very gracefully, styling her grey hair in a dramatic pattern, and defying her wrinkles with blush and eye make-up. The woman wore so much finery that she looked like a lady in waiting to the queen. The soldiers looked filthy, their uniforms hastily stitched together.

"Speak," the woman ordered, "or are you bewitched?"

"I am an advocate of the church," I said, turning back to smash at the boards. "They sent me to investigate claims of witchcraft against these children."

"I am Signora Magdalen Olympias Castillo de la Negra," she announced proudly. "My husband is mayor. He gave me the authority to guard these prisoners. This structure is a house of witchcraft. This house along with all of its inhabitants shall be burned to the ground."

"No," I said flatly, waving my knife. "The church demands these children get a trial. I shall be speaking for them."

Signora de la Negra stepped forward and replaced her pistol in its holster. "I saw the damning evidence myself. Are you calling me a liar? Father Tartalo puts a lot of faith in my testimony."

"What did you see?" I asked, turning back toward my work.

"Sebastian Marquette caught a wild goat and slaughtered it in the classroom. They marked themselves with the blood of their sacrifice." She pulled out a fan a second too late to hide her thin lipped smile. "Are you saying that my feminine wit got the better of me? What else could such a ritual be except witchcraft?"

"The church demands —"

She motioned to the soldiers and I heard the sound of screaming coming closer. I watched two men drag a young Mexican nun behind them. They had shattered her nose, giving her a mask of blood. Every time she begged them for mercy, they struck her across the face.

"The church has already fallen victim to their witchcraft," Signora de la

Negra said. "You shall have to trust in Father Tartalo's wisdom and my husband's mercy. This house of the devil shall be destroyed tomorrow."

"Please," the nun begged, "they are only children." She blinked away the blood to get a better look at the Signora. "Please, I know that I am not bewitched. Every time I fed those children, I returned to the church and performed an act of contrition. Jesus forgave me. He wants you to show these children mercy."

"Silence her!" Signora de la Negra ordered. "If you have to, cut out her tongue. Silence is a virtue the Lord demands."

Etienne screamed out an apology to the nun, blaming himself for everything. A brute took out his carving knife, his hands racing up the woman's body.

"Release her!" I yelled, pulling out my short sword. "I have the authority of the church."

"This is the frontier, boy," the noblewoman said. "You have to earn respect. We do not simply hand out authority to little boys simply because they figured out how to tie on a white collar."

Mairu's spirit granted me swiftness and strength, and I felt his blood racing through my heart as I moved. I shattered the lower jaw of one of the guards that held the nun and pulled my short sword on the other, nicking his throat.

Signora de la Negra pulled out her gun, but I shook my head. "I am an officer of the church. If you kill me, they will hang you." She thought for a moment, contemplating whether she could get away with my murder. I decided it best to hit her harder. "The church shall seize all of your husband's assets. When you are executed, your family shall be left paupers. All of the village of Magdalen shall belong to the church."

She put her gun away, her face and voice cold. "I will speak with Father Tartalo about your behavior. This will not be tolerated." I held my breath until the Signora and her soldiers were long gone.

"Thank you, Father," the nun said, kneeling at my feet. "I swear that these are good children. I have known some of them for years."

Sheathing my knife and sword, I walked over to the front door and channeled the Jentilak strength, pulling boards off the hinges and then smashing the front door open with my shoulder. "I am going to need blankets, food, water, and fresh clothes for these boys," I told the nun. "Do you think you could find some?"

She nodded, smiling. "Bless you, Father. I do not know why people believe these poor children could actually be witches."

Sebastian Marquette stood up, tears streaming down his face. "Because we are witches. I worship the goddess Mari."

[55]

"The creation goddess of the Basques," I said. The children and the nun looked at me, surprised. "I was raised in that region." I thought back to the Jentilak magic that saved my life. "I think I might be a witch."

"That is impossible," the nun said. "You are a man of the cloth. You cannot be a witch."

"The Bible is filled with stories of prophets, healers, and men who possessed magical powers," I said. "Moses turned his staff into a snake. Solomon used the sign of the stars to turn back evil. Even Jesus cast out demons and turned water into wine." I thought back to my homeland, where some of the elders still invoked Mari at festivals. I never thought of them as witches, merely a different faith like the Jews and Moors. "Maybe a man can be both a priest and a witch."

"I swear on your God and my goddess that I never wanted to hurt anyone," Sebastian said. "I am not responsible for that monster out there."

"I know," I said. "I met Gaueko. No one controls that beast."

"How did you survive?" Etienne asked. "I thought he could swallow a man whole or drag you the Underworld."

"A miracle," I said. "Let us hope that I have not used all of my miracles up, because you boys need one."

****

Signora de la Negra returned with more soldiers but without her satisfied smirk. "I have orders from Father Tartalo to transport the witches to a proper prison where they will await trial." The guards began grabbing the boys, who started screaming and crying. Etienne clung to me, and I drew my short blade on the man who tried to jump him.

"You wanted them to have a trial," the Signora said. "I suggest you get these witches to cooperate." Her smile returned. "I do not want to have to hurt them. Resisting arrest can be considered an admission of guilt."

I got down on my knees so I could look the boy in his face. "I know that this is scary, but I will be there to help you."

After a moment, the boy nodded and held out his hands so he could be bound. "Please, don't leave us," he whispered in French.

The Signora pointed to Sebastian Marquette. "Place that one in metal irons. I want to make sure that he cannot escape."

"The boy can barely walk — "

She talked over me. "Tie him to my horse. Father Tartalo demands to speak to the former schoolmaster directly. He has new evidence in the case."

"What is this new evidence?"

"Father Tartalo ordered you to come to his office as well, boy," she told me. "He wants you to see the evidence, since my word is not considered valid. I expect an apology after the execution." She kicked her horse, forcing Marquette to run after her. She jerked the rope, taking pleasure every time he fell.

Her humor faded when she realized that I managed to keep up with a galloping horse without breaking a sweat. "I owe you, Mairu," I whispered.

****

Marquette and I choked when we entered the church. It looked like the house of a miller rather than a house of God. Several nuns scrambled around, avoiding my gaze. Father Tartalo reeked worse than garbage in the sun. I tried to focus on any of his features, but his horrible stench overpowered my other senses.

"Are you familiar with Basque witchcraft, Father?" Tartalo said, circling like a vulture and picking pieces of meat out of his teeth. He was crude and filthy, dirt staining his bald head. "I know that Monsieur Marquette is. Why don't you tell the good father who Atxular is?"

"One of the sons of the creation goddess, Mari," Marquette recited tiredly. "He became a priest to save his people."

"I think Father Atxular has let his name go to his head," Tartalo walked up to me, and I held my breath to cut down the smell. "You cannot save them. They are damned. If you do not leave matters alone, you will be damned as well."

"Jesus taught forgiveness and compassion," I said. "He did not torture or burn them alive. As he ministered to sinners, so do I."

Tartalo laughed, and I felt a chill grab my spine. "I was wrong. You do not think you are some mythic hero. The good father believes that he is Christ."

"I know that I have more power in the church," I said. "I speak for Father Ximenes and the entire diocese. I have his ring and his authority."

Tartalo turned toward Marquette. "Tell us what you really think about Christianity, witch. If you lie, I will boil the truth out of you with hot tar."

"I love God, Jesus, and the Holy Mother. I believe in the saints and their righteousness. I believe St. Abanoub, the child martyr, is a shining example for all young boys regardless of faith."

"Amen," I said. "I hardly think he is a threat."

"I expect a loose tongue if you do not want to find out how tar congeals into the crevice of a sinner. It will burn the filth right out of you. I actually saw one witch who started to defecate out of her mouth."

"Christianity would be a beautiful religion if it was about redemption and love," I said. "Some people focus on the positive, but there is a dark side to the faith. It has passages about murder and hatred."

[57]

Tartalo raised an eyebrow. "Do you really think this boy can be saved?"

"The worst thing the Christians brought was Satan," Marquette said loudly. "Satan follows Christians everywhere, corrupting everything around him. Gaueko used to be a trickster, but the Christians turned him into the worst of the demons. My father thought it was just about what people were taught. That is not true. I met the Dineh people – "

"Dineh?" I asked.

"The Spaniards call them the Navajo. They used to have no concept of Hell, but they are creating a demonic figure out of their former hero, the Slayer of Monsters. Satan does not merely corrupt men but entire nations and their beliefs." He stared at the priest and the noblewoman, hatred in his eyes. "You brought Satan to my ancestors, and you left us no way to fight him."

Tartalo walked over to the boy, shaking his head. "We gave you a means to fight him. All you had to do was abandon everything you ever believed and put your faith in us."

"Go to Hell," Marquette said, spitting in his face.

The priest casually put his hand to the young boy's throat and squeezed it with minimal effort. Sebastian Marquette fell to the ground with a broken neck. "He was getting tiresome."

"You murderer!" I screamed. I drew my sword and the Signora jumped between us with a rapier in her gloved hand.

The sound of an inhuman screech froze us both in place. "What was that?" she asked, looking frightened and out of control. She kept her point up, but she retreated back two steps. Chains rattled as something powerful tried to pull its way free. It let out a low moan of agony and then attacked the doors behind us. The Signora jumped away and held her blade toward the locked door.

Tartalo casually walked over to the double doors and unlatched them. The Signora screamed at him not to, but he ignored her. He seemed to take pleasure in her fear.

I recognized the creature behind the door from my Grandmother's stories. It was the Sorignak. Her body undulated like a serpent and her long, spidery fingers ended in wolverine claws. She had the eyes of a bird of prey, and her entire body was covered in a bear's fur. "You killed our brother!" the Sorignak screamed.

"That is not a demon," I explained. "She is a nature spirit. She probably came here to protect us from Gaueko, the demon wolf."

The sorignak calmed, studying me. "I know you."

"What does it want?" Signora de la Negra yelled, slowly backing away. "How can we destroy it? Should I get some holy water?"

"That creature is bound up," Tartalo answered. "I would be more worried about Father Atxular and why this demon knows him."

"He shares a life essence with my beloved, the prince of the Jentilak," she said. Eyes wide, she clasped her hands over her mouth to keep from saying more. The sorignak turned her attention back to Tartalo. "Witchcraft? You used liars root to make me reveal my secrets. What are you?"

"What is she talking about?"

"You are getting *tiresome*, Signora," Tartalo screamed. For a moment, I expected him to snap her neck as well. "Watch him. I do not know what kind of powers he has. The Jentilak were supposed to be extinct. Gaueko promised me that they were no more."

"Signora," I told her, "you have been tricked." She breathed heavily, playing with the sword in her hand, her eyes darting between each of her potential combatants. "This man is a witch and a Satanist. He just admitted to communing with the demon of the forest. He will kill us all."

"The Signora sadly has fallen victim to witchcraft," Tartalo said. "I shall have her locked up and executed with the rest of them."

"My birthright!" she exclaimed. "You will take away my son's land? What will happen to my daughter and my husband? I will not let you take away everything I worked so hard for!" She stabbed him through the chest with her rapier, her face twisted in a grimace of hate. Her attack pierced his heart, but he barely noticed. The weapon melted like wax in her hand. She screamed as the molten metal slithered out of him and burned her arm. She inched away from him.

"I will take that as admission of witchcraft," he said jovially.

Signora de la Negra stared at me for a few moments. "I was misled, my lord," she whispered, "please forgive me." She grabbed my hand and forced my knife into her chest. She sank to the ground, ensuring a fatal injury by falling onto the blade. As the blood pooled around her mouth, she smiled.

"I do not think I will ever understand humans," Tartalo said, slowly assuming his true form. His face twisted until all that was left were misshapen fangs and one large eye. His body expanded, revealing muscles and pockets of fat. He stood in front of me naked and proud of his miniscule manhood.

"Tartalo the Cyclops," I said, taking a step back.

His mouth opened and his teeth gnashed against each other, filth sloshing onto the floor. "I always preferred to be called Tartalo the Cannibal."

I swung my sword, tearing deep gouges into his flesh. Slime oozed out of his pores, sealing the wounds shut. I thought his stench alone would kill me.

"Come out, little Jentil!" he yelled. "I have missed my favorite meal!"

Tartalo locked his fangs on the sorignak's arm, tasting her with his warty tongue. I lunged at him, sinking my blade all the way to the pommel into his back. Brown slime burned my skin, and I was forced to let go.

"Call for him!" Tartalo demanded. "I want my meal!" I grabbed hold of his leg and pulled it out from under him. The monster crashed to the floor, but seemed to feel no pain. He grabbed me by the throat, his sweat sticking me to him. "I told you to call him, human!" He opened his mouth. "Maybe you want to be the meal."

"Never," I said defiantly.

"What?!" he taunted. "Do you think your god will protect you? He abandoned you, human. Your only hope is the Jentil. Call him."

"I promised that I would not endanger him."

Mocking laughter escaped Tartalo's throat. "Mairu would die to protect his beloved and his brother."

"He will not get the choice," I said, praying for forgiveness for all of my sins and for protection for the sorignak, the Jentilak, and those poor boys in the prison. I knew that penance waited for me for breaking my promise to Etienne.

"Do you know what deus ex machina is?" Gaueko said, walking in on his hind legs. The walls shuddered and creaked. With the horrible sounds of wood splintering, the church shattered around us. Even the floor was ripped away, leaving us standing on sand. Gaueko looked over at me, and I was not afraid. I saw the noble trickster he once was, rather than the monster he had become. "Modern humans believed that the Greek tragedies had gods show up at the end of plays to resolve everything because the playwright simply did not know how to end the play otherwise. The reality was quite different. The Greeks believed that their gods watched everything. It made sense to them that they would end all the action."

"What do you want?" Tartalo said. "You lied to me. You told me that the Jentilak were extinct. How long have you known?"

"I have always known," he said. "You should know that Atxular is my prey. I will not let you have him. Mairu removed my mark, but he is still mine. Give him to me and we shall consider it a misunderstanding." Thunder crashed even though the sky was clear.

"What did you do?" Tartalo asked, his one eye widening in terror.

"I knew how much you liked snacking on the Jentilak," he said, "so I summoned them all here." Shadows grew around him. The cannibal started to scream, but death came too quickly. One quick snap of Gaueko's jaw ended his life. Licking his lips, he savored the rest of the body, pulling the flesh from the bone.

Mairu stepped out of the shadows and ran to the Sorignak. "I thought they killed you, Agyurtzane." When he finished the embrace, he hugged me heartily. "Thank you for rescuing her, Brother. I knew I could count on you."

"I really did not do anything," I said. "Tartalo would have killed me if not

[60]

for Gaueko." I turned to face the giant wolf, but he was gone. I heard his howl in the distance, surprised at how human it sounded.

"He will never stop hunting you," Mairu said. "My spirit grants you long life. Hundreds of years from now, he shall still be stalking you."

"Hundreds of years," I whispered. Marquette said the Christians corrupted creatures like him. There had to be a way to save them. I knew that conversion was not the answer. The infestation began with faith. Gaueko still retained some of his old self. There was a place near his heart that even Satan could not reach. "More than enough to time to figure out how to save him."

Anything for a Tale

by Melia Suez

A young dark-haired man stumbles out of town a short time before dusk.

"Tomorrow is the All Hallows feast on the land of the most influential family in town and I have no tale despite my promise. A new, yet seasonal tale. *New and yet old*, he said. Oh Gods, what am I going to do? I would do anything to not blow this chance to make my name as a bard. Ever since I promised him such a tale, I've not had a single idea that was remotely original and yet based on the old. If I don't have a tale, I will be laughed out of town after all that bragging I did at the pub. Gods, please help me! I'll do anything! Anything!"

"Are you sure about that?"

The young man comes to a sudden halt at the voice. He realizes he is near the old cemetery. He starts to back away, because he can't see who spoke. Suddenly, the shadows near the gate shift to show a man with a beribboned staff leaning against the gate post. "Anything?"

"Yes," the bard states emphatically, "Anything. I have to have a tale for tomorrow or else I'll have to go back to working with my hands instead of my head. Anything."

"So heard and acknowledged," says a feminine voice from within the cemetery. From between two broken headstones, a black hooded, robed figure approaches, surrounded by dogs that are eerily quiet.

"Ah, there you are," says the man at the gate. "Think he will do?"

"He must. We were told to have someone here to record this change in the cycle. He will have to do."

"Wha…" sputters the bard. "I'm right here! Don't talk about me like I can't hear you."

She sighs. "Oh great, he's got a mouth on him….Make it so that he can see and let's go."

Without warning the man steps forward, licks his thumb, and shoves it into the bard's eye.

"Ow!" howls the young man. "What did you do that for?" He rubs at his eye, which is now tearing up. Blinking profusely, the bard suddenly realizes that if he looks through that eye only, he can see clearly around him despite the failing light. The man who poked him still looks common enough, handsome even, except that it was snakes not ribbons on his staff. Then a movement in the graveyard draws his attention. It is the woman walking towards him, and her dogs are mere skeletons. His heartbeat increases. Then the hood on her cloak slips, showing that it isn't hair on her head, but snakes. The bard feels his knees start to shake in time with his heartbeat and quickly closes both of his eyes tightly.

"Oh, crap. He's got no backbone. We'll have to call Bob to carry him and make sure he does his job."

"Wait. Let me talk to him." The man walks over to the bard and heartily slaps him on the back. "Buck up! You wanted a tale. You will have it before the night is out. Besides, you really don't want her to call Bob. He's creepier than she is. Some pet that she acquired recently."

"I heard that!" she calls out angrily.

The young man shakily breathes in and out. Opening his eyes, he says, "I can do it. Without...assistance. Please give me a few moments to compose myself." He then asks, "Bob?"

"Short for beast of burden," answers the man. "She couldn't decide on a name, so I called him Bob. It kind of stuck."

"Hurry up! We are running out of time. The sun is setting. I've got to be in the clearing before the Horde gets there!" she yells.

"Hhhhhorde?" stammers the young man.

"Oh, you'll see. What a tale it will make!" says the man gleefully.

They both start to follow the path the woman makes through the cemetery. The bard stumbles a lot because he keeps closing his left eye. "It will go better and quicker if you keep both eyes open. You need the time to get used to it so that you can see your tale unfold. Otherwise, all will be for naught." So the young man keeps both eyes open, but is horrified at what he is seeing. Everything looks normal with the right eye as they walk through the mist that is rising from the cemetery grounds. But, with the left, he finds that it isn't mist they were walking through, but ghosts. He feels his hair stand up and sweat break out all over his body.

Ahead, on the western edge of the cemetery, is an empty space. This used to be the town's park where picnics were held every Sunday in the summer until the populace got squeamish about eating near dead bodies. On the other side of the space is a field. The last of the harvest had been pulled out of it earlier in the day. Meanwhile, the sun was almost set.

"This is close enough for you," the woman says harshly to the bard. "Are you coming?" she says to the man.

"Nah, I'll stay with the bard. Give my regards." He looks at the bard. "Ah, I see that you have adapted to your change in sight. Good. You won't be distracted by switching between eyes."

The woman harrumphs as she hurries over to the empty area. She marks the space with two torches that appear out of nowhere, just as two female figures are seen leaving the field. While the figures are close enough to see, they are too far away to hear what is being said. Both are beautiful, but one is younger and dressed in pale pink with her hair loose. The other is dressed in harvest gold and nicely coifed. As they approach the torches, it looks as if the older woman is pleading with the younger woman. She just shrugs and gives her elder a hug. Both greet the woman in black, who nods and steps aside.

Suddenly, the sun sets and light races away across the sky. The golden figure continues to plead with the younger, who just steps out of reach in response. As they face the west, sounds, terrifying sounds, can be heard coming closer from that direction. To distract himself from the noises, the bard studies the women. As he watches, the pink of the young woman's dress starts to run and darken until it is blood red in color. Her hair is no longer loose, but elegantly coifed and sporting a crown. At the same time, the other woman's dress turns black and her figure becomes stooped with despair. Her hair becomes disheveled and limp.

The bard realizes, however, that the howling and screaming noises are getting louder and closer. In the sky, he can see riders on steeds that defy description. All that he can make out is a jumble of bones, bat wings, hanging skin, and glowing eyes. Following the riders is a thick cloud that stretches for a long distance behind them. The closer they get the more details the bard can see. That cloud isn't a cloud, but is many individual shapes, ghosts like those that they walked through in the cemetery. They aren't following either, but being herded by the riders. The noise is the neighing of steeds, the shouts of the riders, and the wailing of the ghosts.

So that is the Horde, thinks the terrified bard.

The lead rider suddenly leaves the Horde in the sky. He rides down to the earth holding on to the reins of another steed. Landing, he slides off his steed. Quickly bowing to the stooped figure, the black armored rider pulls off his helm and embraces the woman in red, kissing her long and hard. He hands her onto the extra steed and jumps onto his own while donning his helm. Together, they leap into the sky. Behind them, the woman from the cemetery rides on something that his eyes refuse to comprehend. He concludes this must be Bob. The steeds return to the front of the Horde and continue on their path, toward the cemetery in which the bard is standing.

"What are they doing?!" he screams.

"They are hunting for the souls of those that have not returned to the underworld, whether because of fear, ignorance or reluctance. It's a wild ride," chuckles the other man. As the Horde passes over him, the bard thankfully loses consciousness — all the while wondering if he will wake up alive or as a ghost herded by the Horde.

[64]

"Of course you will live," the bard hears as he sinks to the ground. "After all, this is your tale to tell."

****

A man stumbles out of the town's old cemetery shortly after dawn. He is muttering about horrible alcohol-induced dreams. Shakily, he bends over the pond on the edge of town to rinse his face. He screams at what he sees in the still surface. His left eye is as white as the hair on his head.

From the shadows under the trees around the pond, he hears a chuckle. "You did say *anything*. Be glad it wasn't your life that you gave for your tale."

Yewberry

by Alison Leigh Lilly

N ow it is the end of autumn, I lay my body down.

A hush. The hill is still humming with the day's warmth, the sun sinking into the far shore of the lake. For a moment, I can see it, as though with other eyes, submerged, rippling beneath the waters in arcing liquid wings of flame and dusk, flexing, alternating, a thousand of them, wings sprouting from the round, warm body settling into the depths. Then the vision is gone.

I creep silently along the shore, my bare feet numb and rustling through the long, dried grasses of autumn. The mud is moist and rough on my soles, each step sending echoes of energy sliding up my calves. A thick cushion of warm air lingers among the brittle stalks as if radiating from deeper roots, from the earth itself, untouched by the cooling evening breeze that moves above, circling my knees and waist, wrapping my skirts around me. Already, I can feel the worlds sliding apart, the space between opening. This was a mild day, still, the kind that will come once or twice more before the snows take hold. Winter has a while yet before it's claimed everything, even the steep citadel of noon. But I can feel it coming. The sunlight is low and long against the horizon now, sinking, slipping away; nothing in my power can hold it, nothing will hold it any longer. My body tightens, muscles contracted, but I steady myself and walk on.

Soon, the place I am seeking comes into view across the peaceful, darkening waters: the stunted crabapple tree on the sloping shore of the small island. The lake gapes away on either side of this unremarkable jut of land, a pair of dragon's jaws poised open in perfect stillness. I turn my gaze upward for a moment, breathing deeply, calming myself to the very center of my being. Still, ripples of vibration run through me, escaping my sturdy sense of gravity. Passing over my skin in pulsing miniature bursts of light, the births of tiny stars that flare and die back into the quiet of my body. The sky rumples like a veil pushed up from the horizon in sensual folds of lazuli blues and smoky lavender, and beneath it night is climbing gently upwards. The tree, too, I can see, folds in on itself with age, slumping to brush the wild grasses with the tips of its old limbs. Most of the fruit has fallen, now, and its leaves are dry and stiff. The breeze brings with it the scent of faint, damp rot subtle within the smell of wet and chill.

I let my skirts fall, slipping the cotton blouse up over my head. A button snags on a strand of hair, tugging it free from the braid. I could be undressing for a lover; I feel my own body young and alive under my fingers, undoing each clasp, reaching, stretching to uncover myself. I shake myself loose, the clothes collapsed around my feet. For just a moment, wild fear jolts through every joint and muscle, my whole form going rigid and small under the heavy expanse of twilit sky. I am an animal again, naked and soft and pale, ears pressed flat and twitching, every limb tense. I would run, bolt from the sound of panting, that moment I can hear coming, but fear pins me as if to the air itself and I cannot move. I struggle and break, again and again, against the hot terror. I am shaking, shivering with sweat, and without even the presence of mind to move, suddenly I find myself stumbling. My knees hit spongy earth, the heels of my hands sinking beneath my weight into the bent grass, and I am leaning, wild and staring, over the edge of the water.

Almost as quickly as it began, the terror vanishes. Resolving and dissolving before me, the white face of my body looks up at me from the glassy surface of the lake, watching. Now is the time to do it, she whispers, now, when we are young and alive, when we are full of our own will and our own desire. We must do it, it must be now, tonight. I stumble again to my feet, rubbing my hands against my hips leaving smudges of earth along their curves. I am myself once more, composed and held delicately apart. The animal I am settles down inside me, hot and quivering.

Before entering the water, I search through the folds of discarded clothes, untying the small pouch from the cloth thong that had secured it. Then, I return to the shore.

The water, unlike the ground of hills that surround it, holds no lingering heat from the day. A decisive step and I am in, a shuddering gasp escaping my lips, my mind again threatening to loose itself and plunge upwards, fleeing like light and warmth and sun into the cold void of winter and open ceaseless night. I fight for control. Searching out the furry heat where it curls tightly in the dark recesses of my body. I wade through the biting pain, arms spread skyward and back arched, and then I am clambering up onto land again, the island solid beneath me, my chest heaving with hard breath, the corners of my mouth wet with sobs of involuntary tears. But I am through. The old crabapple tree looms over me, twisted and kind against the starscape, and I lie panting, ripped and rendered whole again in my own aching body.

****

For an hour, perhaps longer, I rest like this, unmoving. My eyes half-open, I watch my breast slowly rising and falling in lazy rhythm. The moon has risen, almost full, over the far hills in the east. Shadows like blue echoes move of their own accord, pass over the undulations of the earth and the flat, glistening surface of the lake that spreads out on all sides around me, studded with reflected stars. Beneath the crabapple tree, my body is growing numb and clumsy, one hand still clenched reflexively around the small pouch. No flint or matches, fire is impossible even if I wanted it, and there is now no way home, no way back to the safety and warmth on the opposite shore.

After a time, I pull myself up to lean against the trunk of the tree. The exposed skin stretched taut across my spine and shoulder blades rubs against the bark, but I am close to wandering now, and can barely feel the sensation. It must be now, and I am young, and I am so alive... Words stumble through my tiring mind without direction or sense. Undoing the pouch, I tug at the damp fabric, gently.

Inside, the berries are wet, full and bright; they seem to glow, radiating like perfect red embers in the darkness. One or two are smashed, their juice slick and sticky on the skin of the others and seeping through the fabric. I imagine, with that vertigo again of some other sense, that I can feel it warm and pooling in my open palm, that I can smell the vague metallic smell of blood.

I raise a berry to my lips and take it tenderly into the deep, warm cave of my mouth. I roll it with my tongue, breaking skin, sucking until I feel the flesh and juice sliding down my throat, cool and burning and stinging sweet. Then, when there is nothing left but the single, unbroken seed, I slip it out between my lips again and set it on a small stone nestled near me in the grass. I do this again, and again, slowly and carefully, until each new berry seems to break open with an unbearable softness, some scarlet slow-motion explosion that rocks my mind gently further and further from the moorings of my physical form.

When every berry is gone, and the ritual almost done, I reach for the seed-covered stone. With another rock, I grind the seeds until they are shattered and gritty, the meat of their insides exposed. They will not find my body in the morning. My clothes will lay crumpled on the far shore, ghostly pale and stiff with crystal frost. I press and grind the poisonous seeds, and lift the stone to my mouth. They will wonder, perhaps, where I have gone, but they will never find me. Now, it is at the end of autumn, I lay my body down. I run my tongue over the cold, rough stone. Fear and desire well up at once, almost overtaking my quickening heart except for the certainty, the calm knowledge: it is too late. The cold and the poison have already begun their work, have already taken hold. I feel my body slipping, sinking, my mind unwinding into the black dome of endless space. Nothing in my power can keep it now. I see myself, still and pale blue, naked in curves and passed over by the shadows of the shivering tree limbs. The worlds are parting, creaking with the sound of ancient wood, gliding farther as every breath comes more slowly, more shallow than the last, and my soul is reaching, stretching to uncover itself, sliding into the opening space between.

****

How could I say what happened then? That was another life, another being, darkness and wind and the beating of wings. There had been a need — that was why it was always done, really, this suicide, this little death — a need to put an end to the rules of things, to step out of skin, beyond the confines of gravity. There was, in me, a deep capacity to suffer, and no reason for it. Only the tense need to sink, to follow it down, until even obscurity and pain could have no more power over me than a stiff current of air. And I rode them, sacred winds, I rode them far to the horizon. Flattened, feathered and unfurled against the swift, unflinching line of time and season, I outflew need. It was long since I had forgotten how to desire.

Want, longing, anticipation were so long forgotten. I had followed my need down into a darkness where even need itself could not hold, but dissolved, guttering like a spent sun, and there I lingered, hovering, a white shadow blotting out the stars. Sometimes the memory of desire passed below me like a twisting ribbon of river through a shrunken landscape, but I was a spirit moving over the waters, pale mist claiming the darkness, ruling over the empty world. For how long? How could I know? What is time without desire to mark it? How could I say what existence then was like? To articulate death to the living, to carry the memory of it over. No, it is impossible to tell.

I remember a dream, only, a memory of memory. That's all. I moved through dream, through thrumming song, murmuring pain and wind that moved in groans and echoes, the familiarity of formlessness, the arbitrary descent into form, all this I glided on, singing. And the world could not hold me, could not grasp me or keep me still.

But then, there was a touch. Like a warm, slow breath. And I seemed to hear my name on the wind, the wind that had always been empty and utterly wild. Now, there was shape to it. Air that moved through the body of some new and unknown being, carved out of noise by throat, teeth, parted lips. There was voice, and the voice grasped and held. I snagged. My body stirred.

****

My body stirs, though I am yet far from it, watching. Pale and wasted, it seems at first only a jumble of bones, the limp corpse of a swan, long neck kinked, pinched off awkwardly between vertebrae, feathers scattered and bedraggled with reddish mud and rain. Wrinkled folds of white and shadow turn in on themselves, a figure smashed and stranded on the shore of the tiny island hunched low in the center of the lake.

Mist rises from the hard clear water, and barely a breeze disturbs the senseless form of my body where it lies. Someone sighs, exhales. One long pinion shifts under the movement of this warm, slow breath – uncomfortable and stiff, still embedded deep in my cold skin. I can feel it. I can feel it, pulling, twisting with every turn of the air, weightless and hollow like a needle sewn into my flesh. I can feel each one, my body punctuated by hundreds, my body, that soggy vulnerable thing crumpled beneath the twisted dark limbs of the old tree. Another sigh, long, unrelenting, and each quill responds again, piercing hot and sharp in a symphony of pain, all the way to muscle, to numbing bone. A rolling, clenching nausea ripples through me. I moan, my body moans, and we breathe ourselves startled and quick together in one sudden moment.

It is dawn, or just past, and the light presses everything flat and immediate, robbed of shadow, without depth or color. My eyes barely open, I search blearily the abstract images of morning as they close in around me; the tree branches above me, the clenched pink buds that clot along every twig against a background of low, gray clouds. Every part of me aches with cold, each toe, the arches of my feet, my calves sloppy with disuse, my hipbones peaking like mountain ridges, collapsing into the starved valley of my stomach. My fingers, my brittle wrists suspended at the ends of strange, thin arms, the weight of my own chest pressing down to meet my spine, my throat caved in and retching, rattling with breath. I am sick, sickened of myself, and anger rips through me hot and resentful, disgusted with form, raging to tear open the flimsy walls of my capillaries, the limpid membrane of each shivering cell. But even anger has a body now, and I am weak with it. Too weak to sustain disgust, to feed my own wretchedness. Heat soaks out of my body and into the ground, smelling of urine, as I slip back into the rocking dark of sleep.

****

I was mistaken. When I awake again, someone has brushed away the last vestige of snow and rotting layer of leaves I had drawn around me as a cloak of feathers in my delirium; someone has cleaned my limbs and face with cool handfuls of water from the lake, rubbed grime and frost away until the skin beneath is flushed and slightly raw. It occurs to me that, yes, after all I'm alive. I am alive.

My body is still unfamiliar, long and hard in the grass. I test my muscles, the utter ends of each nerve, clenching and relaxing, listening for the twitch of response. Sensation trickles and slides underneath my grayed translucent skin, dark serpentine waters wearing away at an encasing of ice. The world is full of the sound of melting, the pulsing, rhythmic falling and slipping of water into the ground. My throat cracks open like an egg and fluted notes escape, drop, catch a current of air and leave me breathless. Again, someone sighs, who isn't myself.

He crouches a few yards away, gazing out across the water. Delicate tongues of green reach up and uncurl around his firmly planted feet, new grass and the gathering liquid-pearl buds of snowdrops suspended heavy from the tips of their bent stems. He is worn and sleepless as though from long illness, but the sun is warm on his broad back and bowed head, burrowing long, light fingers into the hair along the nape of his pale neck. Even from here I seem to feel his blood rushing steadily through his veins, murmuring with a deep vitality.

At first I don't think he sees me, but then he turns. I do not move. Perhaps I still cannot. He comes slowly to lean over me, watching intently, his breath held in suspension, strung up and utterly vulnerable. Behind him, the mid-morning sun burns dense in a wet sky, pouring thickly over his shoulders, seeping into the wispy waves of his hair. Everything smells of verdant earth and the sweetness of blossoms. He brushes a few downy feathers away where they have sprouted again around my collarbone – but no, they are the round, silky petals of the old crabapple tree. He breathes out and they scatter easily from my skin. Will he do anything but exhale? His eyes circle a darkness, each iris pitted and blue, and though mine have been open, I close them again, as if to fool him, or coax him.

Still, I do not try to move. I wait. Shut against sunlight, I move my thoughts, wandering into each extremity of my awkward body, seeking my edges, liminal where they touch against the world. Then subtly, gradually, so that I hardly know their beginning, his fingers too are tracing my consciousness, breaking open each new nerve, sensation trickling into every corner of my frame as he ventures rough hands, warm and large and solid, along each cusp and cup of my body. I lead them, those quiet hands, with the waking of my mind, shuddering sometimes at their resistance and turning then to follow.

How long do we go on? They will say for an eternity, a brief moment. For a moment, his lips climb the pale slope of my neck the way a new sun swells and bursts suddenly above the hilltops, then his tongue circling the ruddy altars of my nipples in holy prayer, his mouth drinking in light like milk from my breasts and, through me, from the earth itself beneath us. They will call him a child, a young god, a lover. I fill with shining undulations cresting and spilling over in birdsong. Sunlight pools around us, rolling in giddy tides. He pushes my heart to beat, my lungs to work, he draws the blood down to every end of me, breathing hot on the animal sleeping in me, dark and soft with fur. They will say, when I slip back again into the space between worlds slipping open, he follows me down, cleaving them and clinging one to the other, bringing aching brightness, drawing everything together, pulling my body, breath, pulling us upward into life again.

They will say, for they will not find us resting where we lay, so this is spring.

Like Herding Cats
by Gerri Leen

Loki looked around the boardroom as the Council of Tricksters refused to take their seats. Chaos. This was utter, freaking chaos. Normally, he lived for chaos; it was his element. Trouble was, it was all these jokers' element, too.

He tried again. "We have a lot on the agenda. Carnivals, if you'll all remember." There was nothing any of them liked discussing better. And it was time to elect next year's patron saint of the Fun Fair – saint being a term so not appropriate in this case.

The gods still ignored him.

"Come to order, damn you, or I'm going to go get Thor's hammer." He waited.

And waited.

And waited.

Finally, he felt a nudge at his elbow. Eris looked up at him, her ugly little face twisting into what she probably thought was a winning smile. She held up her hand; a golden apple in it shone under the expensive track lighting.

"Let me?" she said, her voice cracking.

"Oh, all right."

She laughed and jumped onto the mahogany table with a grace that Coyote would have envied if he'd been paying attention instead of hitting on Kuku Lau and Laverna. Eris hurled the apple onto the table, and instead of turning into a big pile of applesauce, it went: BANG! And then it bounced up, still whole, and hovered over the table. Written on it in day-glow neon that lit up the gilded fruit like a Vegas marquis sign was: "For the sneakiest."

Loki smiled. He'd been worried about opening the Council up to the deity of discord, but so far she was working out. As Eris jumped off the table, the others clustered around, oohing and ahhing over the apple.

Eris winked at him. "Don't care what kind of gods they are, they fall for it every single time." Then she sat down, her assistance apparently at an end. That she'd helped at all was pretty amazing, since her mandate was to work against, not with, anyone. This many centuries into a gig, though, a person mellowed.

Loki clapped his hands. "Okay, take your seats, and let's start this meeting."

"Nice apple," Hermes said, faking a yawn as if once you'd seen one golden apple, you'd seen 'em all. But Loki could hear the wings on his sandals warming up.

"It is a nice apple. And it's not for you." Loki glared at him until he heard the wings shift into idle. Then he sat, checking his notes while the others fidgeted – no doubt thinking up sneaky ways to steal the apple right in front of him.

He saw movement out of the corner of his eye. Iktomi had changed into his spider shape and was moving across the table, heading for the apple. It would have been sneaky if he'd actually been spider size. But no one could miss the man-sized arachnid. The manic giggling wasn't helping in the stealth department, either.

"Brother, you are one whacked-out god." Coyote grabbed the nearest leg and hauled Iktomi back to his seat.

Loki sensed a movement overhead and said, "Raven, don't even think about it." The last time Raven had flown over, he'd shat upon Loki's head. Being adorned with Raven-doo was rumored to be good luck, but it had been awfully damned unpleasant wearing the stuff while trying to chair a board meeting. Especially when the board was made up of these yahoos.

Raven flew around him and landed on the back of a chair. Kitsune, who had taken the next seat, gave Raven the eye, her lush red tail swishing violently through the slit in her violet kimono. Even in her human form, she couldn't get rid of the tail. She licked her lips, her fox-sharp face becoming a little softer.

"Not in the mood, you," Raven mumbled, then looked away. But he kept looking back.

It was hard to say no to a fox-woman – Loki had never managed it, much to the irritation of Sigyn and Angrboda. His wife and mistress were used to sharing him with each other, but they really hated it when he took things outside the family. "So, any old business before we start?"

No one was paying attention to him, still. They were all studying the apple.

"Eris, if you don't mind."

"Sure, boss." She did something with her tongue and the tip of her nose – Loki looked away, but not fast enough to miss the red tip going into a nostril – and then the apple disappeared to a chorus of disappointed groans.

"Old business. Does anyone have any?"

"Yeah," Saci said, pounding his one leg with his misshapen hand. "Why do you always get to be in charge? We're all equals here, but I don't see us banging the gavel."

"I don't have a gavel." Loki held up his hands, showed that nothing was up his sleeves – he was willing to bet the trickster dwarf couldn't say as much. "See, no gavel."

"You know what he means," Kokopelli said, stopping his infernal flute playing long enough to spit the words out. Then he went back to playing; it was useless to ask him to stop. Besides, the alternative – him playing with that other long, tubular thing the tourist boards in the southwest had elected to excise from the official image of Kokopelli – was highly unsettling.

Kitsune batted her long, curvy eyelashes at Loki. "I think you're doing a wonderful job. Please continue."

Loki looked away quickly; he knew he couldn't resist her. Even if he had been the only one who could see through Balder's sweetness-and-light routine. Well, almost the only one – it had been his bad luck that the other one had been that stupid, freaking mistletoe. What a load of trouble friend mistletoe had gotten him into when it convinced him to take down Balder. And everyone blamed Loki, of course. No one thought to blame the foliage.

"Can we get on with this?" Tezcatlipoca asked. "I want to talk about the carnivals." He'd been campaigning heavily to be the next ruler of the funhouse. As the god of smoke and mirrors, he seemed a natural. But he frequently went a little too Aztec when he was in charge. People tended to frown on heart-removing rituals in the middle of the midway, even if the special effects accompanying the carnage were first rate.

"Okay, carnivals." Loki pulled out the report Hermes had pulled together. The man was a whiz on the computer. Then again, the king of spam and spyware ought to be good with the tech. "Bad news. Injuries are down. Way down."

There was an assortment of excuses and promises to do better.

"On the other hand, we've got serious upward mobility in the inflatables injury." He winked at Legba, who smiled, his teeth gleaming from his wrinkled black face, like the moon on a bayou night. It was the smile that caused trouble, that loosed loas and made a voodoo party sing. Loki was suddenly nostalgic for the wild times they'd had in the French Quarter. "Snaps to my old friend for unleashing the idea of private rentals of the Moonwalk on the general populace. Little Johnny's birthday party hasn't been so lethal since the invention of the slip-and-slide."

"That was mine," Coyote said, grinning and thrusting his muzzle in the air to give a howl of victory.

"The trampoline still beats them all," Saci said, glaring at Loki.

"Yes, yes, it was great." Loki felt, as he always did, a surge of competition with the Brazilian. "But we're talking carnivals, not backyard fun."

"You were, too, talking backyard fun. You commended Legba on transitioning the moonwalk from the midway to the lawn. Maybe we should think of taking the trampoline from the backyard to the carnival?" Saci looked around the room, smiling at the nods he got. He was also campaigning heavily for king of the carnies, and since a certain cable network had made it fashionable for the vertically challenged to run freak shows, Loki's nemesis actually stood a chance of winning the vote.

"There's more to carnivals than death and maiming, you know." Laverna smoothed her toga. "The days of con games on the midway are over. People sit at home with their little boxes full of horror and mayhem. They have their own coliseums. What do they want with a beanbag thrown at a weighted-down milk bottle?"

Nobody paid her much attention. She'd been bitching about the demise of the festival scam since the fall of Rome. But her con men had slunk to the edges of the empire, ensuring that even if her beloved empire had foundered, the confidence game would go on.

"We need to reinstate the shell game," Kuku Lau said.

"With real shells, no doubt?" Coyote, who'd apparently struck out with the Polynesian beauty, gave her his *you'd never survive in the desert* look.

Kuku Lau returned the favor with her *I swim with sharks, what do you do?* look.

"Ooh, here's a nice factoid." Loki held up a graph. "Crime's up in the amusement parks."

"Thank me for that," Coyote said. "I've got a system. And Hermes has been consulting."

"How did you find the time to break away from all your cyber crime?" Loki was still a little sore that Hermes' identity theft plan had taken off the way it had.

Hermes just looked smug – he always knew the value of the restrained comeback. There was a reason he was the messenger of the gods besides the goofy sandals.

"Midway crime is up, too." Loki didn't let them celebrate. "But attendance overall is down."

Nods from around the table.

"We need to find a way to reinvigorate the lowly carnival," Laverna said. "We need to give it more...respectability."

"That's the problem," Legba said. "We did that and called them amusement parks. No hucksters. No freak shows. No outdoor pisspots."

"Now we have theme parks, and clean, pretty spaces, and lots of sparkling white tile in the bathrooms." Kuku Lau looked like she was about to gear up for a speech – Loki suspected she was hoping for the write-in vote – but Kitsune broke in.

"What we need" – she looked over at Hermes, winking and making him blush – "are carnivals on the internet."

Everyone looked at her.

"Somewhere fun. Where people can wander innocently while we fleece the hell out of them." She blinked coyly, her hand to her mouth as she giggled. But her tail was lashing.

"I love that idea," Kokopelli said between notes.

"Me, too," Raven said, grinning at the fox-woman. "In fact, I'd say that's such a great idea that Kitsune should be in charge of carnivals."

"Do I hear a second?" Hermes asked, shooting Loki a triumphant glance, as if he was getting one over on him.

"Second," Loki said, smiling innocently.

Hermes frowned.

"Now wait just a damned minute," Saci said, jumping up and hopping on his one leg, his tanned face turning roughly the shade of his red cap. "There are others in contention this year."

"Motion on the floor," Kitsune said with her *butter wouldn't melt in my mouth* expression still plastered on. She glanced over at Loki, her eyes assessing him – would he support her?

She wasn't his arch rival; that was to the good. And she wasn't likely to build pyramids to the sun, cut out living organs from the fair goers, or call down serpent gods. And she had the sexy thing working for her big time. Loki slowly nodded: yes, he'd support her.

She leaned back in her chair, a satisfied smile on her face. "Time for a vote."

Tezcatlipoca looked flummoxed. "But –"

"All in favor raise your hand or paw – or whatever works," Raven said.

A round of appendages came up. Loki coughed, and Iktomi put down the extra legs he'd raised.

Loki did a quick count: the foxy tart had won. "And the new queen of the –"

"I protest!" Saci leapt to the top of the table – pretty impressive for a one-legged dwarf – and began to sputter out a whole lot of profanity in Portuguese.

"Loki, this is your doing! Every year something happens to keep us from our true place." Tezcatlipoca brandished his ceremonial dagger, encrusted with fire opals and gold leaf. Loki knew from experience the thing hurt like hell going in and didn't feel much better when Tezcatlipoca yanked it back out again.

Kitsune winked at Loki and slid her chair back, probably to get out of range of Tezcatlipoca's blade and Saci's spittle.

Loki looked from one angry loser to the other. For once, this hadn't been his doing. But no one was ever going to believe him — just ask the freaking mistletoe how easy it was to duck blame when good old Loki was around.

"Should I...?" Eris gave him a grin that was starting to look more and more winning. She held the apple under the table between them, where only he could see it. Her voice, still all crackly, dropped another notch, as she said, "I'd hate to see you hurt just because they don't like how the vote went."

"Me, too." He watched as more of the gods readied their magic or their weapons or some combination of both. This was about to get out of hand. He stood up. "Well, the decision's made. I'll see you all next month."

They reacted as he expected. All eyes turned to him. And most of the eyes weren't very happy.

"Remember that apple? It's for whoever can catch it." He nodded to Eris, and she flung it far over their heads.

The apple hit the ceiling, and the plaster transformed into the night sky. Then the darkness was pierced by the glare of a thousand neon lights. The Vegas strip. Oh, how he loved it there.

"Nice choice, sweetheart."

She preened. It was, for the most part, not a good look on her.

The gods took off after the apple. All except Kitsune, who gave him a strange look.

"What? I supported you."

"Will you support me when I'm running for your position?" With a flick of her tail, she transformed into a fox, and dashed after the others.

Loki took a deep breath.

"She's dangerous," Eris said, rubbing his arm in what, he had to admit, was a mighty sensual way.

"Yes."

"I have friends. They have friends. Not all of them like foxes."

He glared at her. "Is one of them called mistletoe?"

"No."

"Then maybe we should talk."

"I think we should do more than that." She was looking prettier and prettier. It must be true what they said: personality — and the ability to clear up what could become a rather large problem — did make a person more attractive.

Eris led him from the room, out into the Vegas night. The gods were running here and there, causing general havoc wherever they went as they chased after the golden apple, which seemed in no great hurry to be caught as it zinged hither and yon.

"It's not even real gold," Eris murmured. "It's not even a real apple."

"I know." Loki watched them for a moment, then he took her arm and led her toward his favorite casino – he was in the mood to mess with the odds at the craps table. "But they fall for it every, stinking time."

[Note: Previously published in Renard's Menagerie *#3, July 2007.]*

Unlock

by Ashley Horn

An hour had passed, and still I stared at an empty screen. "Be fulfilled; write for your Gods!" the ad said. And I couldn't manage even a sentence in Their honor.

I dropped my head onto the desk and closed my eyes, the headache that had been haunting me for the last two days pounding in my temples. What kind of writer was I that a short story overwhelmed me, and what kind of priestess that a small devotion of my time was too taxing?

"Lindsay?" My roommate Stephanie poked her head into my room. "How're you doing?"

"Not good," I told her honestly. I waved weakly at the computer as she walked closer. "I've got nothing."

She patted my shoulder. "You've still got a week or two. Don't worry about it; you'll think of something. Have you tried meditating?"

"Not yet, but that might help." I picked up my head off the desk, took a drink of my tea, and pulled up my meditation playlist. "Thanks."

"No problem." She smiled, a little dimly, and leaned on the corner of my desk. "If you could keep it down, though? I've been dragging all week, and I think I'm getting sick again. I'm going to get some sleep."

I stood and gave her a hug. "No problem, Steph. Sleep well, okay?"

She nodded and left, closing the door behind her. I turned my music down so that only I could hear it, pulled my yoga mat out of the closet, and unrolled it on the narrow strip of floor between my bed and my desk. It kept trying to roll back up on me — what I get, I suppose, for resolving to keep up with it every day and then not touching it for three months — so I weighted one end with my pillow and the other with a rolled blanket to prop my feet on. Then I turned out the lights, lay down, and closed my eyes.

I waited. The music played, with its light flutes and piano and rainstick. Or maybe it was a sistrum. I could never tell. Maybe I should have put on one of the nature soundtracks. Nah; they tended to grate after a while. Or maybe music in general was a bad idea, since my headache only seemed to be getting worse.

I waited, and, did I remember to lock the front door? Maybe I did? I really ought to go check, or, no, Stephanie probably had when she went to bed. She usually did.

Then my foot began to itch, and then I had to sneeze, and then the music started in the dorm next door.

"Gods," I muttered to the ceiling, beating the back of my head against the pillow, "why can't I concentrate on anything…" I settled myself on the mat again. Getting frustrated wouldn't help me.

One, I pulled in a long, slow breath; two, I pushed it out, trying to eject my headache with it. One, in, and I saw in my mind the familiar swirls of lavender energy rushing into my body to soothe me. Two, I pushed the energy down into my toes, felt them go lax and begin to glow. Three, I let the breath out again, just as slowly, along with the inky black tendrils of my headache. Four, I rested.

One, in; two, feet; three, out; four, rest. The pain slowly receded, leaving behind it a cool, clean openness that I filled with my light. One, in; two, ankles; three, out; four, rest, I breathed, until all of me glowed and I lay completely relaxed.

Unlock.

The word pealed through me like the chime of a crystal bell, and my eyes shot open. A fog of brilliant Nile blue billowed around me, bright against my dark ceiling.

I tried to cry out, to roll, but my body lay unresponsive, heavy under the new energy. *What are you doing?* I screamed in my head. *What's going on?*

Saving you, the resonance intoned, and then, again, *Unlock.*

I struggled against the cool presence, but my body didn't listen to the orders my mind screamed. The weight settled into me with my breath and spread through my body, filled it until I was pushed out. I landed beside myself, lightly as a wisp of smoke.

"What just happened?" This time, the words came out easily. "What did you do? What are you?"

I watched as my body sat, turned to me, and considered me for a silent moment. Then I met my own eyes, and a jolt coursed through me. The eyes in my face were as warm and black as the night sky on a moonless night, and in my heart they felt as far-seeing as time itself.

"I am He That is Thrice Great."

I saw my mouth move, heard the words uttered in my voice, but it felt much bigger, ringing in my soul as it had before. The being in my body considered me, wordless, for a moment more.

"I have much to do and little time. Walk with Me; you will serve as My vessel," He said, then pushed to our feet. We picked up a red feather from the altar on my dresser, an assembly of garage sale goods that reminded me of my Gods. I scrambled to follow us as we opened the door and stepped out into the dark central room, a protest on my lips.

"We haven't the time," He told me, and began gathering materials from the makeshift kitchen Stephanie and I had set up on milk crates next to the window. "I will answer your questions once My task is completed, if we work quickly enough to allow it."

We gathered a bowl of water, and added salt and rosemary to it.

When we were satisfied with the mixture, we turned to me. "Remember how this was made," He said in the voice that wasn't quite mine, "you will need to know it again someday."

We then dipped the stalk of the feather into the water and began to write, or maybe to draw, on the wall. The shapes like feathers, people, and animals glowed in the same deep water blue as the energy around us, and pulsed like a heartbeat. We continued for what felt like hours, writing around the walls, doors, and windows until every surface of my dorm bore our shining, pulsing symbols.

"And now your roommate," He said, and I threw my insubstantial self in our way.

"She's sick!" I told us. "You can write on whatever you want, but leave her alone!"

We dipped the feather in the water again, walked through me, and opened Stephanie's bedroom door. "As I said, I am saving you, with or without your consent." We ducked inside, and I followed.

"Linds?" Stephanie's eyes flickered open, and she raised her head, looked back and forth between the bowl in our hands and the soft, strange expression on our face.

"Sleep," He said, and, without another word, Stephanie laid her head back down on the pillow and fell asleep again.

"How…" I began, but we shushed me and stepped up closer to the bed.

"Look," He said.

Stephanie lay in bed, the covers pulled up to her ears — she usually slept in a sports bra and shorts — and her CD player clicking softly because it had run out of tracks to play. Seeing her without the constraints of my physical eyes, she looked paler. She oozed a dull yellowgreen light that pooled around her and seeped into the rest of the room. I must have been staring, because I didn't realize that I'd come up beside us until He spoke.

"In a day, maybe a little more, this poison would have leeched into you," He said, flicking droplets of water at the area around Stephanie. The sickly glow faded and receded, and we continued chasing it with the water until it withdrew into her skin. "Then you would both have died. Sit there with her while I make this room protected."

I knelt by the bed and passed my incorporeal fingers over her face; she didn't even flinch. "What's wrong with her?"

We were already scribing over the inside of the closet door, but we peered out at me. "Stress. It's a common problem, usually simple to treat, but hers has compounded into feelings of worthlessness, and eventually it would have become depression, and then....You've already begun to catch it. Hence the intervention."

We returned to writing the glowing blue hieroglyphs around the room, and I to keeping Stephanie company in her eerily still sleep. Had she always looked so tired, and when had she gotten so stressed that it started to get to her? Hadn't we, just a week ago, traded stories to read, and hadn't I told her that I thought her work was amazing?

When we'd finished covering the room, we came to my side, dipped the feather into the water again, and gently pulled the covers off of her.

"You can't do that," I told us, and tried ineffectually to put the blankets back; we smacked my hands away and I actually felt the sting.

"I have no desire for either of you to die; move aside."

We glared at me so intently with those deep black eyes that I backed away, and we rolled Stephanie, unstirring, onto her back.

"In an ordinary situation, this would be painful, but I've anesthetized her." He told me, and we began to draw the thin, glowing blue lines onto Stephanie's skin.

We wrote up her arms, down her legs, palms and soles and forehead and stomach. Then we rolled her over again, and covered still more of her. The process took longer than the entire rest of the dorm and, as we worked, the pallor of her skin darkened, becoming closer to her natural coloring. Then we stepped back, surveyed our work, and nodded.

"It will take more than My handiwork alone, and the process will be slow. She'll need you, but she should recover." We then turned the feather around and began to write upon our self. "And so should you."

"I ...." I shook my head and watched as we wrote on my body. On the back of my hands and upon my forehead and chest, there glowed a hieroglyph like a long-beaked bird, a series of lines, and a seated man. "Thank you."

"You're welcome," He said, and we pulled me into an embrace. "Write in My name."

And then my world went black.

I woke in the late afternoon, back in my own bed. On my altar, I found the water bowl and feather, and on my computer screen there was a single word on my program screen.

Unlock.

Aunty Zee

by Diotima Sophia

The drums – the three drums – carried their rhythms out into the night. To most, it would be a vaguely discordant music, perhaps reminding them of an old TV show. To some, yet more evidence of *what our society was coming to?* To some few – an increasing or decreasing number? She was never sure....to some, the drums would spell out a clear message. Of that select few some would follow the sound, and join. Some – perhaps the wiser? – would go inside, bolt the doors, and take precautions that would only be effective against one who chose to let them be so. The thought of all these different groups – these different reactions to an essentially primal sound – amused her. She knew it would amuse him.

But then, so many things did that: amuse him.

They'd been preparing for days. The preparations were careful and costly – stinting to save a penny could cost more than one might be willing to pay.

Herbal infusions had been steeped. Pots had been cleaned and signed. Flour decorated the bare ground in intricate patterns – that last had taken the most time, as she'd insisted the verve be just so, exactly right. The newer members' attempts simply were not good enough. Not for this, not tonight.

In exasperation, she'd given the flour to the old, old woman who had been with her for so long. Muttering the time honoured, "You just can't get the help", she'd asked the aged hunsi, creaking with arthritis, to do this one service for her.

Zennina had looked at her – that hard, piercing stare going right through – and bent to the work without discussion.

Not without a word, of course – this was Aunty Z, after all. Every movement was accompanied by some comment, some proverb, some bit of advice. As she passed by, tying her hair up in the expected white kerchief, the old woman looked up at her and murmured, "pig as muma...."

Well, she didn't really need telling that what she was planning wasn't wise – but she also doubted that her decision was down to her (relative) youth. Though it could be one reason she'd get away with it. If she did. She realised, however, that as usual, Aunty Z had a pretty good idea of what she was thinking.

Finally, it was time. The drums beat. People danced, some of their own accord, some to the music of the drums, some tipsy with the presence of the loa.

Legba had been saluted and welcomed, as was fitting. The night took on a certain formulaic cast. The second eldest of the women led the rituals, intoned the songs in English, in Spanish, in language. The assembled group answered her, some with conviction, some with fear, and some just learning the words, not yet feeling them.

The words....

They danced around the carefully erected tent – just poles hung with sheets, but she'd been insistent, so there it was. All eyes strayed to the tent at some point – no one knew what she was planning but they assumed it would happen there, behind the sheets.

And indeed, at the height of the clamour, she slipped into the tent.

Only Zennina was sharp enough to see her slip out again, into the trees behind the tent – but Aunty Z had been expecting something of the kind. After all, how was this sort of thing ever straightforward?

Well, the girlchild was her own foolish self. Zennina did her best to keep the others occupied. Her best was quite good enough.

And no one but Zennina noticed when she rejoined the company. The others would swear that she'd been there all night.

Eventually, dawn arrived, silencing the drums. The tent was taken down by the exhausted dancers. The pots presented to the directions and carefully stowed for the journey back to the city. The designs on the ground were already scuffed. Now they were deliberately obliterated – some invitations work best with a "limited time offer," as the ads say.

Bead necklaces, so proudly worn during the night, disappeared under conventional clothes. Soon all that was left of the evening's proceedings was a churned up piece of waste ground, between the copse and the car park.

And her car.

She'd stayed, of course, to see everything done properly. Partially this was her responsibility, partially it was simple common sense. Rumours they could withstand, but even in this pseudo-tolerant age, some things would not be easily overlooked by the neighbours. Or the press. Or the ASPCA, come to that.

She wasn't alone. Zennina waited by the car.

"Grandmother" (the title was honorific, not familial), "you should be long gone – home, asleep".

"Humph!" No one – ever, in creation – could put as much information into a single syllable as Zennina could. That exclamation told the listener: *I'm tired, I'm cold, I'm too old for this*, and not by any means least, *You're a fool, girl!* All these meanings and more she understood, but acted only on the one which meant, *Open this car now, miss!*

The drive back wasn't long, but it was silent. Very silent. A deliberate silence, you might say, formed not by a lack of talking but by a dearth of words where words might have been.

Eventually, she stopped and bought coffee for both of them, hot, sweet and strong. As they sat sipping, the old woman finally broke, and spoke.

But instead of the questions she'd been preparing for – what had she done, why had she done it, what did she hope to gain – and the diatribe listing the reasons she was incredibly foolish, Zennina surprised her yet again.

"You's a fool, girl, for all you're clever. But… him hog, him wash."

To say she was startled was an understatement. Her coffee spilled all over the dashboard and narrowly missed her skirt. She'd expected reproaches, not to be praised for seizing an opportunity!

"You think Aunty Z not see? Girl, I see and I know….And I been seeing for a month. More. 'That girl', they say, 'how good she visit family passed on – she take flowers e'ry day.' But you got no one passed on here" – and pointed.

She hadn't realised that she'd parked across the street from the cemetery – and Aunty Z smiled to see her realisation.

"And I not asking what you want. I don' want to know. I do know," Zennina said, turning to her, "what you did, girl. That's dangerous – but you always was headstrong." The old woman reached out, and turned the younger woman's face this way and that. "And pretty, I'll give you that. But I do got one question, girl."

Bewildered by this entire conversation – all her prepared defences useless, as she'd expected to have to explain and justify something Zennina apparently not only understood but did not disapprove of – she nodded.

She'd answer.

"What you take with you, when you go? Y'had something in your hand going, and not coming back. What you take?"

The stare was now intense. Even if she'd wanted to, she'd not have dared to lie.

"Pigfoot. I took a pig's foot."

Aunty Z stared at her.

The stare lengthened.

Then the old woman's laughter split the tension in the car, and carried out to the morning rush hour. She laughed till she cried.

"Oh girl, yes, you clever. And you came back intack."

She nodded.

Zennina smiled. "You learned well. Him Baron, he take wid him what he hold, when he leave."

Aunty Z squeezed her hand, her whole, intact, warm, firm hand, and said, "Take me home, child. I'm old and need sleep. Ain't you got not respect for y'elders?"

But all the way home, and all the way up the stairs, she chuckled gently.

"Him Baron – he got trouble now."

Godwin's Law

by Jason Ross Inczauskis

I looked at the assembled group of people. It was a decent turn out, better than I'd expected, if not as great as I would have hoped. In total, there were ten of us present, which was actually pretty impressive given the short notice that had been given. There were even a couple faces there that I'd never seen before. The sign-in sheet was passed around so that everyone could put their contact information down. Once it had returned to me, I rose from my chair with a smile.

"Hello, everyone," I said. "Welcome to the very first meeting for this chapter of Pagans For Peace. I would like to thank you all for coming. Now, to get things started, why don't we all go around and introduce ourselves. Just tell everyone the name you want to be called, a little bit about yourself, and maybe a bit about your own spiritual path." Everyone seemed okay with that idea, so I decided to start. "For those of you who don't know me, my name is Jonah Doveheart." Of course, Doveheart wasn't my real name, but it was the one that I had chosen to use. "I work at the organic food store over on State Street. In my free time, I support various charities and causes. As far as my spiritual path goes, I have dedicated myself to the Goddess Aphrodite, because I know that only through Love can a good future be found."

I sat back down to allow the others to do the same. Most of them weren't telling me anything I hadn't heard before. My best friend Carl was a college student who fancied himself a shaman, though I'd personally say that he's more of a stoner that sees indulging in his favorite plant as a spiritual calling. My girlfriend, Silvermoon, was a vegan, a Wiccan, and a volunteer at the local animal shelter. The Twins, Cheryl and Jade, weren't really twins, or even related for that matter, but everyone considered them such anyway, mainly due to their tendency to dress alike and finish each other's sentences. Both of them were devoted heavily to Isis. Gloom was an androgynous individual that favored the goth look, as well as anything involving magic or Hekate. In the year I'd known them, I never did have the guts to ask whether they were a boy or a girl, and I didn't expect that to change any time soon. Teresa ran the New Age store where we were holding the meeting, and was focused on the Celtic pantheon. Her husband, Richard, worshipped the Norse God Baldur, though he was quick to explain to the newcomers that not everyone who worshipped the Norse Gods was a racist. He needn't have worried too much about that stereotype, though, as it turned out that one of the new guys, Walter, already worshipped them. It was the last new face's introduction that started the trouble.

"Hi," the young man said, standing up. "It's really nice to meet you all, and I'm really excited to be here. My name is Michael Ward. I'm still deciding what I want to do with my life, so I haven't declared a career yet. I did just get back from four years overseas with Army, though, and I'm still thinking about reenlisting. As far as my spiritual path goes, I'm still kind of figuring it out, but I am firmly dedicated to the Great God Ares, and have been for about six years now."

I don't think he could have gotten a more shocked silence from us if he'd suddenly grown an extra head. Only Walter and Richard seemed completely unfazed by his announcement, and quickly moved to shake his hand and welcome him. Walter was amazed to be meeting someone who dedicated himself to that God, and Richard just always seemed to be perpetually unfazed by the things that happened around him.

I was amazed myself, but not in a good way. "Ares?! You worship Ares?!" I practically shouted.

"Yeah," Michael said, leaning away from me a bit, clearly feeling uncomfortable now. "What's wrong with that?"

"Ares goes against everything Pagans For Peace is supposed to stand for! Ares is a God of War, for Christ's sake!" By this point, I was shouting.

Teresa shook her head, then quickly excused herself to go and busy herself in the shop.

"Calm down, honey," Silvermoon said quietly, laying one hand on my shoulder. "You're getting all worked up."

"I know I'm getting worked up, but I've got every right to, don't I? I mean, the group is called Pagans For Peace, not Pagans For Slaughter." Silvermoon sat back down with narrowed eyes, and I knew that I'd have to apologize for taking that tone with her later.

"You don't know a damned thing about Ares," Michael said in a calm voice that didn't match the obvious anger on his face. "I want peace just as much as you do. Maybe even more."

"Yeah, that a fact?" I asked, my volume lower, but my tone no better. "The only peace Ares offers is the peace of the grave! He's a monster! He's the God of Hitler!"

"Don't say things you can't take back," Richard said quietly, though I didn't pay any attention to his words or his disapproving tone.

"Ares is not a monster, and he sure as hell isn't Hitler!" Michael exclaimed. "He is a vital force in this world. You think he's evil, but he's not!"

"Of course you'd say that," I said. "You were a soldier. He condones all the slaughtering, raping, death and destruction that you and your Army buddies were enjoying every day overseas. Of course you'd try to defend him. He's a God that lets you do whatever the hell you want to do, to whoever you want to do it to. But that's just not something I can tolerate."

"That's not the way it is!" Michael said, his anger clearly growing with each word that I said. "I was serving my country. You think war is fun? It's not. War is hell! It is a horrible, miserable experience that you couldn't even begin to understand. I'm not a monster, and neither is Ares. I'd thank you to stop accusing us of it."

The Twins quietly got up, and headed towards the door. "We're just going to go," Jade said quietly. Cheryl picked up where she left off. "There's clearly some issues that need to be worked out here." I barely registered this, though, as I was too focused on my argument.

"Come on, Jonah, leave the guy alone," Walter said. "Nobody's slamming your choice of Gods, why do you need to slam his?" I wasn't really paying attention to him, either, though, and his words went unheeded.

"What's to accuse? You've admitted to it. We all know what war is like, and we all know the kind of people that choose to go to war. You can't defend it by saying you're just serving your country. A country worthy of service wouldn't need soldiers. You're right about one thing, though. Ares isn't Hitler. He's worse than Hitler. He's the one that creates people like Hitler, who thirst only for blood and war. And he's the one that takes people like you and turns them into Nazi terrorists. People like you that get off on slaughter, torture, and pain."

Michael jumped to his feet, his fists clenched. He'd half lunged towards me, and I suspected that he was about to punch me. I decided I'd let him. It would just prove my point. He stood there, trembling with rage, but closed his eyes, and didn't swing. Maybe he was worried I'd press charges against him, and was trying to count to ten in order to keep from hitting me.

"Dude, Godwin's Law!" Carl shouted into the midst of us, leaping to his feet.

"That's a stupid internet thing, Carl," I said. "It has no bearing in real life." Carl practically lived on the internet when he wasn't stoned, and was always bringing up various memes that he encountered.

"No, it clearly applies here. You brought up the Nazis, just as predicted with Godwin's Law, which clearly states that inevitably all arguments will eventually devolve to the point that references to Hitler or the Nazis will be used." Carl spoke of it as though he were a lawyer arguing an actual law rather than an internet meme. "That means argument over, and you compared him to them, which, I might add, also means you lose the argument." At the time, I had no idea that that Carl was right. I felt like I was triumphing over Michael. I felt like I was winning a battle for peace. I didn't know how wrong I was.

"Shut up, Carl! I'm comparing him to the Nazis because he's like a Nazi!" Carl put his hands up, shook his head and sat back down. He was never the most confrontational being.

"Jonah, you're overreacting," Richard said. "Why don't we all just calm down and talk about this rationally?"

"Because he's polluting the group, Richard," I said. "Pagans For Peace has no place for warmongers among its ranks. His hatred is ruining everything we stand for."

"I'm not the one being hateful," Michael said quietly, apparently much calmer now as he opened his eyes. His hands were no longer clenched into fists.

"You are hateful by your very nature," I replied. "Don't expect us to give you a medal just because you actually managed to go a whole five minutes without killing someone."

"You know what, fuck this shit," he said, shaking his head. "I don't need to stand here and take abuse from you with a smile on my face. If I want that, I'll go to the good Reverend's house. I'm out of here." With that, he stood up and left. I wouldn't even say he stormed out. He seemed hurt, but completely at ease as he left.

"Wow," I said, chuckling nervously. "Well, that was unexpected. Now, shall we get back to business?"

"I think the meeting is over, Jonah," Richard said. Walter nodded in agreement. Silvermoon wouldn't even meet my gaze.

"Okay," I said. "I guess that's fair. We'll try to get things on track next week."

The others got up, and prepared to leave. Walter glared at me, Silvermoon still wouldn't look at me, and Gloom just chuckled as they walked towards me.

"Good meeting," Gloom said. "I haven't been that entertained in quite a while." I couldn't tell whether they were being sarcastic or not. They shook my hand, then departed quickly.

"Dude, you really need to take some of my medicine," Carl said. "It'd do you a world of good." He turned to go himself.

"You know, Carl, that only counts as medicine when you've got a prescription for it!" I called after him. He didn't laugh, though, or even look back.

"Can I have a word with you?" Richard asked quietly, standing right behind me.

"Sure," I said, as I waited for the others to leave.

When they had, he sat back down in his seat, then gestured to one of the others. I shrugged, then sat down across from him.

"Jonah," he said, after thinking of his words for a few moments. "If you're going to try running a group, you need to learn a little more tact when you disagree with someone's choices. Do you understand?"

"I've got tact, Richard," I said.

"I didn't see it tonight. You also need to learn some consistency. If you're going to call your group Pagans For Peace, then you've got to give everyone a chance, at the very least. You didn't even let Michael explain himself. You just went off on him. For no reason."

"No, Richard, I had a damned good reason. We're supposed to be a group honoring peace. How can we do that if we've got someone worshipping war in our group? He was a source of corruption in the group waiting to happen. I just acted before it became a problem."

"It became a problem, Jonah. Half the group walked out tonight because of your argument, and you were the only one that seemed to have a huge problem with him. You should have given him a chance. Maybe gotten to know him a bit better."

"I know him. I know everyone like him. Soldiers aren't good people. If they were, they wouldn't be soldiers."

"Well," Richard said, more clearly irritated than I'd ever seen him in the entire time I'd known him. "I see you know all about it, and don't need someone like me to tell you about it. Why don't you go on home now?"

"Look, Richard...." I began, but he interrupted me before I could finish.

"Go home, Jonah. And by the way, about twelve years ago, I was a soldier, too. Think about that." With that said, Richard walked out of the room to go and help Teresa with the shop.

I was shocked. You think you know a person, but I guess there's always more there than you realize. Still, I figured he was right about it being time to go home, so I left as quickly as I could so as not to disturb them any further. I was kicking myself the whole way home. The irony of the first meeting of Pagans For Peace being more or less cancelled on account of fighting was not lost on me. I was thinking that I should have just asked Michael to leave politely, rather than having argued with him. That would have been better, and more fitting with the vision of the group. My friends probably wouldn't have been angry with me, either.

I got back to my little apartment, and tossed a frozen cheese pizza into the oven. I quickly took a shower to help calm myself down. I didn't soak much, as I always tried to watch my water usage to avoid wasting any, but it still helped to calm me down a bit. I was out well before the pizza was done cooking, and had plenty of time to pour myself a drink and go to talk to my statue. It might seem a little silly, but I do that on a fairly regular basis. I walked into my living room, then stood before the altar I'd made for

Aphrodite. The altar was large, but mostly bare. There were always fresh flowers on it, and there was an offering bowl that frequently needed to be cleaned, and a few shells that I'd acquired over time. In the center of the altar was a white resin statue of the Goddess with gold leaf highlights, and it was this statue that I used as a focus for my attentions when I was trying to talk to her.

"Well, tonight I screwed up," I said to the statue. "I let my anger get the best of me. I really shouldn't have, but he was a follower of Ares, and it just pushed my buttons to have someone worshipping the enemy coming to the meeting. Still, I could have handled it a bit better, and asked him to leave without making a scene of it. I hope you can forgive me, for not using a more loving approach to get rid of him."

The statue didn't answer, of course, but I didn't really expect it to do so. I just felt a bit better getting it off my chest. When the oven chimed, I went to get my pizza, then came back and clicked on the Discovery Channel to watch a nature documentary while I ate. Tonight's show was looking at the endangered piping plover, and I chuckled a bit while watching the little bird running back and forth with the tide. The next show was about the conservation efforts to save the panda, which is usually a subject I find quite interesting, but tonight I dozed off in the chair while watching it.

When I opened my eyes again, I could hear the sounds of cheering coming from the television. I looked to the screen, and saw that apparently a war documentary had come on. The scenes were flashing between stock footage of war scenes and the speeches of world leaders, including Hitler. Of course, there were speeches from other leaders, ones that even I'd consider the "good guys" in comparison to him. Still, I had no interest in watching a war documentary, so I hit the power button on the remote. When that didn't work, I cursed the batteries, then stood up and went to hit the power button on the television itself. The parade of black and white tanks currently on the screen didn't vanish. By this point, I was beginning to feel nervous, and it went from there to outright fear as I pulled the plug without any apparent effect on the images on the screen.

"What the hell is going on here?" I asked, backing nervously away from the set. My retreat was abruptly cut off as I backed into something warm, solid, and far larger than me. The scent of sweat and metal washed over me. A shiver ran up my spine as I spun around to see what was behind me.

"Hi," said a very large dark haired man dressed in Ancient Greek armor. His eyes, the color of bronze flecked with red, somehow managed to seem kind and cold at the same time. He smiled at me with gleaming white teeth from beneath his helmet. Then he hit me.

Okay, hit might have been an understatement. That word implies that he punched me, and maybe I would have staggered back a bit. I think pulverized might have been a bit more appropriate, given the circumstances. I soared across the room, and felt a sickening crunch as I continued through the wall. I felt like every bone in my body had snapped, and that somehow I was still alive. I hit the parking lot, rolling across the pavement until someone's bumper stopped me. My mouth filled with blood, and I spit out a tooth.

The God slipped through the hole I'd made as I exited, and stalked over to pick me up. As he walked, his armor fluidly changed from Ancient Greek to modern U.S. Army fatigues. "You're very aerodynamic," he said, pulling me to my feet and steadying me, holding on to make certain that I didn't fall over. I howled in agony at his attention, and was quite positive that I had numerous broken bones as well at this time.

"Ares...." I managed to choke out.

"Oh, you recognized me," he said. "I'm glad. Means I don't need to introduce myself."

"It's Michael, isn't it?" I asked. "He asked you to punish me so that he didn't have to do so himself."

"No," Ares said. "The only thing Michael asked me for during your little tiff was help controlling his anger. No, I'm here because I took an interest in you."

"So you just show up and try to kill me for no reason? Typical."

"Oh, quit your bitching," Ares said. "I wasn't trying to kill you."

"Oh really? You hit me hard enough to send me through a wall!"

"You call that little love tap a hit? That was just me making a point. I didn't do anything to you that you haven't done to someone else." With these words, his appearance changed, and now he wore a patchwork suit of chainmail that looked like it had been damaged and repaired repeatedly over a long period of time.

"I've never hit anyone in my life!" I yelled at him.

"Maybe not physically," he said. "But you sure know how to make people hurt on the inside."

"But you...." I trailed off. My pain was gone. There were no broken bones, no blood in my mouth, and even the tooth was back where it belonged. Looking back toward the apartment building, there wasn't even a hole in the wall anymore.

"That's right," Ares said. "You're dreaming, kid. That means that the little scratch you just got was all on the inside. A wound just like the ones you hand out. The ones you got just won't hurt as long as the ones you gave."

"What do you mean?" I asked.

"Think about poor Michael," he said. "You treated him like a monster, but you don't know what happened to him. War isn't fun, Jonah. Do you know what it was like for Michael over there? No, you don't. You've never been in an armed conflict, so how could you? You don't know what it is like to wake up every morning knowing that it could be your last. You don't know what it is like to stare death in the face every day." As he spoke, the parking lot began to warp.

The darkness of the parking lot was abruptly replaced with the blinding brightness of a noonday sun. My hand came up to shield my eyes, but the damage was already done. As I stumbled, I reached out to find something to steady myself with, but there was nothing there. I fell to the ground, the hot grit biting into my skin. Sweat poured out of me, stinging my eyes even as I struggled to clear them so that I could see.

"Ares?! What the hell is going on?! Where are we?!" I didn't hear any response. "Ares?" I asked a bit more softly.

I began to crawl, despite the grit biting into my hands. If I could find some shade, I could try and regain my bearings. As I crawled, a shadow fell over me, and I heard a click from above. I opened my eyes, and looked upwards into the Arabic features of the man pointing a rifle at my forehead.

The Arab soldier smiled at me, and in the voice of Ares began to speak. "Tell me, Jonah, have you ever stared down the barrel of an enemy's weapon before? Have you ever known that your life was separated from death by nothing more than luck and the split second it would take for that trigger to be pulled?" With that, the trigger was pulled, and I flinched as my ears were filled with a deafening explosion.

I gradually opened my eyes, squinting against the sun still. Fifty yards away, an American stranger lay dead on the ground, his head blown apart by the Arab's rifle. Gunshots rang out, and soon the enemy soldier lay dead beside the American.

"Didn't think so," Ares said, now wearing the form of an American officer. I looked around, and was surprised to see that my friends, wearing American military fatigues of their own, were gathered around us. Richard gazed out over the desert, scanning for any enemy movements. Cheryl was busy bandaging a wound on Jade's leg in the shadow of a totaled vehicle. Silvermoon and Carl were both reloading their rifles. I could see Gloom in the distance, scouting ahead of us. Looking down, I was stunned to see that I was dressed the same way they were.

"What...?" I began to ask.

"You want to understand Michael and people like him? Try being one," he said tersely.

"You mean I'm going to have to kill people?!" I yelled, perhaps a little too loudly.

"Of course not," Ares replied. "You get a choice in the matter. You can fight the enemy, or you can stand there and get yourself or your friends killed instead. World of possibilities, really."

"It'll be okay, Jonah," Carl said, trying to reassure me.

"How can you say that, Carl?" I asked. "Ares dragged us here to kill or be killed!"

"Yeah, but if we stick together, everything will be o—" We dove for cover as bullets rained down upon us. Carl's body fell to the ground, now ragged from bloody bullet holes, the pool beneath him spreading out through the desert soil.

I came up behind the battered vehicle, breathing a quick sigh of relief that I'd only been grazed. I glanced out, and reached for the gun that I'd dropped when I took cover. I stared at his body, and shuddered. "That could have been me," I said quietly, closing my hand around the gun and pulling it to my chest. The guilt and relief fought their own war within me.

"Feel pretty lousy, don't you?" Ares asked from a few feet away. He had a couple bullet holes in his own body, but was busy reloading his weapon. Cheryl and Jade were both pressed closer to the vehicle. I didn't know where the others had taken cover, but I silently prayed that they'd be safe.

"What do you think?" I asked, a little angry that he'd ask me such a stupid question at a time like this.

"I think that you're thanking the gods that it wasn't you, and you feel shitty about your friend dying instead. Pretty normal reaction to seeing a dear friend brutally torn apart by tiny slugs of hot metal. Michael felt the same way."

"Michael went through this?" I asked, feeling pity towards him.

"Multiple times," Ares replied. "He lost a few good friends over here, and he prayed to me for the strength to carry on despite their loss."

"I guess he's been through a lot," I said quietly.

"Damn straight," Ares said. "He's been through more than you can even imagine. You've never cried for killing an enemy soldier. You've never spent a sleepless night wondering if you were evil because you no longer cried for killing the enemy soldiers. Michael has been there. Can you understand that?"

I shook my head. "I don't know what that's like," I said. "But, it's his fault, really. He knew what he was getting into when he signed up."

Ares laughed. "Do you think anyone knows what they're getting into when the go to war? If they did, do you think that there'd be anyone who signed up for it that wasn't exactly what you accused Michael of being? Michael wasn't some psychopath. Michael signed up to suffer those things because he believed that through his sacrifice, the world could be a better place for everyone. That's what he saw it as. He was giving himself up so that other people wouldn't have to."

"Why should anyone need to do that?" I asked. "If people didn't go to war in the first place, then nobody on either side would need to sacrifice themselves."

"Beautiful thought," Ares said. "It would be great if it worked that way. Sadly, it doesn't. As sad as it is, there are some people out there that want war more than anything. People for whom life is not sacred. Refusing to fight them won't make people like that rethink their position. All they'll think is how much more convenient it is to be killing people who won't raise their weapons in opposition. People like Michael don't go to war because they want to kill. They go to war so that there's somebody to stop people like that. Then, people like Michael come home to a hero's welcome for doing so. Unless, of course, there's someone like you that greets them. Then, they're informed about how evil they are, and get treated like crap for trying to make the world a better place."

"I guess I never looked at it that way," I said. At that moment, I heard the click above me. I whirled around and saw the soldier leveling his rifle towards me. I screamed, raising my own weapon and firing without thinking. The soldier's head split, and my face was splattered with warm blood as the full weight of the soldier came crashing down upon me. I quickly pulled myself out from under the corpse, crawling backwards as quickly as I could, breathing heavily and trying to calm my racing heart.

"Now, just imagine, going through all that crap, then coming home to a welcome like yours," Ares said.

I couldn't respond at first. I was still shaking from the experience, just staring at the bright desert earth at my feet. It took several false starts before I was able to get a response out. "I... I... I'm... sorry..." I finally said. "I... I didn't know..."

"I'm not the one you need to apologize to about that," Ares said.

"No," I agreed. I raised my eyes to him, and saw that now he was wearing the uniform of a New York City police officer. "But wait, if even you think war is so horrible, why do you do it? Things like that are your fault. You're the one that makes everyone fight. You could stop it."

"Jonah, don't be stupid," he said. "Humans fight. It happens. If I withdrew from the world today, you know what the humans would do tomorrow? They'd fight. About the same old thing, about new things, it doesn't matter. Even you, self-proclaimed Champion of Peace, fight all the time." The Champion of Peace comment seemed to be sarcastic, but the rest of his statement seemed quite serious and sincere.

"No, I don't," I protested. "You're the one that made me kill that soldier! I'm all for peace!"

"No you're not, and I'm not talking about the soldier," he said. "I'm talking about the way you live your life. You say you want peace, but what you really want is a world where everyone agrees with your personal vision of a perfect world, and actively works to bring it about. You're not willing to kill for it, but you don't hesitate to fight for it."

"But I don't fight...." I started to say.

"Yes, you do. Remember when you became a vegetarian? What was it you said to your brother?"

The battlefield melted away, replaced by our family's table from our Memorial Day barbecue three years before. I watched myself sitting there, enjoying a heaping plate of potato salad, coleslaw, and vegetarian hot dogs. Then my brother sat down across from me, his plate loaded up with hamburgers, ribs, and a chicken leg.

"What the hell is wrong with you?" I'd demanded.

"What's your problem, man?" my brother had responded. "You've been bitching at everyone all damn day."

"I'm just trying to help," I'd said. "But you're a cold-blooded murderer if you put any of that crap in your mouth."

"No, I'm not. This is food. It's called eating, not murder. I've had it up to about here with your animal rights crap. I'm an omnivore. Deal with it."

"You two stop fighting," my Mom had said. Her plate had more side dishes on it, but even she had a chicken breast on it.

"Look, I'm the only one in this family with anything resembling a moral conscience!" I'd yelled. "I can't just sit here and watch you all destroying innocent lives! I tried providing alternatives, but nobody wants to do the right thing but me. Don't invite me to any of these 'family barbecues' until the animal sacrifice is eliminated." I stormed off, and in the three years since, they had listened, and hadn't bothered inviting me.

"Those were fighting words, not peaceful words," Ares said.

"I..." I sighed. "I guess you're right. Maybe I did try to change them too much too quickly."

"What about this?" Ares asked, his clothing shifting once more, this time into blood-spattered Medieval armor with a cross emblazoned across the chest. The scene changed, and I saw me and a couple of my friends running away from a leather goods store. The windows had been broken, and much of the merchandise had been spray-painted.

"Was that really a peaceful act?"

"I guess not," I said. I couldn't believe I was getting a lesson in peaceful behavior from the God of War. I could feel myself turning red, but there was nothing I could do to stop it.

"No, of course it wasn't. That was an act of war. And how many protest campaigns have you participated in? How many times have you shouted at people, calling them murderers or monsters, when ultimately they're only guilty of having a different perspective than your own?"

"So what you're saying is that we can't stand up for what we believe in? We can't pursue peace?" I said, not believing what he was saying. "All we've got is war?"

"Not at all," he said, his armor now becoming modern riot gear. "What I'm saying is that ultimately, peace is a process, not an end result. One should fight for what one believes in, but don't try to deny that it's a fight, and don't demonize your opponents. Screaming at someone doesn't make them see that you're right, it just makes them see that you're an asshole, and probably a damned ignorant one at that. If you're going to treat them like an enemy, don't be surprised if they start treating you the same way. If you really want peace as much as you say you do, then acting as though you're superior to everyone who disagrees with you is probably the last thing you should be doing."

I nodded, understanding his point. If I was always offended when I was treated as lesser for my beliefs, why should I have assumed that those on the other side would be any different? "But what about the violence?" I asked. "Isn't there something that can be done about that?"

"Sure there is. It's not for me to do that, though. That's for humans to achieve on their own. I don't control people's actions. I am not responsible for the choices that humans make. I didn't make Hitler order the slaughter of the Jews during World War II, and I didn't make you verbally assault Michael earlier this evening. Hitler made his choice, and you made yours. I'd thank you not to compare me to him again."

"I won't," I said, feeling more than a little embarrassed. I felt like all of this was something I should have known before, but somehow it had never occurred to me. I forced myself to meet his eyes. "If you are not responsible for any of it, though, then why do they call you the God of War?"

"I am not the cause of every conflict, but that doesn't mean that I'm not present for them. Wherever there is war, I can be found. I am there to give courage and strength. I am there to help people stand against their enemies, even when said enemies are the enemies within. I am there to arrange the conflict so that, regardless of whether it ends in success or failure, there is still something to be gained."

"What about when someone dies?" I ask. "How have they gained anything?"

"People die. It happens all the time. It happens during war, and it happens during peace. It is natural. To assume that nothing is gained from death is to assume that you know the nature of life, death, and what comes after. Given your degree of knowledge on the other topics we've discussed tonight, I'm going to assume that you are not blessed with that degree of wisdom."

"No, I know that I don't know what's coming after…I just…I'm having a hard time seeing what can be gained when someone dies…."

"Look, kid," Ares said, a surprising degree of compassion in his voice despite everything that had happened tonight. "I can't tell you what comes after, or anything like that. Not because I don't know, of course, but because it is one of those things that shouldn't just be handed to mortals. It is something that every mortal must experience to truly comprehend. But I can tell you this much: sometimes, even when someone dies, there is something to be gained. A battle lost does not necessarily mean only tragedy. Sometimes there are lessons there deeper than what tactics work and which ones don't. Sometimes a defeat can strengthen a people in the long run, even as it harms them in the short term. It can help bring people together in common cause, who might otherwise have turned upon each other in selfishness. Sometimes the sacrifices made by soldiers can fill the hearts of the common people with courage and hope for the future. Sometimes, when the battles are bad enough, it makes both sides begin working towards peace. It can be a harsh lesson, but that doesn't mean it isn't an important one."

"I guess you're right," I said, barely audible to myself. I couldn't believe that I was beginning to agree with the God of War. My emotions clashed within, pride and anger I had always believed to be righteous battling against my newfound understanding and guilt over some of my previous actions.

"Of course I'm right," he said. "Don't beat yourself up because of it. If it makes you feel any better, consider this. Conflict is inseparable from life, and thus, so am I."

"It is possible to live a peaceful life," I insisted.

"Sure it is," he said from beneath the samurai helmet that had formed around his head. "But not one without conflict. There is conflict at every level of existence. There is no avoiding it. People fight. Animals eat each other. Even plants compete for water, nutrients, and growing space. Conflict is necessary, you see, in order for things to become stronger. Without conflict, life becomes stagnant. Without it, there would be no evolutionary arms race between predator and prey. There would be no challenges for people to overcome, and no need for people to improve themselves. Why would they even bother? Without conflict, people could stop worrying about other people in the slightest, and care only about themselves and their own gain. Would that be the world you'd want, Jonah? A world where people didn't even need to care anymore? Where they could go from birth to the grave without needing to make a single effort in their entire lives?"

"No, that's not what I'd want," I said. "I want people to be able to make themselves better people. I want them to listen to their conscience, and work towards improving themselves and the world around them. I want them to be able to think, and learn, and to fight for what they believe in...."

I trailed off as Ares began to whistle nonchalantly, his eyes pointedly fixed upon me. It took me only a second to register what I'd just said, and I began to laugh. "Well played, War God," I said, once my laughter had subsided.

"Look, kid," he said, wearing leather armor that was studded with little metal beads, "I'm going to point something out to you that you'd probably already know if you'd read your myths a bit better. I know that you are dedicated to Aphrodite, so you've really got no excuse on this one. You do know that the two of us are lovers, right?"

"Of course," I said. "How could I not?"

"Do you know about our daughter?" He paused to wait for an answer, but when he saw me trying to dig through my memories to find the answer, he decided that he'd waited long enough. "Her name is Harmonia. Sound familiar? Through the union of Love and War, Harmony is born. Think about that, Jonah. Isn't harmony something you would generally encourage? Yeah, I thought so. Before you go and bash anyone or anything because of a warlike nature, just stop and consider what sort of harmony might result from the outcome of the conflict. Can you do that for me?"

"I can certainly try," I said. "I can't promise I'll be successful, though. When I get angry, I sometimes don't think things through very well."

"Trying is a good start," Ares replied. "Making amends to those you've already hurt would be a pretty good idea, too."

"I know," I said. "I've got a lot of apologies to make to a lot of people. I just hope I haven't burned too many bridges."

"Good luck with that," Ares said, smiling. His armor burst into brilliant flames, forming a great golden shell around him. When it solidified, it greatly resembled the Greek armor he had worn when he first appeared. Now, though, it was forged of gold rather than bronze, and light poured forth from it as though a star burned within it. It was etched with the accounts of millions of battles, and even as I watched, more etchings appeared, the golden armor silently bearing witness to all the world's conflicts. "I'll see you around, kid. Take care of yourself." With that, the glow intensified, until all I could see was the brilliant light.

My eyes snapped open, then squinted to block out the sunlight streaming through the window. My back was stiff from having slept in the chair all night, but I quickly climbed to my feet to go and pull the curtains closed to block out some of the glare. With that done, I stretched, loosening up some of my joints. As I finished my morning stretching, my eyes fell upon my altar, and I decided that it looked a little bare. "I think there needs to be another statue on it," I said quietly to myself, making a mental note to order one whenever I got online again.

I went to take a warm shower to wash the sweat off from the night before, then began to get ready for my day. I started making a list of the people I owed apologies to: my brother, Silvermoon, Richard, everyone else from the Pagans For Peace meeting, as well as many others. At the top of the list, though, was Michael. There was no question in my mind that I needed to apologize to him, first. I got out the sign-in sheet and my phone, and stared at it for about twenty minutes. Finally, I prayed to Ares to grant me the courage to do what I know needed to be done, and began to dial.

Crossroads

by Rebecca Buchanan

If the coyote whined or yelped, the sound was lost under the scream of the horn and the sickening thump of the impact. The coyote flew, legs stiff, knocked off to the side at a weird angle. The car slowed for just a second, and then accelerated away. With a whimper, the coyote staggered to its feet, fell, clambered up again, stumbled out into the intersection. Fell.

Shoulders hunched, Maggie dug her toes into the gravel of the shoulder. She tried not to see the blood. She pulled her jacket collar tight around her throat. She glanced out at the coyote, its chest rising and falling rapidly, breath thin white puffs. Hastily, she looked away, looked around, up and down the empty Camino Cabra and Calle Picacho, anywhere but down at the dying animal.

It whined.

Out onto the road, one step, two, heels catching. Swallowing, she knelt. The asphalt was cold. Her bag felt heavy across her back and chest. She grabbed at the strap. "Hi." Lame. "I'm really sorry." Lamer. She swallowed again. The coyote's rear legs kicked, catching her across the knees. She winced. Fingers stiff, she disentangled one hand from her bag strap and slowly, slowly lowered it to the coyote's nose. The fur was harsh, rough, a wild swirl of ambers and golds and rusts and blacks and whites. Its eyes rolled towards her. "I'm really sorry you got hit. That guy's an idiot. He was driving too fast. He shoulda known better." She swallowed again, licked her lips. "Oh wait." She heaved her bag over her head and it thunked down on the asphalt. Pushing books out of the way and dog-eared notepads she pulled out her water bottle. "Here. Want some? Will this help?"

The coyote's eyes rolled away from her and then back again. Its tongue lolled out of its mouth, licking at the air.

"Okay, here." She popped the cap, pouring a bit into the animal's mouth, bottle held awkwardly. It lapped at the water, tongue curling. She ran her free hand over the coyote's head. Mom would have yelled at her about fleas and hosed her down with insecticide. Dad would have called her stupid.

"So, listen. You're dying, you know. I can't – I'm sorry, but I can't really do anything about that. But, I was kinda hoping that maybe you could carry a message for me. See, I've been reading these books. About all those old Goddesses, like Hekate and Ereshkigal and The Morrigan. And people used to pray to them. Some people, like my Aunt Sarah, still do. When things are bad. And things are bad for me, right now."

The coyote's tongue darted out. She poured more water, rubbing its ears gently. Blood pooled around her knees.

"So, could you carry a message for me? Please? To Hekate. You're a coyote, so I think she'd listen to you. You're her kind of animal. Could you please tell her that things are really bad now. Getting worse. Dad's drinking again. The hard stuff. Mom's yelling at me again. She hit me last week. She hasn't done that for a while, but...well, I don't want her to hit me anymore. I want Dad to stop drinking. Can't I just go live with Aunt Sarah again, like last summer?" More water. "If you could just take that message to Hekate for me." The coyote choked, wheezed. "Thank you. And I'm really sorry you got killed."

A violent shiver, a wheeze. The coyote's eyes rolled away, and it stilled.

Maggie stayed for a few more minutes, rubbing its ears. Eventually, shivering, she stuffed her water bottle back into her bag. Pushing her sleeves down over her hands, she grabbed the coyote's rear legs and dragged it out of the intersection. Over the shoulder, around the scrawny ponderosa, over a few clumps of burrograss, and over to the base of a yucca. Back to the ponderosa to pick up a few branches scattered across the ground. She laid those across the coyote.

"So ...." She twisted the zipper pull on her jacket. "Sleep well."

Back out into the street to grab her backpack, just before a car roared through the intersection. Hugging her arms tight against the increasing cold, she trudged down Picacho. Around a corner and up Camino de Cruz Blanca. A few houses here and there. A police cruiser sped past. Her feet were beginning to hurt. Around another corner and up Camino Ocaso del Sol. More houses. Another cruiser. She frowned. Around a curve in the road, and she saw the lights flashing. Two police cars, three, an ambulance. Neighbors on their lawns or peering out windows. A few pointed at her, shaking their heads, or looked away.

Maggie stopped, chest tight, knees locked. The lights hurt her eyes.

Something blocked her view. She looked up, squinting. Badge. Mustache. Hat.

"Are you Maggie?"

She nodded, head loose and wobbly.

"I'm sorry, but there's been an...incident. Is there someone we can call? Someone you can stay with tonight – for a while?"

Maggie nodded. Her knees unlocked. She fell.

[Author's Note: An older version of this tale was previously published in Luna Station Quarterly #005.]

Reunion

by P. Sufenas Virius Lupus

Apollon didn't look forward to travel on this occasion.

His yearly snow-and-skiing holiday in the Hyperborean lands was certainly something to look forward to, when he could get away from it all for a short while, at the very least. He was never nervous leaving Delphi in the hands of Dionysos while he was gone; after all, he knew that, even if Dionysus held the biggest orgy *ever* there in his absence, he at least wouldn't trash the place.

This was something else altogether. This was a "family reunion" of sorts, but one which the extended family would not all be attending. (Tragic, really, as he would have loved to spend some time on Olympos at that season.) This was a "family vacation" of sorts, when they'd be getting together for a short while at their time-share in Naukratis. His mother would not be there, nor would his twin sister (and in any case, Artemis had her hands full these days, working in close connection with Kybele and doing a bang-up job of being constantly mistaken for a Jewish virgin).

And strange though it sounds, Apollon didn't like the location at this time of year. The midday sun on the Canopic branch of the Nile was worse than the most heinous tales of Sekhmet sober, and all he could think about was Phaethon and his spectacular demise. He was a winter-holiday type, not a sun-holiday fan. And just as high tourist season was swinging into full gear, he'd have to be there, and be traveling.

Unfortunately, Golden Arrow service wasn't an option for this trip either. If he was going, it would probably involve Helios; and, he at last made up his mind, he *was* going, so Helios was duly notified. Then, two weeks before, he changed his mind; then a few days later, he changed it back; then, the following week, he changed it again; and finally, after spending a long time on the phone with his father Zeus after a flurry of text messages, he felt guilty enough that he decided he would go no matter what. When Helios got the news, he met the decision with as much equanimity as any of his previous confirmations and cancellations. "Great! I'll pick you up that morning!"

"Thanks. Incidentally, what are you driving these days?"

"You'll just have to wait and see! Bye for now!"

Perhaps it was his memories of the past that made him anxious. There was that time when Typhon was raging abroad, and many of his extended family members took a prolonged vacation in Egypt — if "vacation" is the same thing as "enforced exile"— and he himself had assumed the form of a raven. But wearing black in a country known for its hot sun, and not being able to bring a change of attire, was miserable, to say the least. That had to rank up there as the worst vacation ever. Whenever he thought of Egypt, he thought of that incident, and beads of sweat formed on his forehead.

Fortunately, this time he did have enough notice and leisure to pack a suitcase properly for the occasion. But, like many nervous individuals who learn to be ready for anything, he found that he was over-packing — a shale grey casual suit for the cocktail party, a more formal white suit with a long jacket and a golden yellow collarless shirt in case they went out for a fancy dinner or a night at the opera, three haute couture but nonetheless informal shirts (each costing an economic-crisis-inducing amount of money), his very fashionable pre-stressed jeans, the impeccable cargo pants, the nice messenger pants (a gift from Hermes last Thargelia), the white linen pinstripe shorts, the more psychedelic board shorts with the big green snakes on them (a gift from Asklepios on the same Thargelia), seven tank tops, four pairs of shoes, six pairs of socks, five belts, eight pairs of underwear, and (because there was still room) several swimsuits ranging in coverage from form-fitting squarecuts down to a white semi-sheer thong (which Hapi sent as a gag gift for Thargelia, but Apollon personally found incredibly sexy)…and, it was just an overnight trip. If anything about this trip was going to be stressful or uncomfortable, it was not going to be his lack of clothing for any conceivable occasion.

Apollon heard a horn outside. It was not a human's expelled breath through a ram's horn, it was something that probably resulted from a person pressing too enthusiastically in the middle of a steering wheel.

He went outside, suitcase in hand, and saw Helios in his latest chariot: a gold Humvee. Helios was waving proudly from the driver's seat, and the same ever-loyal, ever-present horses, Aktaion, Lampos, Erythreus, and Philogeus, were reined to the front bumper. Helios rolled the passenger side window down.

"So, what do you think?"

"A Humvee? Really? I mean, seriously…."

"Yeah, it's nice, isn't it?" His response was like Helios thought he was the center of the universe, not noticing at all the sarcasm in Apollon's response.

"Helios, what will the other gods think?"

"Probably that they're jealous and they wish they had one themselves. I can't wait to see the face of Re as I drop you off — he'll turn green with envy!"

The midlife crisis of a sun is never a pretty thing to watch, and Helios was no exception. This had been going on for centuries, and was not in the least helped by the fact that he had at last eclipsed Gaia as the acknowledged center of the solar system (conveniently forgetting, of course, the more recent revelations that there are suns beyond number in the cosmos). After that, it was conspicuous consumption central around the solar palace. Even so, at least the horses looked somewhat proportional to this vehicular monstrosity; back when it was the solar Spanish galleon, or the solar ocean liner, or the solar bullet train, or the solar Space Shuttle, the horses looked insufferably silly tethered to the front (not to mention quite overworked). Apollon tossed his suitcase into the back seat, sat on the passenger side, and before his door was fully closed, they were off.

He wondered who else might be there. Aphrodite was on break from filming her latest television series, *Porneia in the Polis*, and she'd definitely be there; father Zeus of course, and his principal wife Hera (who, though she seemed to bear no resentment toward Apollon, nor his mother or sister, after the unfortunate incidents surrounding their births, was still a bit overbearing in her hospitality); and his half-brothers, Kastor and Polydeukes, who he always mused would add up to a full brother if they were combined together, but he certainly preferred them separate. They'd no doubt be waiting at the end of the driveway when they got to Naukratis to see Helios' horses. Maybe if things got very uncomfortable, they could go for a late-night row on the Nile with Apollon, and if things were very *very* uncomfortable, perhaps a case or two of that good red Egyptian beer would also go with them. But as for others, he wasn't certain. This uncertainty vaguely disturbed Apollon, but also excited him slightly. He was not in Delphi, he couldn't foresee — or even predict — what was going to happen.

He could hear his father's booming voice in his ears already. "Son, I really think you should consider going into the lightning business." Wasn't it good enough for him that Apollon was doing the oracular thing? "I'm proud that you're carrying on that family tradition, but this is different. I'm not going to do this forever, I want to retire, and since Zagreus didn't work out the way I had hoped, I need someone who I know will do a good job, someone who has never let me down. Don't let me down now, son, don't let me down." They'd had this conversation a hundred times before, and it was only a question of when it would happen again.

It was mere seconds since he shut the door, and they had already arrived. Apollon remembered the old days, when his arrival at some location would have been preceded by some of his old staff — the Muses, the Graces — preparing the way for him and organizing the festivities to honor his epiphany; but these days, they all had careers of their own, successful corporations to run, lots of projects in the works. These days, Apollon was mostly on his own. He still made sure he visited all of his old boyfriends at least once a year, and those were occasions to celebrate, even if it was only Apollon and whichever boy it happened to be doing the celebrating. But these get-togethers were different, where he was one god among many, and some people at the party might not even be kind enough to introduce themselves if they were standing in front of him....

Morpheus had been right, though. Apollon's need for popularity, and to be the center of attention, wasn't fair to all of his extended family, and didn't square with his wishes to be overlooked by his father when it came to certain things. He was ambivalent about it, and sometimes he just wanted to lash out and attack someone, like he did in the old days. Morpheus pointed out to him last week in their session that in this sometimes unpredictable wolfish madness, he took after his father. And Apollon knew he was right. He was more like his father than he cared to admit; and, just maybe, it was flattering that his father wanted to give him those extra responsibilities. It might not be so bad to be king, as it were. There was a reason Morpheus was so highly regarded when it came to being a therapist, and he was worth every drachma — and he'd better have been, at a hundred thousand of them an hour!

Not five seconds had passed since they were in Delphi, and Apollon already missed it. The surging Nile certainly had its charms, but would never be the soft trickling of the Castalian Spring and the sounds of the wind across the peaks of Parnassus. Like he had guessed, Kastor and Polydeukes were there, waiting for them — or, more accurately, waiting for Helios' horses — and Apollon got out of the ridiculous vehicle, retrieved his suitcase, and stood there in silence as his half-brothers ignored him in favor of Aktaion and Philogeus. They looked different this time: Kastor had let his hair grow almost over his eyes, and was wearing an almost-too-small black t-shirt and ridiculously tight and low black jeans with a studded metal belt (and was that a lip ring?), while Polydeukes had bleached his hair blond, had it cut high and tight, and looked as much the jock as he ever had in his white tank top, red basketball shorts, and white reversed baseball cap.

"Hey, boys."

"Oh, hey Apollon!" Polydeukes turned and smiled at him, but Kastor still stroked Aktaion's mane. Polydeukes socked him hard in the shoulder. "Hey, dummy, say hi to Apollon!" Kastor rolled his eyes, turned toward him and said in the most dejected and unenthusiastic voice possible, "Hey."

"You'll have to excuse him — he's doing that 'emo' thing, 'I'm not okay,' and all of that. I swear, some people just never get over dying...."

Apollon tried not to laugh. He knew Melpomene had been busy producing lots of younger bands those days, but he had no idea this would become popular among his family.

"It's all right, Polydeukes — I think it's cute." Kastor suddenly beamed at this, and as Apollon passed the two, he tousled Kastor's black stringy hair.

"Thanks a bunch, Helios! I'll see if I can get a ride back with Boreas or someone."

"Well, if you can't, give me a call! It isn't as if I can't go backwards whenever I want!"

"Interesting idea, Helios; but let's just not go there, shall we?" Helios turned away with horses and Humvee in a wild frenzy of waving, a flurry of laughter, and flash of golden light. Apollon could swear, as Helios glanced toward the Sahara, that he saw a glimmer of sadness in his eyes. With Phaethon long dead, he knew that Helios wasn't sure who (if anyone) would ever take over for him when he retired. He suddenly thought about his own father and how envious Helios must have felt towards Zeus, and about his own children. Perhaps he'd pay Asklepios a visit in Memphis while he was In Egypt — he certainly had clothes for another day.

Apollon went in to the lavish estate that was the Greek's timeshare in Naukratis. There were people all over, and the first person Apollon recognized was Amasis, the owner of the timeshare and their host for this party every year, who was not looking particularly healthy. There was a boy leading the old pharaoh, with one arm around his shoulder as the old man leaned precariously on an ornate walking stick. Suddenly, Apollon realized who the boy was: Tutankhamun. Apollon approached the two.

"Greetings, Amasis. I see you're looking well!"

"You don't have to lie to me, sonny, I'm decrepit but not senile!" It was so unfair, this Egyptian custom — Amasis' tomb had not been seen for millennia, and he was thus suffering greatly in the afterlife, whereas Tutankhamun's tomb was known worldwide, and he looked like he just stepped out of the baths after a good workout. (Sure, there was the unfortunate incident involving the lost penis for several decades, but young Tut never was much of one for the gymnasia, so who would have known?)

"Well, even so, I can't thank you enough for throwing this party again this year. It's nice to get together with old friends and family, if only briefly," replied Apollon.

"Nonsense, sonny! I know you'd rather be somewhere else! You just come here out of guilt every year because of my benefactions all that time ago! Don't think I don't know it either! You'd rather be in Delphi, and I know it…and guess what? So would I! I always liked your people…."

"Now, now, now, Ahmose, don't misspeak." Tutankhamun shook his head.

"If I didn't respect my elders, Tut, I'd smack you across the mouth! Now, where's that waiter?"

Ganymede, in a ridiculous white collar and black bowtie, with a shiny black vinyl pair of hot shorts (and nothing else), came up to them with a gleaming silver tray. Apollon knew that his father insisted he wear such things at official functions like this, and the prince of Troy wasn't at all comfortable in it. "Here we are, Amasis: a nice bowl of foul* for you."

"Dammit! This is a party, I want celery sticks! I want crackers! When is that damn Imouthes going to be done with my teeth?"

Tutankhamun looked at Apollon and rolled his eyes as he ushered Amasis away, with a beleaguered Ganymede following closely behind. Apollon noticed the fuzzy rabbit tail on the hot shorts at that point, and felt embarrassed on Ganymede's behalf. His father was shameless beyond belief.

It was then that Apollon noticed Aphrodite, looking radiant as ever, in a dress that he could have sworn was made from kelp and seashells held together by filaments woven by a golden spider. It was stylish beyond conception, conservative enough that it could have worked even in Rome, and yet there was more of her skin showing beneath it all than perhaps even poor Ganymede in his bunny suit.

"Dolphy! It's good to see you!"

"Goldie, you're looking quite the dish!" The two air-kissed on both cheeks.

"You don't have a drink, Dolphy! We must do something about that. Waiter!"

Ganymede arrived again with a tall flute of champagne, and a tray of hors d'oeuvres. Apollon took the drink, and then inquired, "What are these?"

"Wild boar on flax crackers with cream cheese and olives."

Apollon looked at Aphrodite angrily, and she returned the look — he was thinking of Erymanthus, she of Adonis.

"Wild boar? In Egypt? Really!" Apollon snapped at Ganymede.

"Look, I don't set the menu here, I just serve stuff. That's all I do — *serve stuff!* Don't get mad at me, the old cow decided what was going to be served!"

"It's all right, darling; we'll have a word with her." Aphrodite caressed Ganymede's bare right pectoral, and he seemed to relax a bit. "And by the way, sweetie, how have things been with you and the old man?"

"Tsh! Like he even gives me a second thought these days. Like I said, all I do is serve stuff."

"Well, here, let me give you a little something." Almost as shameless as Zeus himself, Aphrodite reached down the front of Ganymede's hot shorts. The young immortal's eyes nearly popped out of his head with surprise and the look on his face went blank but happy. "There! Now, later tonight, I guarantee you'll have a hotter time with His Brilliance than when the eagle snagged you!"

Ganymede blinked about ten times rapidly, and a hint of a smile crept over his lips. "Thanks!" he whispered hoarsely, lowering his tray to waist level

[110]

to hide what was protruding beneath and walking rapidly and rather stiffly back to the kitchen.

Apollon tried to recover the conversation. "So, putting all of that aside for the moment, how have things been?"

"Oh, you know how it goes. Hundreds of dating websites, some more specialized than others, and yet the only thing that seems to work every time is Craigslist — and even then…!"

Apollon smirked. "Still, the quizzes are fun."

"Aha! Just as I suspected! Have you had your hands in those, Dolphy?"

"Why Goldie? You're accusing me of such a thing?" Apollon faked shock to a degree that Dionysos would have given him his own personal goat as the prize for the performance.

"Dolphy, come on! I know you're big into this whole 'Know Thyself' thing, but these are really ridiculous. 'What Twilight character are you most like?' Really!"

"If people aren't going to do things the right way, then at least they can work within the structures of this time, no matter how silly they might be … or, rather, how silly they, in fact, most certainly are." Apollon rubbed his fingers against his shirt and looked down as he continued. "Besides, I'd talk if I were you — Craigslist." He looked Aphrodite directly in the face and raised an eyebrow. "Need I say more?"

Aphrodite smiled, shrugged, and changed the subject. "Well, have you seen my new show?"

"*Porneia in the Polis?* No, I don't have television in Delphi." Apollon left out the fact that he didn't need television in Delphi, because he could see absolutely everything there; but he knew that Aphrodite wanted to brag a bit, so he let her.

"Well, you must come over sometime! In fact, if you'd like a cameo in an episode, I'd be delighted to arrange it, darling! Producer, director, writer, and star has its privileges, you know! We've got Kybele as the dedicated business woman who has a child despite her lover being castrated; Helen as the perfect little rich wife, who leaves her first husband for a more risky second one — and let me tell you, that's a stretch! — ; and, we've got Hebe as the star, sort of. Well, she's really into shoes. But then of course there's me. I'm the publicist who sleeps around a lot."

"Goldie, I'm sorry to raise this issue, but I thought this was supposed to be a dramatic comedy."

"Oh, it is, darling, it is! It's hilarious! Sex and relationships are an endless source of amusement and hysterical laughter!"

"Actually, I meant the 'drama' part. I thought, in other words, that this involved actual acting, you know, like pretending you're someone or something else?"

"Oh, please, Dolphy! Acting? That's Dionysos' thing, and anyway he's not in the show. But you really must come and see us shoot it sometime!"

"Well, I'll think about it." Apollon paused, and thought of Rhodopis, the high-class call-girl that caught the eye of Charaxus, the brother of Sappho, all those years ago. She was intimately connected to Aphrodite, and yet her gratitude went to Apollon, and for it Delphi was well off in iron spits for many years. Now that would have made for an interesting dramatic series, but Aphrodite would never produce it — too much resentment over his outshining her, he mused quietly.

"Goldie, I need to have an audience with His Brilliance and Her Married-ness, I think, but I'll catch up with you later." Aphrodite air-kissed Apollon again before he walked through the crowd. All of the world with its mass of humans and their mundane problems looking for advice were far more interesting to Apollon than the endless family drama that was the daily lives of the gods.

At last, Apollon made out his father in the distance. He had that unmistakable mane of salt-and-pepper hair and that well-groomed beard, and those piercing blue eyes as clear and blinding as ever, but he really needed a lesson in proper attire for such occasions (as if his insistence on Ganymede's outfit was not an obvious sign of that). He was wearing a purple Hawaiian shirt with green oak leaves and streaks of yellow lightning through them, and very light grey, far-too-baggy cargo shorts, and flip flops. Flip flops? Hera was next to him, looking for all that like a housewife of the mid-1960s, with a bob haircut, a while lily just above her right ear, a short sleeved tight magenta blouse with brilliant blue peacocks on it, and turquoise trousers with a huge white belt. Still, she had the figure and the grace to be able to pull it off, somehow.

"Dolphy! It's been so long! Mwah!" Hera kissed and hugged Apollon in a somewhat ostentatious manner, and yet he knew that she was utterly sincere. "You must come and visit us on Olympos one of these days!"

"I will, Hera, I will."

Hera whispered quickly in Apollon's ear. "Your father misses you, and can't stop talking about you."

"Well, son, it's good to see you." Zeus nodded and put out his hand.

"Oh, come on, Dad! This is not a Mithraic family!" Apollon threw his arms around his father, fully a head taller and considerably wider than himself, as if he were Olympos itself in a bad shirt. Zeus gave in, and embraced his son.

"So, son, I'd like to talk with you, but maybe we can wait until later. Hermes is out in the back manning the barbecue, and I think you should come and stake out your piece of the ox before all the good bits are gone."

"Dad, can I ask you something meanwhile?"

"Of course."

"How is Kastor? I mean, the whole emo thing is cute and all, but I'm a bit worried about him. Polydeukes doesn't seem to be very happy with the whole thing either."

"Hmm, yes. There's no accounting for such things, I'm afraid. He's immortal, and of course I respect that; but you know as well as I do that he's not really mine the way Polydeukes is. Uncle Poseidon has done well with looking after both, of course, but Kastor just isn't like us at the end of the day. Tyndareus was his father, and nothing can change that."

"Dad: they're identical twins. Kastor is every bit as good as Polydeukes."

"Well, perhaps, but he died, and it's only because his brother loved him so much that he's even here at all."

"You know, you're a real jerk when it comes to dying. You snatch up Ganymede so that he never dies, and yet because he was mortal at one point, you've got him waiting tables for you. Zagreus dies, and then all bets are off for who succeeds you. Kastor dies, and you can't be bothered to take an interest in him. No wonder he's depressed! And if that weren't bad enough, Hermes fools around with Polydeukes, and yet not one of the gods pays any mind to Kastor, despite him being every bit as attractive as his brother. I'm really surprised you didn't just eat him when things started to work out poorly."

"Apollon! Really, this isn't the time or the place for this conversation!" Hera was visibly shocked and taken aback, though no one else was paying attention, and Apollon was not declaiming. Even in anger and criticism, he was moderate.

Zeus actually looked hurt, and for the first time in ages, was introspective. He looked down at his flip-flopped feet, shook his head slowly, and was silent.

"Look, Dad, I love you and I will praise you forever, but it would be nice if, just once in a while, you looked at things from a perspective other than your own all-knowing one. How do you think Ganymede feels? How do you think Kastor feels? And just because your children didn't castrate you — though heavens know we all thought about it from time to time — or you didn't eat your own children, still, that doesn't mean you automatically get the 'Father-God of the Aeon' award."

"So, son, what are you suggesting?"

Apollon didn't know what came over him, but in his excitement, he began to speak without fully knowing what he might say next. "It's nice to have this party every year, but why don't we actually use this time for something, I don't know…useful? Why don't you try and get to know Kastor a bit more on this occasion? Why don't you put aside thoughts of all your lovers (despite the children of several such affairs being here in front of you), and pay attention to your wife like you should on this day? As nice as it is to have a party for everyone here, why don't we make it more about 'us'? I mean, let's face it, Aphrodite has enough money right now to buy and sell most of the cosmos without making a dent in her bank account. Why can't she be convinced to actually buy this estate, rather than having it be a timeshare that isn't really our own? I'm sure Amasis would be fine with that, and I think it would make things a lot more interesting with our Egyptian friends. Why don't we actually," and here Apollon gulped a bit before he continued, "act like we live here rather than just vacationing here? You know, get rid of the pork, start treating the justified and deified dead like they're our equals rather than our inferiors…why don't we even drink Nile water instead of importing our own? It might be a real learning experience!"

Hera, though not opposed, was in some disbelief. "But I thought you didn't like Egypt, Apollon."

Apollon couldn't believe he was saying it. "It's not a bad place — anyplace can be home as long as you act like it is. And Typhon is long gone, so let's leave that whole mess behind us. Let's actually try and make this a home, and make ourselves a family, rather than whatever it is we have going now."

Zeus began to smile slightly. "Hmm. So, this occasion might be a housewarming party?"

"More than that, Dad — it's a homecoming."

Zeus shook his head and beamed. "You never cease to amaze me, son. You know, I really think you should consider going into the —"

Apollon interrupted, "Now, Dad, just because we're a family and will be acting like one doesn't mean that I'm going to go into the family business."

Hera looked pleased. "I'll get Aphrodite, and we'll make the arrangements with Amasis immediately."

"But meanwhile," Apollon cautioned, "not a word to anyone. I want to tell Kastor about this myself."

Zeus slapped his son on the back, and Apollon stumbled forward slightly at all the might of the heavens striking his shoulder as he walked outside. He saw Kastor and Polydeukes by the pool, with Polydeukes dunking his feet in, but Kastor standing awkwardly with his hands in his jeans pockets looking down and away from his brother.

"Polydeukes, go have a word with Dad. He's wanting someone to go into the lightning business, and I think you might be the man for the job."

"Really!?! The real thunderbolt kind, not just ball lightning (damn kids' toys)?!? *I'm in!!!*" Polydeukes hopped up in a blink, and was away into the house. Kastor just stood there.

"Hey Kastor."

"Hey."

"So, sit down. I'd like to talk with you."

The moody youth went from standing up straight to sitting cross-legged without bending over, and looked at Apollon, who settled on the ground in front of him.

"Do you like it here?"

"It's okay, I guess." Kastor was noncommittal. "I wish we were in Rome instead."

"Well, how would you like to live here, semi-permanently?"

"Huh?"

"We've talked it over, and we're going to buy this estate from Amasis. It won't be a timeshare any longer, we'll own it. We'll all still make sure we're here at least once a year, but we'll own it the rest of the time, so we can use it whenever we want."

Kastor's eyes widened a little. "So, if we own it, does that mean I can have my own room? And I can decorate it however I want?"

"Of course! Anything you like!"

Kastor smiled, but then suddenly remembered himself, and tried to impress Apollon with his profound depths of sadness. "Yeah, that would be cool. I'm kinda tired of having to always share a room with Polydeukes. In Rome, I don't have to do that. I get sick of being treated like I'm just like him, you know? It's really hard being a twin."

Apollon laughed aloud, perhaps a bit too much. "Gosh, Kastor — no, I don't know what that's like at all!"

Kastor looked down, embarrassed at first, but succumbed to laughter eventually as well. "Yeah, sheesh — sorry, I kinda forgot. You must think I'm a big idiot."

"Not at all! It's all right, it's all right." The two continued to laugh. "You know, you're awfully cute when you laugh. You're awfully cute all the time, but especially when you laugh."

Kastor was surprised. "Uhh…thanks …?!?"

"I'm sorry — does that make you uncomfortable?"

"Well, no, it's just that I think you're being nice by saying that. I mean, you're family, you kinda have to say things like that, don't you?"

"Did Hermes 'kinda have to' get your brother a horse and be his lover?"

Kastor was suddenly conflicted. "Are you asking what I think you are?"

"If you think I'm asking if you'd like to be my lover…" Apollon paused for greater effect, "then you'd be right."

Kastor smiled in a dazed manner, but then suddenly became grave. "But wait, isn't that kind of, I don't know, weird? I mean we're family and all…."

Kastor was definitely the more human of the Dioskouroi, for good and ill.

"Yes, it's true: we're family, but it isn't like we have the same father or something."

Kastor realized how right Apollon was about that. "Oh, yeah! ... Well, sure! But, aren't I supposed to resist a bit?"

Apollon laughed again. Kastor reminded him of Hyakinthos so long ago. "You can if you want, but I find just cutting to the chase is a bit better. It saves time needlessly postponing the inevitable. Plus, this isn't human society, you don't have to play by any of their rules. You're an adult, a veteran, an independent person; you can do whatever you like."

"Well, I think I'd like to kiss you." Apollon was pleased at this reaction. The two kissed somewhat gingerly, tenderly, briefly, and then Apollon put his hand on the back of Kastor's head, and pressed him into his shoulder in a long embrace. They held each other for a moment, and then stood up.

"There will be plenty of time to get to know one another in every way possible later. But there's a party to attend to now, and we don't want to miss the best parts of the barbecue." Apollon put his arm around Kastor's lower back, and escorted him back toward the gathering of the gods.

"Oh, guess what?" Kastor seemed rather excited. "Later on, Antinous said he'd like to take us on a boat trip up the Nile. Wanna go?"

"Hmm," thought Apollon, looking back toward the four-foot-deep pool. "Well, let's see if we can talk him into a late night dip in the pool instead."

* *Author's Note:* foul *is an ancient Egyptian soup traditionally made with lentils. Modern variations include a greater variety of vegetables and other beans.*

Over the Rainbow

by Eric Scott

Dottie's mother's hair, once black as the Wicked Witch's habit, had been sprouting gray strands for forty-nine days. They swallowed her head like lichen, silver patches betraying her constant harried smile. Kate's eyeglasses magnified the new creases in her skin. A tiny, aching stumble had crept into her steps. They were little things, things most people wouldn't notice, but Dottie did. Dottie noticed everything.

She and her mother hadn't spoken since they got on the highway nearly an hour before, when the sun had just crested over the horizon and cast the road and the Mississippi River beside it in pomegranate-orange. The radio was set to NPR, too quiet to make out: white noise.

Kate stared through the murky windshield and occasionally glared at the defroster. Cold February wind kept the glass clouded. Dottie, for her part, held onto the pecan pie in her lap and ran her caramel finger across the window pane, tracing runes in the fog.

Kate coughed. Dottie knew what that meant: she'd been rehearsing whatever she was about to say. Dottie had spied on her mother often as a girl, watching her mouth soundlessly into her bathroom mirror, framed by chipped white wood. The news that grandma had died, the talk about boys and sex, the announcement that her parents were getting a divorce – each had been preceded by the same hesitant cough. And Dottie had always known the words before her mother began to speak.

"Honey…Thank you for coming," Kate said. "It would have meant a lot to Linda, I know it would."

"You don't have to thank me," said Dottie. "She was practically my second mother."

"I know…." Her mother hesitated. On the radio, somebody asked a question about the power-train of a 1993 Toyota. The hosts burst into laughter for no reason Dottie could explain. "Well. I know it's awkward for you. Andy and all. And this might seem silly….Just another thing the old people have to do."

Dottie shook her head. "No," she said. "You're saying goodbye. There's nothing silly about that."

She was lying — a little, anyway. She understood that her mother was grieving, but they had already held a funeral for Linda Walstead, nearly two months ago, in the field outside her home. She'd watched Linda's husband, Peter, set up the altar, had listened to Linda's children, Lucy and Andy, call in the elements. She'd been there when their little tribe said their goodbyes, spread the ashes, and closed the circle.

They said goodbye with red balloons. Each person at the funeral – more pagans than she had seen at a sabbat in years – had one, lighter than air, with a white string hanging down. As the sun set, the family went back out to the altar and shared a round of Linda's persimmon mead. She had finished bottling it the week after Yule, just a week before her death. In a year's time, it would have been fine; then, it was sour, too pungent. But they each passed the bottle and each took a drink, even Dottie, who hated alcohol. They drank it and pretended to love it, because they had loved her.

When the bottle came back empty to Peter, he sat it on the ground and looked up at the rusty gradient of the sky. He started to speak, his voice a shaky tenor. "A man once said," Peter began, "that the quality of heart is not judged by how much we love, but by how much we are loved by others." He paused, swallowed. "Well, look around you, and judge the quality of this heart." He raised his balloon high above his head with trembling fingers. "Goodbye, Linda."

He let go of the balloon and it rose up, up, up into the sky, and then there were dozens trailing after it, an ocean of red that seemed like it might never end. And then at last the balloons were just a red blotch in the sky, and soon, not even that. They floated away into the Summerlands, Linda Walstead floating with them.

Dottie thought it had been a nice enough funeral, even though she cringed when Peter mentioned The Wizard of Oz. But it was over. Why go through it again? Why not let the dead lie?

"Any idea what we're going to do?" Dottie asked.

"Not sure," said Kate. "I think we're doing some kind of Buddhist ceremony."

"Buddhist?" said Dottie, confused.

"You know Pete and Linda. They always were willing to take anything that hadn't been bolted down...."

Twenty minutes passed before her mother came to a farm bounded by a picket fence. An open gate led to a driveway that curled uphill through a copse of trees. Next to the gate was a sign on a pole:

THE WALSTEAD FAMILY
WELCOMES YOU TO
THE ELYSIAN FIELDS
2917 Zimmerman Rd.

Above the words, a serene image of the sun with a human face stared out.

Dottie looked at the smiling sun as the car wound its way past, remembering the day they'd put it up, her memories as clear as a lakewater reflection.

The Walsteads held their housewarming party on the festival of Lughnasadh, the first of August. Fifty-four people showed up, the biggest crowd a festival had ever attracted: the regulars came, the regulars' friends came, old coven members who had moved away for work or family came, all to celebrate the Sun King's feast and to make sure for themselves that Peter and Linda Walstead were still alive.

Peter let Andy, ten years old and already tall and lanky, drive the final nail into the sign outside the Elysian Fields. When it had been driven in all the way, the fifty-four pagans clapped and grabbed each others' hands. They started to sing "Sumer Is Icumen In," the men pumping their arms in rhythm, just like in The Wicker Man. Dottie had been among them, a little girl in a gingham dress, laughing and clapping and exulting in the thrill of something she could not yet name: the turning of the wheel, the fruit of life, the splendor of Wicca.

Dottie remembered the joy she once felt, and shuddered to think she had ever been so young.

Peter was outside the house smoking a cigarette when they pulled up. He looked across the Elysian Fields and took in one fiery breath. The morning sun blazed on the duck pond at the bottom of the hill. A thin film of water had started to appear across the gray ice. Peter looked at it for a moment after Dottie's mother had turned the engine off, as though he did not notice them, but finally he turned and smiled. Dottie realized that his golden mustache, which she had known him to wear her entire life, had faded to white.

Dottie's mother took her daughter's hand and squeezed it. "I love you, honey."

"I know, Mom. I love you, too."

Her mother opened her car door and clambered out with little grunts of pain and stiffness. Dottie had come to associate them with her parents' generation. Kate pulled Peter into a matronly hug that lasted for over a minute; Dottie tried to ignore the sound of sniffles.

"Hey, Kate, Dottie," said Peter. "Good to see you two here."

"It's always good to see you, Pete," said her mother, releasing him. "We missed you at Candlemas."

"Oh, I know," he said. He dropped his cigarette to the concrete driveway and crushed it. "I tried to make it, but I just got caught up in things." Dottie knew he didn't expect them to believe him. He looked over at Dottie with a broad grin. "C'mere, kiddo. It's been awhile."

Peter hugged her, as he had hugged her so many times before: every six weeks, a turn of the wheel, a long hug from Uncle Pete. The faint air of cigarette smoke that clung to his flannel shirt didn't make her cough or wrinkle her nose; from him, it smelled comforting, safe.

"Lucy and Andy are in the house," he said as he let her go. "We'll be up in a minute."

Dottie walked through a green door into the house's garage, where Andy's truck was parked; Peter's white Ford pickup sat outside. She could hear a knife chopping through vegetables, smelled ham in the oven. Three months ago, it would have been Linda in that kitchen, ready to kiss Dottie's cheek and put her to work peeling potatoes, but no more. The garage was dark, and when she flipped the garage's light switch, nothing happened.

"Hey! Your light bulb must be burnt out," she called. Her footsteps murmured like ghosts on the creaky stairs.

"It's not the bulb," called a male voice. "The electric went out about seven A.M. Good thing we still use gas out here." Dottie came out of the stairwell and into the earthy tones of the kitchen. Andy, still tall, lanky, and blond, leaned on a stone countertop, eating a slice of green apple. "Figures that mom would bump into the power lines on her way out..."

"Yeah," said Dottie. "This is my last meal on earth and you're going to do it right, goddammit! I don't want you microwaving anything, and if anyone even touches the television, gods help me I'll haunt you myself!" she said in her best warty hag's voice.

Andy didn't chuckle. He looked bad, like he hadn't been sleeping. The word, she decided, was weary: bone-weary, world-weary, like he was tired and had been for weeks.

She paused, already out of words, and realized the frustrating silence between them had not faded since she last saw him, at the funeral. "How have you been holding up?" she asked, at last.

Andy swallowed the last of his apple slice. "Jesus, how do you think I'm —"

"Dottie!" called a voice from the dining room. "Is that you?"

Andy rolled his eyes and checked on the pot of stew. Lucy bounded into the kitchen, a tall pale girl who could have passed for a Valkyrie if she hadn't dyed her hair a dark shade of violet. Her long skirt swirled around her, every step a salsa dance. She kissed Dottie on the forehead.

"Hey, you," said Dottie. "What's up?"

"Not too much," said Lucy. "I got in about nine last night. Train got held up for like, seven hours. It was crazy."

"You wouldn't have these problems if you stayed in Saint Louis...." If Dottie had been the sort of person who smirked when she teased people, she would have smirked then; but she wasn't, and didn't.

Lucy grinned. "And maybe if St. Louis had a half-decent linguistics program, I would have."

Dottie leaned on the counter, looking at her two old friend, the Green Man and the Valkyrie. "It's practically a family reunion. Too bad Lou isn't here." Dottie saw Lucy's face twist in discomfort and regretted mentioning him. "What?"

"Nothing," said Lucy. "Nothing. I just feel weird talking about him. He would have wanted to have been here."

"He'll be out of jail in a couple of months," said Andy. "And then I'll punch him in his fucking jaw, the dumbass."

Lucy shot her brother a look, and turned back to Dottie. "Anyway. Enough about that. Come on, I'm still setting up the table."

Lucy dragged Dottie through the doorway into the dining room. She caught a last look at Andy before being crossing the threshold: he lifted a spoonful of soup to his lips. His face soured. "Something missing," he muttered, and started looking through the spice cabinet.

****

The dining room was one enormous altar, from the statue of the Buddha atop the mantle to the chorus of deities whose figures littered the room: Athena and Pan, Odin and Freyja, Ma'at and Thoth. A painting of the Kabbalistic Tree of Life hung next to an image of Krishna playing the flute; a hundred holy symbols, all made of silver, hung from the chandelier in the center of the room. The dining room was also the library, walls lined with bookshelves stretched from floor to ceiling. Books crammed every shelf: mythology, rituals, magick, a small collection of early editions by Crowley, Gardner, Austin Spare. Hidden away on one of the shelves were three round, silver picture frames: one of the Wicked Witch of the West, one of Glinda the Good Witch, and between, a smiling portrait of a woman in a green dress, her chestnut hair brushing against her shoulders. Dottie wondered whose idea it was to put Linda between the two witches.

The dining room table, set with a sanguine cloth, had been filled by plates and dishes of food; they, too, were a part of the altar, the food of the sacrament, the gifts of the Goddess.

The five of them sat around the table, Peter at the head. He closed his eyes and took a deep breath, then reached for Kate and Lucy's hands. Lucy's fingers crept into Dottie's and their hands came to rest on the table. Dottie looked across the table to Andy and stretched her hand out to him. His grip was cold and formal.

"There's a belief among the Tibetan Buddhists that the end of life comes in stages," said Peter, slowly. "That there's the period of dying, when you know that this life is coming to an end, and you begin to see a bright light...."

And then the stage just after death, when the soul is still present, has not yet shed its attachment to this world and lingers on. They believe that the soul can linger for forty-nine days before, at last, it passes on to whatever fate waits for it....The disintegration into the peace of Nirvana, or their reincarnation into this world, once more.

"The Buddhists hope for Nirvana, but I know Linda would have wanted to hop back on the wheel and go around again," he said, a sad smile forming beneath his mustache.

Lucy sniffled. Dottie, not knowing what else to do, squeezed her friend's hand and felt a brief squeeze back. "We're here today to say goodbye, one last time, as her soul makes its final survey of all that it knew while it was known as Linda, and then passes on." Peter looked at his son. "Andy, would you start us off with the elements?"

"Sure, dad." Andy breathed in through his nose and held it. His hand loosened a little: it felt a little more like it had when Dottie held it years ago, back when she thought she was in love with him. For the first time since Linda died, he looked at peace, like the Green Man. "Spirits of east, spirits of the air, we call you into our circle today. Breath of life, winged winds, carry mom's spirit to us now. So mote it be." Everyone echoed him: "So mote it be."

He swallowed and gave Dottie's mother the faintest squeeze. Dottie had learned what that meant when she was a little girl: Go on. Your turn.

Dottie's mother, in the south, called in fire. She tripped over her words, asked the spirits to see Linda through her rebirth, like a phoenix. Lucy, in the west, called the spirits of water with an invocation that sounded like something out of Yeats, asked for her mother's swift passage across the Styx. After each of their invocations, the table resonated with repetition: "So mote it be."

Dottie felt Lucy squeeze her hand, and she closed her eyes, wondering what to say. She chewed on her lip and pondered it, then felt Lucy squeeze her again: Your turn. Didn't you feel me the first time?

"Spirits of the north, spirits of the earth....Spirits of the ground, where we'll all return someday. We were made from your clay, will one day be again in your sacred womb. Be with us here today." She paused. "So mote it be."

"So mote it be," said the family.

She opened her eyes and saw Andy looking at her. He rolled his eyes, just barely, and then turned away.

Peter gestured to the dishes. "Linda loved to cook, so we made as many of her favorite dishes as we could...."

"We brought pecan pie and green salad," said Dottie's mother. "Linda threatened to stop talking to me, that one year I forgot the pie." She smiled at the memory.

They sat there for a moment, until Lucy poked Dottie in the shoulder. "Well, come on. Pass me some of that ham."

Dottie thought the food was a little odd for the occasion, more suited to Christmas at a grandparent's house than a Buddhist farewell ceremony. The Walsteads had made ham, a vegetable stew, green beans with bacon slices, and lentils. Dottie realized, once she took a bite, that the lentils were made with Indian spices, which gave the meal a little more Buddhist credibility.

Her mother and Peter did most of the talking, little anecdotes that they had both told many times before but needed to hear out loud again. Lucy listened and sometimes added a memory of her own: the food fight Linda started one Midsummer when she was a girl, where Andy and Lou, too young to know better, started throwing apples and pears instead of mashed potatoes and ice cream; the first ritual she'd help her mother write, that Samhain when she was seventeen, a ritual done by candlelight to the sonorous chiming of hand bells. Andy kept quiet.

Dottie didn't say much, didn't feel like she had much to say. She had known Linda her whole life, but always as her best friends' mother, never as a friend or an equal. She had always been in the background, an adult doing adult things, while she and the other children lived in a world adjacent but never fully connected.

That feeling did not fade away, as she thought it might, when she grew into a woman; they remained divided, the elders and the children. Eventually Lucy and Lou moved off to college, and it was just Dottie and Andy, the last two, alone. Perhaps that was what convinced them they were supposed to be lovers. Then that broke apart too, and the only person left was Dottie....

Linda was like a fairy or a land-wight: something she believed in, but only at a distance.

Dottie's mother began to cut up the pecan pie and divvy the slices between the five. They ate it silently, an unspoken compact in the air acknowledging something sacred in the act. When Dottie chewed on the first bite of pecan and crust, she realized that this pie would be the final dish they would share with Linda's spirit before that knot of attachments and memories scattered itself forever. It must have been a powerful moment for the Walsteads. She wished she felt the same.

When the pie was finished, the last bits of food eaten and the knives and forks laid to rest on the tablecloth, Lucy reached for her father and Dottie. Without words, the table joined hands again, and Lucy cleared her throat. "I think we should have a chant," she said. "One of mom's favorites."

Dottie's mother nodded, and closed her eyes. Everyone did the same but Dottie, who watched her mother start to sing. "We all come from the goddess," she called, her alto voice more suited to stories than songs. "And to her we shall return, like a drop of rain flowing to the ocean."

Their voices joined hers, and they chanted for longer than they had in any ritual. The words faded away, became a tone-poem, an endless circle of notes that revolved throughout the dining room, each "ocean" drifting directly into the next "we all come from the goddess," each repetition sung for fear of being the one to at last declare an ending, to finally say goodbye.

****

She half-expected to find him with his legs crossed, chanting the names of the gods, like she'd found him so many times before. But the Green Man was nowhere to be found. Instead, Dottie saw Andy in his black coat and blue jeans sitting on the edge of the duck pond, a burning cigarette clenched between his teeth. He looked out at the gray ice, growing thinner in the afternoon sunlight, and raised the cigarette to his lips again.

"When did you start smoking?" she asked.

"About the time I started playing in bars," he said. "It comes with the territory."

Dottie blinked. She hadn't known he was in a band, much less one that played gigs. "Oh," was all she said.

"If you're going to give me the safety lecture, spare me. Dad's already told me half a dozen times."

"I wasn't going to lecture you. You're a grown man, you do what you want." She sat down next to him. He didn't turn to look at her. "You're testy today." He gave her a look like skunk spray and returned his focus to his cigarette. Dottie frowned and patted him on the back for a moment, to no response. "Come on," she said. "Don't act this way."

"How would you prefer I act? Completely oblivious? Smile and pretend like I'm happy? Fuck that." He flicked the ash from his fingers, watched it settle on the melting face of the pond and ripple outward. "I don't feel like hiding today."

Dottie swallowed. "I'm sorry about your mom."

"Thanks," he said in a dead tone.

Crows cawed from the power lines that lined the road outside the Elysian Fields. Dottie took her hand from Andy's shoulder. "Do you want me to leave you alone?"

"Doesn't matter, either way," he said. He drew in one last drag and stubbed the cigarette out in the dead grass. "It's not like you're really here to begin with."

"What's that supposed to mean?" she asked. He didn't answer; instead he went for his pocket, to pull out his pack of cigarettes again. Dottie swatted his arm. "No, I mean it. Answer my question."

"I mean, like usual, you're mixing up being around with being here. You pat me on the back and tell me it'll all be okay, and you think that's real sympathy." He finally got hold of his pack and shook another cigarette out. "You know you didn't even mention Mom when you invoked earth? Her goddamn final goodbye and you didn't even mention her."

Dottie blinked. "I'm sorry that I messed up an invocation, but...."

"You didn't mess anything up, Dottie," he growled. "You said it perfectly. Would have gone over great at Full Moon. But this was supposed to be different. Supposed to be more than just some ....empty ceremony."

"So Full Moon is just an empty ceremony?"

He grunted. "Yeah, most of the time, it is."

"You're starting to sound like me."

"No call for that kind of talk," he said, finally flicking open his Zippo. "That's fighting words in most states."

She sighed. "Come on. It's your mom's last day on Earth....Do you want to be like this for it?"

"Of course I don't want to be. But it's how I feel." He coughed, and sounded almost exactly like his father. "I just....Dottie, I hadn't cried in years. Years. Not when my grandparents died, not when my dog died. But fuck, I can't help it anymore." He put the cigarette between his teeth and rubbed at his eyes. "Heart condition. Completely unexpected fucking heart condition. Gave out on her just like that, no notice, no nothing. I sure as hell wasn't ready for her to go."

They heard the sound of a door shutting, then the voices of their parents and Lucy. The voices were too quiet to make out, though. More stories, Dottie guessed; it seemed like their memories of Linda were black holes, no moment too small to escape. The three got into Peter's truck and pulled off deeper into the Fields.

"I wonder what they're up to," said Dottie.

"Lucy hasn't seen the chickens yet since she got home. Expect they're going out to the coop." His breath swirled around his nose, a mixture of smoke and fog from the cold air. "My dog," he said, softly. "You know, that's what I kept thinking about at the funeral. The day we had to put Jackson down. He had fallen down over in the wheatfield, and couldn't get up.... And he was too big to pick up and put in the truck. Called the vet out, had him put under and then put down. I was sitting there next to him, petting his fur, while the vet put that last needle into him....Chanting under my breath, 'hoof and horn, hoof and horn, all that dies will be reborn.' Believing it. Needing to believe it, because there was nothing else to do.

[125]

"And when were standing out in that same field, watching those balloons fly away from us, I was saying the same thing.... 'Vine and grain, vine and grain, all that's cut will rise again.' Everything comes around in cycles, everything that dies comes back. No bullshit eternity. No such thing as forever." He looked at the burning stub in his fingers and took another drag, then stamped it out. "And I didn't believe it, Dottie. Such a beautiful sentiment, but at the end of the day, my mom's gone, and she ain't coming back. Hell, if the Buddhists are right, the best thing could happen to her is that all those little bits of soul that thought they were her have realized they were wrong, and they've finally let go of the illusion...."

Andy looked at her then, for the first time since she'd walked into the kitchen that morning, looked directly at her. She saw lines in his face she'd never seen before, saw his hair starting to thin into a widow's peak. She saw his father's face hiding behind his own, a statue chipping its way into being. She saw the dead cigarette in his hand, saw the mud on his work boots, saw the cracks of crimson traced in the whites of his eyes.

She saw an eight-year-old boy in a white wooly sweater, chasing after his sister in her green dress and shiny new shoes. She saw the girl carrying a two-foot-tall red Power Ranger doll. She saw herself, a seven-year-old with latté-brown skin, standing next to the Yule Tree and laughing at the sight, not yet so stern as the woman she'd grow up to be. She saw the girl in the green dress run directly into Linda Walstead's legs, who scolded her and made her give back the doll. She saw the boy stick his tongue out at her as soon as his mother had vanished into the other room and mutter, "Thanks for the help, Dottie."

She saw a young man standing in circle at an August Full Moon, saw him sneak his arm around her waist as the coven watched The Wicker Man on Uncle Geddy's television, saw him lean in, eyes closed, to put his mouth to hers for the first time. She saw them standing in Uncle Geddy's backyard, pressed together, felt something like the moon rising in the pit of her body.

She saw him naked, his thin, bony body lit up by a circle of mismatched candles, that weekend when Dottie's mother went to Chicago on business and together they performed the Great Rite. She saw their bodies moving in rhythm to some primal beat they had never heard before. She heard herself call him Pan, call him Kernunnos, call him Horned One; she heard him call her Isis, call her Venus, call her Goddess.

She saw him at his mother's funeral, a red balloon floating away from his fingers, mouthing words she only now understood.

And then she saw him again, Andy Walstead, Andy the Green Man, sitting by the duck pond, watching her with a dead cigarette in his hand, this old friend, this person she once shared her whole world with. She saw him raise his hand to his face and wipe away any hope of tears.

"What?" he asked.

"Nothing," she said. She reached for his hand. It was cold, but so was hers. They sat like that for a moment, listened to the crows and the chickens and the sound of Peter's truck as it ferried their family around the farm.

"It's going to be okay," said Dottie, and for once, she believed it.

Mother Blood Sky

by JD Revezzo

Crimson-pink, the sun broke over the horizon as the gods' war council met to decide, and Mother Blood Sky watched them warily, hopeful, fearful of what the day would bring. She could no longer stand back; she'd had to do something! They must challenge this destruction, or their world would not survive.

"Come, Exalted One; give us your perspective," the gods said.

In the space of what the humans would term a mere breath, Mother Blood Sky gave them the overview they sought. It wasn't a pretty story, but she spun it out vividly, recounting every detail. It was a tale full of hatred; a lament of shameful deeds; a tragedy of gratuitous destruction that ripped their hearts; a report that, with its end, left them bereft. Her kinsmen's hearts bled disgust and dread.

Her hand shook as she took the missive they held out to her, and she wondered if she should retract all she'd said.

Impossible. Their anger demanded retribution.

Her challenge accepted, the heavy oak doors creaked as they opened before her exit; her boot steps echoed over the smooth stone floor. Outside the beauteous palace, the ting and din of hammer against metal and stone met her ears as she hurried away. The scent of animals followed her to the gate.

The courtyard was soon behind her, and she set out on her path. She ran, down through winding forest paths, followed them breach to the edge dividing her world from prying human eyes. Picking a golden-orange leaf from one of the tall Sweet Gum trees nearby, she wondered how they would look upon this day, in years to come. What stories their historians would tell. What would they say? Would it be the day the sun had darkened? The day all hell broke loose from its moorings? Or would they see it as the day their patriotism was again tested? How long would that feeling last? Would it become one more link in the chain of nonsense that ruled their lives? Or would it mean something to them? As much as it meant to her, the council, and their men?

She wondered what treaty terms the survivors would ultimately accept — if there were any left.

She studied the delicate leaf, wondering if they were making a mistake. What if the council had misinterpreted the signs? Had she? Maybe those beings weren't so dense after all. Could it be that they truly didn't see the grand design, that connection between everything. No. It was clear they'd seen and rejected it. They loved to foster complications, to create them where she and her people saw none. Why, they were still fighting over the power of their arbitrary calculations!

All the while, what was real, and precious — the thousand intricacies within the simplest of things — became completely lost in their squabbling.

Mother Blood Sky knew these things had led the council to rule against them, but the here and there of it was behind them. There was nothing to be done about it now. Resolve was all that remained. The council was livid, she beyond so, and everywhere along the borders of her glade, the humans rushed to and fro in their playthings of metal and glass, whiling their lives away, typically oblivious to the dangers mounting against them. They skittered along like mindless automatons, so happy in their righteous anger, so intolerant in their bliss. The thought of their deeds turned her stomach sour, even as it tugged at her tears. They were poor fools, every one. But they could never repair the destruction they had wrought, she knew, even as she wished she had never spoken up against them.

Would the humans understand what their lethargy, their hate, their ridiculous love of dominion, their superstitious natures, their soul-sucking greed had cost them?

Poor fools! Let them take to the skies, if they would, the seas if they dared, anywhere they thought they could find refuge. Let them find out if the windfolk and the seafolk were just as angry as she and the council.

Cradling the leaf in her hand, she whispered, "Tell them it is time, little brother. Tell them it is time to move out." Lifting her hand to the winds, Mother Blood Sky watched as a tiny whirlwind descended to touch her palm, whisking away the special missive, dancing it out to its destination like a red-winged fairy of hope.

Out it spun across the field, to flit playfully over the rush and roar of their iron beasts, to spiral away into the concrete savanna. Caught momentarily on a windshield, against a wastebasket, releasing itself, it became the prey in a playful chase, and was soon caught and cradled in a little girl's hand who cried, "Look, Mommy, the leaf has a little baby!" when she noticed the peculiar pocket etched within, glittering like luminescent tin. When a wind gust broke the child's grasp, the missive flitted away to land at last in the hands of those for whom it was meant.

The message received, the signal cry rang out, a whisper so powerful, it hushed the winds. Mother Blood Sky's captains looked down upon the battlefield: cities glittering and drab, sprawling and claustrophobic. Lifting hands of strong resolve, they gave the signal. "It is time!" And a battle cry echoed across the glade.

Beneath signs that read *Hollywood* and *Welcome to New York*, at the steps of

[129]

Salisbury Plain, the threshold of Dublin, the shores of Tripoli, before the ancient Japanese torii, and the walls of the Forbidden City. Outside the domes of the Kremlin and before the Brandenburg Gate. In the shadows of signs for Orlando, and Dallas. On the African plains, and at the ports of Hudson Bay, Havana, Jamaica, Bermuda. Across the blazing desert sands and in the shadow of every oasis — everywhere the humans massed, the wolves howled and lions roared. Tigers turned away from their usual prey, sharks and crocodiles gnashed strong jaws at unsuspecting humans, snakes and spiders rose up to strike, and carrion birds swooped down.

A thin tendril of sunlight cracked the horizon and kissed the red gold of Mother Blood Sky's armor, the steel of her immortal weapons. Clouds overhead deepened, gray rolled to black, smothering the horizon, winds cracked tree trunks, ancient and strong, thunder shook the Earth's foundations, threatening a storm the likes of which no living being had ever seen ....

And the humans below panicked as they watched the signs of doom unfold, and the Juggernaut swooped mercilessly down....

[Note: a previous version of this tale appeared in Twisted Dreams Magazine, *October 2010.]*

The Myth-Shifter

by Star Foster

New Colony Assimilation Project
Sext4; 12th Armstrong, 5397 QST
Classified Status: Lvl 8
Authenticity verified by Cpt. Karal Byun, IN 67544892
Attachment: Communication records between Aberrog and Bengar

Report Received: Gen. Jant Aberrog on the Triax Colonies, Cannult system

Greetings in peace and liberty,

As I mentioned in my previous report, the planets Berron and Fyand were colonized successfully and assimilation of indigenous population is proving successful. Fyand is on schedule. Berron is developing rapidly and you should receive your first mineral shipments by Sext6.

In my previous report, I had stated our next goal was the colonization of Beta Prime, but further research indicates lower than expected resources combined with a hostile population. To maintain project momentum I chose to skip Beta prime to focus on Noirraill, a small planet with a fertile environment. While lacking in major minerals, metals and fuel gasses, the agrarian advantages it offers the system, as well as the NCAP, make it an important strategic colony.

The vanguard landed on 36 Yuri, 5397 QST. The population was at HG stage with minor agrarian activity. Military strength at .01. Government was minor tribal model. Religion of primitive solar/lunar variety. Economy rating .01. No unusual traits presented themselves to myself or the vanguard at this time.

Initial contact positive. Population open to trading; free with supplies and information. Sexuality open and uninhibited. A central village with a large market was targeted as the most strategic for dissemination of savior myth. Vanguard made the decision to use colonization model Alpha7. Priestess-Captain Oudra Bengar and two acolytes took up residence on planet while vanguard remained on ship, except for intermittent trading expeditions.

As of 42 Yuri, 5397 QST the colonization was on schedule. PC Bengar provided regular reports of the religious mysteries, astrological myths and agrarian cycles of the population, as well as the interpretations and cult of her team. The mythic shift was on schedule and one of the acolytes was beginning the savior exercises.

On 1 Tereshkova, 5397 QST report received from PC Bengar that the savior exercises were proving effective, but that the new interpretation of myths and astrology were not taking root. She requested additional time to indoctrinate the priesthood before the vanguard began Phase II. I granted five additional days and sent another package of hallucinogens to aid her work.

On 3 Tereshkova, 5397 QST I received a report that the acolyte chosen to lead the savior cult had fallen prey to local disease. Several additional days would be required for the martyrdom and shift of power to the other acolyte to be complete. PC Bengar advised that a time of general mourning had been declared, with villages that had been visited by or heard of the deceased acolyte gathering to pay respects. She advised me that all commerce had ceased for the duration of the mourning period and that the vanguard would be seen as unwelcome by the inhabitants.

I advised PC Bengar that the cease of economic activity during tragedy was a counter-productive practice and advised that she realign this tradition to our colonization plan. I requested daily updates on her progress and immediate notification when the vanguard could land unhindered.

My next communication from PC Bengar was on 8 Tereshkova, 5397 QST and read as follows:

"The acolytes have perished. Eaten. The tusked one will not conform to your wishes. The blood of the proud fills his cup. The dire truth does not bend. The dire truth consumes. Tempt him not to wrath. He is jealous of the fruits of his fields; he counts his bison covetously."

PC Bengar having a spotless record of myth-shifting in planetary colonization, and knowing my own experiences with her in the NCAP, I found the message alarming. It was my theory at this time that the message had come from a native priest and that PC Bengar was in danger.

I immediately assembled a rescue team and sent them planetside. I received a confirmation of landing and then complete silence. Our communications team, who never before failed me in anything, were unable to pickup any communications or beacons from the planet.

I assembled my officers to form a plan of action. The majority agreed that the most experienced members of the vanguard would reconnaissance in cloaked gear before further action was taken. I decided to lead this force, leaving Major Ravid Ashumel in charge of the vanguard fleet.

Once planetside we found the pod used by the rescue team, empty, with no indication of any malfunction. The pod's power packs didn't give off any energy signals, nor were there any other energy signals, other than those of the recon team, picked up the entire time we were planetside.

Upon entering the village we encountered a large gathering of people, all silent. On a platform in the market we saw PC Bengar flaying the skin off one of the members of the rescue team. He appeared to be dead, but we were unable to get close enough to get an accurate scan or to positively identify him without being detected. Several Terran skeletons were hanging from poles around the market, wrapped in bright ribbons. Inspection of the two we were able to get detailed visuals of revealed knife marks consistent with butchering. We continued to observe the platform from a distance.

Once PC Bengar had removed the skin from the crewman a large man bearing thick curved horns on either side of his head and tusks curving out of his mouth mounted the platform. He was hairy, to the point of seeming to be covered in coarse fur from head to toe. He gave a strangely loud, animalistic bellow, at which the crowd seemed to surge forward as a silent wave.

PC Bengar then chose three young women from the crowd, helping them up onto the platform. The man with horns danced in a sexual manner with each woman in turn, after which they were allowed to saw off the legs and arms of the flayed man to take with them. The horned man remained on the platform, penis erect, and bellowed again. This time the people gathered cheered; a deafening sound. PC Bengar kneeled before him weeping and swaying. Two men removed the remains of the flayed crewman. We were unable to follow.

When the crowd finally dispersed it did not take us long to find PC Bengar's quarters in a large, almost empty temple. We found her in sexual intercourse with the man from the platform. The tusks and horns were on a shelf but the hair was genuine. In the corner what was left of the bodies of the acolytes had been mummified and covered with unknown symbols. The hallucinogens were unopened and there was a bottle of a potent alcoholic substance open by the bed.

I de-cloaked to debrief PC Bengar and she began screaming "God-killer! God-killer!" repeatedly. The hairy man moved to attack me but was quickly dispatched by a cloaked teammate. Attempts to debrief PC Bengar proved futile. Attempts to sedate her or calm her were useless and before we realized what was happening she fell on her own knife, the one provided to all myth-shifters upon completion of training.

We are uncertain still of what went wrong in such a simple colonization exercise. Our scans did not reveal any toxins, hallucinogens or any other substance in PC Bengar's body to suggest a chemically altered state. While we left the bodies as they were found, we did take large tissue samples from PC Bengar, the two mummified acolytes and the hairy man. Half of the samples will remain with the vanguard medical lab, and the other half are included with my report. I have also included all planetside visuals, and all communications between myself and PC Bengar.

While we are still uncertain of the cause of the incidents on Noirraill, we do still believe it is of strategic importance to NCAP. Its agrarian potential is vast. We feel that traditional methods of colonization are inappropriate given recent events. I am requesting permission to remove all humanoid life forms from the planet by biochemical means.

I am also requesting a new Priestess-Captain for the myth-shifting team, and at least three additional acolytes. By the time they arrive the biochemical cleansing and the settlement of new colonists should be complete. We will need a PC for the colonization of Yeerai, as the indigenous people's cooperation will be necessary, at least at first, in order to efficiently exploit the resources there.

I do not expect the NCAP to be adversely affected by this unfortunate incident in the long term. We are still on schedule with other colonies in the system and have encountered no other setbacks.

I also hope that this incident does not tarnish PC Bengar's record. She was a fine officer who had manipulated the religions of hundreds of planets successfully. I am honored to have served with her and, though I do not know the circumstances that led to her break with her training, I believe that when she landed on Noirraill she was loyal to the NCAP.

General Jant Aberrog
Commander of the NCAP, Ford Sector

The Resurrection of Samhain

by Quincy Allen

I can't believe that old bugger Kyteler actually bought the thing. Earth must really be short on cash." Lieutenant Quintin Hayes scanned the lased crater before him and fed in the data to an analyzer at his hip. The pit, a perfect cylinder, was three hundred meters across and twenty meters deep. A ring of portable force-field generators resembling little Kilroys, their noses dangling over the edge, lined the perimeter at ten meter intervals and kept the sides from caving in. The deep-green turf of the region, an inches-deep carpet of what looked like curly jade hair, ran right up to the edge of the pit. Numbers slid by on Quint's visor: dimensions were accurate out to five decimals; latitude and longitude were dead on right down to the microsecond; the geological magnetics were as near a match as they were likely to find on Stranach IV. He lifted his stratavisor and rubbed tired eyes. "And to ship the damn thing seventeen parsecs out here ...." he said into the comm with disbelief. "What kind of money does that take?" A low-hanging autumn sun still cast warm light, but things would start to get chilly when it dropped below the horizon.

"You don't have that many zeroes in your head, Quint," Captain Maggie Dunne kidded, laughing lightly as she stood in front of the lasing-rig control-panel and held her finger over the sys-check icon suspended in the panel hologram. Maggie reflected back to his arrival in an over-burdened, one-way transport pod two months earlier. They'd detected his transponder and received a brief message about what he was there for. When he landed, he had a short list of equipment, including the force-field generators, the lasing-rig and a tidy set of orders to prep for the arrival of Kyteler's new acquisition. "Did the numbers check out on the hole?" She asked in a rigid tone, all business once again.

"Green across the board. The geo-magnetics came in at a ninety-seven-percent match, and we only needed ninety-five. It's double-solid." Quint took one last look at Maggie's distant figure at the far edge of the pit and turned away, heading back to their small encampment. The tight coils of vegetation, Stranach IV's equivalent of grass, were spongy under his feet, and he wove his way around the sparse maze of short, multi-colored blooms, fronds, stalks and boles of the native plant species that covered the rolling, alien country-side around him.

"Roger that. Running the sys-check and shutdown on this pig." She pressed her finger through the projected icon and pulled it back.

"Awwww...don't say that," Quint complained. "Machines are people too, you know. You could hurt its feelings."

Lifting its seven ton mass off the ground on repulsor beams, the gray, egg-shaped rig powered up with a deep humming sound and began swiveling, extending and then retracting the half-dozen lasing arms that extended out of its cerametal carapace. Maggie stepped away from the unit and let it go through its sequence.

"Machines are machines, Quint. You're mental."

"Wrong on both counts, Captain. I'm an engineer, and that lasing-rig has more intelligence than a dog if you'd just give it a chance." Quint reached their small group of inflatable shelters and hopped up on a fallen log that bordered the camp. He lowered his visor, selected magnify and scanned back towards the pit, picking out Maggie's floating form. Her slim figure was flying back towards him, passing directly over the pit. He adjusted his visor again to zoom in past her to the colony ship that squatted in permanent retirement to the right of New Dublin where 2,000 Irish colonists had been living for four years. The Unified Systems Council based on Mars had granted Stranach IV to the Irish Culture Polity as a culture-integrity world ten years before. The colonists were tucked into the belly of the colony-ship *The Monsterrat* and in cold-sleep on their way to Stranach a year later. *Monsterrat* was Ireland's only colony in the Caribbean during the expansion years of old Earth. Quint spotted the harvest rigs in the fields to the south of the town as they went about collecting the last of the season's harvest.

"Dog-smart or not, it's still a machine," Maggie came back with an amused tone. She stared down into the pit below her as she sailed over it like a ghost, suspended in the field emitted by her grav-belt. She scanned for irregularities along the bottom of the pit. "Now get the stove up. I'm starving," she added.

"Roger that," Quint replied and stepped off the log. By the time Maggie was touching down by her shelter, he had water boiling and was dropping in a chopped assortment of the local roots and vegetables followed by a few pinches of spices that were also native fare. He was a much better cook than Maggie, and he seemed to have a natural culinary flair for working with the local flora. They waited a few minutes in silence, just watching the pot boil.

"That smells great!" she said finally as she stepped up behind him and put her hands on his shoulders, her hands instinctively starting to massage them.

"That feels better," he replied, leaning back slightly into her. "This stuff won't take long if you want the tubers to be al dente."

"You're the chef. Impress me," she ordered and kissed his neck.

"I'll impress you once we get into your shelter. As to this, can you go grab us some bowls?" He kept stirring the pot.

"Pretty sure of yourself," she accused as she stepped away and reached into a container holding their supplies.

"You just let me know when you have a complaint, and I'll put in for a transfer," he retorted then lifted the pot off the stove.

"You don't have any place to transfer to, lieutenant," Maggie said, smiling. She held out a bowl in each hand, allowing him to spoon in some of the stew. With the vegetables chopped the way they were it looked like any stew one might find on old Earth. He set the pot back, turned off the flame and they sat down next to one another, leaning against the fallen log. The comfortable silence lasted as long as the meal, and when they finished, they both set their bowls aside. Maggie leaned in to Quint's shoulder as he put an arm around her, and they watched the sun start to slide behind a far-off hill. The gray dungarees of the Colonial Engineering Corps were warm, but the nights were getting colder as winter started to set in.

"So, when does it arrive?" Quint asked, squeezing Maggie and grabbing her hand.

"In two days: on the thirty-first." She squeezed back and cuddled in closer as the temperature dropped.

"Seriously? It's arriving on Halloween? How prophetic."

"The old man doesn't do anything without a reason." She stood and pulled him up behind her, heading for her shelter. "And you better get used to calling it Samhain, not Halloween. You're on an Irish world with Irish colonists who want to get back to their roots."

"Sir, yes sir!" Quint said like a fresh cadet. He kissed her lips, stared down into beautiful green eyes and pushed a lock of fiery red hair off of a freckled cheek. "Did I ever mention how much I love red-heads?"

"Call me 'sir' again and you'll have to love another." She glared at him but couldn't hold it. The glare turned into one of her witching smiles that never ceased to melt his heart; he was powerless before that smile. She held open the door and slapped his butt as he went in.

****

"*Balor*, rotate X aspect point-two-five degrees starboard." Quint stared down into the descent display that tracked the incoming chunk of Terran soil and tried to ignore the blasting wind that pressed down from above. He dared not look up at the black shadow slowly dropping out of the sky towards him. It was large enough to blot out both moons now, and he could almost feel the hundred million metric tons of earth suspended in the *Balor*'s tractor beams. That he was sitting in darkness only made the situation that much more unnerving.

[137]

The sun had set an hour earlier, so he sat in darkness in the middle of the encampment as he guided down Duncan Kyteler's prize artifact. The darkness didn't hinder his work, however, and he just barely managed to keep his hands from shaking. His eyes would never have left the screen for something like this anyway; the bonus for hitting the mark on the first try was incentive enough to do a perfect job. "Track point-eight meters to 183 degrees ...." Quint's voice sounded almost panicked in his ears, pitched way too high. He could only hope the crew didn't' give him too much grief when they were finished. "Steady....Track point-two-three meters to 240 degrees...." His teeth started to ache as the perimeter of the starship's drive-field crossed over him. He felt its sub-sonic hum, and the vibration threatened to shatter his skeleton and turn it to fine powder. "I'm in your field, *Balor*. Go to hover and maintain descent on tractors only."

"Roger that, ground-control," a man's voice said casually into the comm.

Sure, Quint thought, it's easy to be relaxed when you're sitting on top of that thing rather than stuck underneath the damn thing. Quint gritted his rattling teeth and kept his eyes on the monitor. "You're on the mark...package passing zero elevation...negative one meters...." A high-pitched whistling filled his ears, and a blast of air washed over him as the huge earthen cylinder slipped into the pit with less than two millimeters clearance all the way round. He maintained focus as one of the shelters blew over on its side. "Negative two meters...." Quint thought his teeth were going to jump out of his skull. He reminded himself of the bonus: I can buy new teeth...hell, a new head with that kind of money. "Negative fifteen...negative sixteen...Okay...slow descent ninety percent and increase field-dampers three hundred...."

"Roger that, ground." Quint wanted to slap the guy for being so cool.

"Easy...you're almost there...slow descent another ninety-percent...you've got centimeters...." Quint felt a gentle tremor flutter under his feet as the package bottomed out. The ground beneath him seemed to let out a tremendous, satisfied sigh as the bedrock once again took up the weight that had been stolen from it by the lasing-rig. The air stilled and the hum receded as the *Balor* drifted north, away and up from the surface. The drive-field receded, and then it was silent. Quint's skeleton and teeth stopped feeling like they were being shaken apart.

"Package delivered, ground-control," the man above said. "Nice guide-in, by the way. As good as I've seen."

"Are you kidding me? I damn near crapped my pants."

Laughter came through the comm. "Kid, take my word for it. I've been doing this twenty years. You're a natural. You ever decide to get off that rock, you look me up. I'd give you a job in a Mercury minute!"

"Thanks, *Balor*," Quint said sincerely. "I may take you up on that some day. Ground out."

"Roger that, ground. Have a better one." The comm went silent.

Quint pulled the comm-unit off his ear, shut down the terminal and pushed back on his chair, falling back onto the soft, green turf. He held up his hand before his eyes and could see it shaking slightly in the darkness. The only thing that kept him from freaking out completely was that he was now a rich man. The bonus would be enough for him to live quite comfortably on Stranach IV for the rest of his life – and without farming.... *Dea-Domhan*, he corrected himself. He'd have to remember it now that the colony had finally decided on a name for their new home. Maggie had told him that Dea-Domhan meant good earth, and he wished she were with him. She'd said that she had preparations to make for the celebration of Samhain. She had at least left him with a flask of imported Irish whiskey to celebrate a successful guide-in or lament a failed one. He pulled the flask from his pocket, twisted off the cap and held the flask up in salute to the retreating shadow of The *Balor*'s massive shadow as it blotted out the stars on its journey back into space. He tilted the flask into his mouth as he lay on the soft turf and took a couple of long swigs that burned sweetly as they went down. Quint closed his eyes and breathed deeply. He was exhausted, and the adrenaline was starting to wear off. Before he knew it, he was sound asleep.

****

A chill as deep as the grave seeped into Quint's body, startling him awake. It was an unnatural cold very different from the normal cold of the on-coming Dea-Domhan winter. He opened his eyes when his ears picked up an eerie, rhythmic chanting coming from down the hill towards the direction of where The *Balor* had delivered its payload. The cold deepened, and for the first time since his arrival he could see his breath as he exhaled into the sky. A ghostly shimmer at the corner of his vision forced him to turn his head and stare into the darkness as a tingle of fear gripped him. There was nothing there, but the cold didn't abate. He stood up and put his frozen hands into his armpits, turning towards the project site.

His eyes widened and his jaw dropped to his collar. He found himself suddenly questioning his sanity and an even greater fear tightened itself around his insides.

He could now see where the chanting was coming from. The area down the hill was surrounded with lit torches, and a great bonfire shone brightly at the center of the newly arrived circle of massive stones. The bonfire was surrounded by circles of people in white, hooded robes, and there were hundreds of them. The bone-chilling cold seemed to fade, and the temperature returned to normal, abating his fear somewhat.

"What the hell?" All he could do was stare in disbelief. Stonehenge, Kyteler's prize, was there just as it should be, but everything else made no sense at all. As he stood staring at the spectacle, he caught an occasional glimmer of faded bluish-white forms, looking almost like glowing smoke, meandering through the sparse vegetation of the area moving away from the bonfire.

One of the hooded figures detached itself from the edge of the circle and started walking up the hill towards him. He instinctively reached for his service-blaster and realized that they didn't issue them on colony worlds where there wasn't indigenous fauna. He spotted a few more ghostly wisps receding into the darkness away from the flame as the hooded figure approached.

Quint struggled with a severe flight-or-fight conflict, but finally curiosity won out as the hooded figure entered the small clearing of the encampment. Delicate hands lifted up and pulled back the hood to reveal beautiful green eyes, fiery red hair and freckled cheeks.

"Quint ...." Maggie started, but she didn't know quite where to begin.

Quint grasped on to the tangible reality of the woman he loved as an anchor in the sea of confusion that threatened to wash him away. "You mind telling me what the hell is going on?" He didn't know if he should be angry, scared or just chuck it all and go crazy right then and there.

"This is what it was all about, Quint. I meant to tell you, but there wasn't any way. You'd have to see it to believe it...from the beginning." She reached out her hand and smiled in the bewitching way that always hooked his heart.

"Uhh...and what is this, exactly?" They moved closer and held each other. He latched onto the solid footing of her embrace, and the seas of confusion around him calmed.

"Kyteler...he died just after buying Stonehenge from the Earth government. They needed the money and his lawyers were able to make the case to the Unified Systems Council that Stonehenge was a piece of Celtic heritage. He had himself buried there amongst the old graves around the monument. He wanted to live forever, and this was his only option."

"You haven't answered me," he said a bit more pointedly than he intended. Perhaps it was caused by the wispy ghost of a woman slowly walking by wearing clothing that looked like it came from the Dark Ages. The air chilled once again, and they could suddenly both see their breath in the night air.

"Good, old-fashioned, Irish ghosts: a new Irish world needs Irish ghosts. Stonehenge let us wake them here. We brought Kyteler back from the dead a short while ago along with the others." She kissed him gently and hugged him. "Welcome home, Quint," she said and never let go of him.

Appendix A
The Nature and Functions of Thoth in Egyptian Theology
by Edward P Butler

The concept of theology guiding the present essay understands it as an active process of inquiry. Theology in this sense demands that we carry out for ourselves the process that begins, not from arbitrary intellectual categories, but from myths, and results in a conception of the intellectual revelation that is unique to a pantheon, because it is drawn solely from the relationships immanent to it. In this way, theology grounds itself in working with myths and symbols in the multivalent state these have prior to any arbitrary delimitation of their reference. Conserving the symbol's integrity in this way unlocks its productivity, because fresh inferences can always be drawn from applying formal structures to new domains, once those formal structures have been discerned.

Investigating a deity in this fashion requires finding the mythemes (units of myth) and relations that are generative, as opposed to static attributes that are the result of such an inquiry, whether or not we are aware of the process. A productive mytheme for understanding Thoth's nature is his responsibility for healing the *wedjat*, the 'Eye of Horus', after Seth injures it. The Eye of Horus, whose graphical form seems to incorporate aspects of the eyes of a human, a hawk, and a leopard or cheetah, is called the *wedjat* [*wḏȝt*], or 'Sound <Eye>,' from *wḏ*, meaning healthy, flourishing, or prosperous or, as a verb, to proceed or attain. Its hieroglyph depicts a papyrus stalk, and hence it is also literally 'green', with all of the other meanings seeming to flow from the metaphor of vegetable growth. The *wedjat* is one of the most multivalent symbols in Egyptian thought, being used to represent everything from the moon to Egypt itself, but if we seek the center of its varied usages, it seems to be that the *wedjat* represents the beneficial power contained within offerings to the Gods of every kind. Whatever is the substance offered or otherwise utilized in ritual, once it has been ritually activated, it becomes the Eye of Horus. One can see this formula, for instance, throughout the Pyramid Texts, where the most varied offerings and ritual items are identified as the 'Eye of Horus' in the act of deploying them. This is not to say that ritual items are not associated with other mythemes in this text and in other Egyptian theological

[143]

and magical works. The *wedjat* is, however, the most universal symbol in Egyptian theology for any helpful substance or object, a general term for any amulet, as well as being a very common amulet in its own right. It expresses the double nature of Horus as a healer and as one who has been healed, for the 'Eye of Horus' refers virtually always to the eye that was wounded and healed, not to the other. Thoth's regeneration of the *wedjat* forms the basis of a ritual bond between these Gods, and thus between the functions of wisdom and sovereignty, but also between the effective use of knowledge and the stability of the cosmos itself. Thoth is also frequently credited with the reconstitution of Osiris (e.g., in PT utterances 368, 448), but it is not clear that this association is primary relative to the healing of the *wedjat*, for reasons discussed below.

The dispute between Horus and Seth concerns whether the cosmic sovereignty is to be accorded to brute force—or more charitably, sheer animal vigor—or whether the principle of legitimate succession is to be acknowledged on a cosmic scale. If Horus' claim to the throne of his father Osiris is found to be legitimate, despite the general divine recognition that Horus is not as strong as Seth, then the order of the cosmos, that is, nature as such, can in some way vindicate what is mortal. What is mortal will then be more than merely the by-product of natural forces of growth and change. Horus is the legitimate inheritor of Osiris, whom he has never known. Osiris is everything mortal in its mortality. Civilization depends upon the kind of bond existing between Horus and Osiris. Thought and communication depend upon the possibility of persons who are absent, and thus 'mortal', to one another, being able to possess 'the same' idea. In the sense that it is truly shared, the idea is in this way essentially absent, or 'mortal'. The bond between Isis and Osiris is of a different kind altogether inasmuch as Isis and Osiris are wholly present to one another; this relationship is not at stake in the conflict myth. In the same way, the conflict between Horus and Seth is of an entirely different symbolic value than the conflict between Re and Apophis, in which Seth is the savior of the cosmos against the force of entropy. One conflict can allude to or cite another, but this is a fresh symbolic equation, a full sentence, so to speak. The conflict of Horus and Seth concerns, in effect, whether civilization is to receive the authority of nature or is to remain its by-product. The resurrection of Osiris is in this way only finally accomplished through the acceptance of the legitimacy of Horus (and it is in this light that it involves the Isis/Osiris relationship).

In the conflict between Horus and Seth, which can never be regarded as simply and wholly resolved, Thoth, although clearly Horus's partisan in the quest for the sovereignty, was nevertheless understood to heal both Gods of their injuries, the eye of Horus and the testicles of Seth. Thoth thus represents something of value to both domains. Thoth also embodies a certain conflictual bond between the two combatants. In one key incident, Seth has used a homosexual encounter between himself and Horus to attempt to disparage Horus (i.e., as the passive participant and thus apparently subdominant) before the divine tribunal deciding the issue of the cosmic sovereignty. Seth is tricked, however, into ingesting lettuce contaminated with Horus' semen, which shows its presence within him by the emergence of a luminous disk from Seth's head. This disk is given to Thoth, and is taken to be the lunar disk often depicted on Thoth's head. In this way, wisdom is produced from nature because of a preexisting 'seed.' A prominent theme that can be discerned from the fragmentary Demotic 'Book of Thoth' (on which more below) is the idea that wisdom is continuous through the whole of nature; thus the text says at one point, "Is a learned one he who instructs? The sacred beasts and the birds, teaching comes about for them, but what is the book chapter which they have read? The four-footed beasts which are upon the mountains, do they not have guidance?" (B01, 1/6-7). Thoth's bond with Seth can also be seen from the fact that in certain images of balance and totality, such as the *sma tawy*, the 'uniting of the (two) lands', in which Seth represents Upper Egypt and Horus represents Lower Egypt, there is a tendency later in Egyptian history, as Seth falls into disfavor, to replace him with Thoth.

Another aspect of Thoth's role in mediating between Horus and Seth can be seen from the terminology used to refer to it. Thoth is generally characterized as 'separating' [*wp*] the combatants, a term which has the sense of separating physically but also of deciding or discerning. The same terminology of 'separating' is used in oracle consultations, where the God being consulted is asked to 'separate' (*wp*) two petitions, that is, to choose the correct claim and discard the other. This function can also be seen, however, less as a binary choice than as a bringing forth from obscurity into determinacy the functions of all the various divine principles. This broader sense of Thoth's activity is brought out in a hymn calling Thoth "the legislator in heaven and on earth, he who sees to it that the Gods remain within the limits of their competency, each guild fulfills its obligations and the countries know their frontiers and the fields their appurtenances," (Bleeker 1973, 137). The term *wp* is also used in contexts that speak of Thoth having distinguished or separated the languages of different countries from one another (see Cerny 1948), in which the principal idea is clearly not of forceful separation, but of the circumstances that allow difference to flourish.

In the tribunal setting, Thoth pleads the case on behalf of Osiris, that is, any mortal as such: "Content are all the Gods…with this great and mighty word which issued from the mouth of Thoth for Osiris," (PT utterance 577). The judgment that decides the legitimacy of succession from Osiris to Horus is effectively one and the same with the judgment of the deceased preceding the resurrection. The involvement of Horus, however, means that this judgment is also essentially in *this* world. Thoth's 'word' on behalf of Osiris is thus by extension every correct act of discernment and every act of justice. One end of this continuum is perception, the other is social action. Thoth is he "whose abomination is falsehood...lord of laws, who makes writing speak...who witnesses truth to the Gods, who so judges that *ma'et* [truth] is upheld, who vindicates the loser, savior of the needy one and his possessions...who rescues the needy from the powerful," (BD spell 182).

The Goddess Nehmetaway is frequently characterized as Thoth's consort (Seshat, also Thoth's consort at times, is at other times regarded as his daughter). Nehmetaway's name means 'Rescuer of the one who is robbed'. Some have seen a reference to her in the deity Plutarch refers to as "the first of the Muses at Hermopolis," whom "they call Isis as well as Justice [*Dikaiosunê*]," (*Isis and Osiris* 352B). The notion of justice here is not purely social, however. Injustice of any kind is always connected theologically to the Osirian plight of the mortal. Egyptian theology at once recognizes that the mortal is inherently victim of an injustice, but also affirms a cosmic process of vindication.

Another important function of Thoth is pacifying wrathful Goddesses, especially Sekhmet and Tefnut. This role is expressed in the epithet *sehetep neseret*, 'the one who pacifies/propitiates the divine flame.' Thoth mediates in this way between the mortal and the divine, for the fiery blast of wrathful Goddesses, which is called *neseret*, forms a barrier of sorts between these realms. There is also a complex symbolic equation underlying this function of Thoth's. The wrathful Goddesses are referred to by the epithet 'Eye of Re,' *irt* R^C. Now, *irt*, 'eye', is written the same as *ir.t*, the substantive of the verb *ir*, 'to do.' These Goddesses are therefore the 'doers' of Re, who execute his will in the cosmos. They are the operational dimension of Re's authority. But the pun upon *ir.t* that makes of them Re's 'eyes' in the world — the eye being not merely a passive witness but an active gaze — also evokes the Eye of Horus. Thoth's action with respect to the Eye of Horus, the ritually effective substance as such, can also be seen as harnessing and rendering beneficial to humanity the power of Re's fiery 'judgment' upon the chaotic forces that threaten the cosmos. The wrathful Goddesses, in particular Sekhmet, are thus often understood to participate in Thoth's regeneration of the *wedjat*. In the Tenth Hour of the Amduat book, for example, the healing of the *wedjat* is shown being carried out by Thoth, in baboon form, and eight forms of Sekhmet, four with lioness heads and four with human heads.

The most well-known myth, for us at least, concerning the wrathful 'Eye of Re' Goddesses is the narrative known as the 'Destruction of Humanity,' from the New Kingdom Book of the Celestial Cow, which I have discussed in detail elsewhere (Butler 2009). At the end of the process recounted in this narrative, humans have come into true humanity, and the 'Eye of Re,' through the process undergone in this text, becomes analogous to the restored Eye of Horus, the *wedjat*. In BD spell 167, "Spell of Bringing the *Wedjat*," the deceased affirms that "Thoth brought the Sound Eye, he pacified the Sound Eye after Re sent it forth (when) it was greatly enraged…If I stay sound, it stays sound." Here the Eye of Re and the *wedjat*, or Sound Eye, are thoroughly identified with one another.

Between Thoth and Re there is such a close relationship that Thoth is commonly referred to in later texts as the "heart [i.e., mind] of Re" (see Boylan 1922, 114f). A text from Esna (Sauneron, Esna V, 266, text 206, 11; III, p. 33; Sauneron in Mél. Mariette, p. 234-5) states that Thoth came forth from Re's heart "in a moment of grief". In very much the same way, humans are said to have come into existence from tears shed by Re (also said of Atum). While this myth has its basis in the similarity between the words for 'tears' (*remi*) and for 'humans' (*romi*) in Egyptian, it underscores the fundamental Egyptian idea of a distance between humans and the natural or cosmic order, a distance even painful on some level for the Gods themselves. This distance is made concrete where it is specified that Re (or Atum) wept because he was separated from his 'Eye', i.e., his agency or 'doing.' When she returns, he has fashioned a new eye, so he places the original 'Eye' upon his forehead, i.e., as the uraeus serpent whose flame is the defense of the cosmic order Re has established. This order involves a painful degree of separation between the natural order and human experience; but the work of healing this rift is immediately taken up by the Gods who occupy the space thus created, Gods such as Thoth, whom Re assists by delegating some of his own power.

The role of diverse Goddesses as 'Eye of Re' is one of the central themes of Egyptian theology, and central to the myth known as that of the 'Distant Goddess,' a particular variant of which involves Thoth. This myth is told with an ever-shifting cast of deities, depending upon its application in a given theological context. Its most cosmic form involves Shu and Tefnut, and is closely linked to the mytheme of the origin of the uraeus cited above, but an original local form of the myth may have involved Onuris and Mehyt. Many temple inscriptions allude to it, but the myth is not preserved in any early narrative form. In the myth Tefnut is induced by Shu to return with him to Egypt from a vaguely-determined foreign land called Bougem or Keneset, regarded as lying to the south and east of Egypt (e.g., Somalia), but essentially a mythical place — hence she is the 'Distant Goddess.' The return of the fiery and wrathful 'Distant Goddess' involves her appeasement and/or purification, paradigmatically at Abaton on the island of Bigêh, the site of the 'tomb' of Osiris.

[147]

The myth of the 'Distant Goddess' is not perfectly understood, but it clearly unites cosmogonic themes concerning the Eye of Re and Osirian themes (i.e., themes more concerned with individual, rather than cosmic or social welfare). It is perhaps not surprising therefore that a variant of the myth involves Thoth. This variant is known particularly in the form of a demotic narrative (translated in de Cenival 1988; a portion also survives in Greek translation, see West 1969) that seems to tell a popularized version. In this text, Thoth takes the form of an animal, perhaps a monkey — in the Greek translation an otherwise unknown 'wolf-lynx'—in order to try to convince Tefnut to return to Egypt with him. She is at first in the form of a "Kushite cat," later taking the forms of a lioness, a vulture and a gazelle before returning to "her beautiful form of Tefnut," (22, 2) to return with him. The motif of cajoling the 'Distant Goddess' is used in this text as a framing device for the series of arguments, fables, and hymns Thoth deploys. Thoth is particularly appropriate to the myth when presented in this fashion because the text showcases the author's command of the most heterogeneous forms of knowledge and rhetoric.

One of the primary ways Thoth facilitates the exchanges across the border between the human and divine realms is, of course, in his function as lord of sacred texts. An important passage from the Book of the Celestial Cow provides Thoth's charter, as it were, in this function. When Re is about to withdraw from his role as immanent sovereign of humanity to take his place on the celestial plane, he says to Thoth, "I am here in heaven, in my place... be a scribe here, have power over those who are here...thou shalt be in my place, my deputy," (Piankoff, 32). Re specifically directs Thoth to create writings pertaining to the netherworld, where those who rebelled and were slain now reside. Here we see the divine authorization for the composition of the very afterlife literature for which Egyptian civilization is so famous. This body of texts serves to reestablish the communication between Re and his most distant subjects which was broken off at the beginning of the myth.

Re proceeds to empower Thoth in his mediating function by a series of formulae (65ff) linked to Thoth's diverse forms — the ibis, the moon, and the baboon. First, Re grants him the authority to send forth [*hꜣb*] the other Gods through spells and invocations and to check their actions in turn, this power corresponding to the ibis [*hꜣbi*]. Next Re bids him to "encompass [*inḥ*] the two heavens with thy beauty and thy light," this corresponding to the moon [*iꜣḥ*]. Finally, Re charges him, as the baboon [*ꜥnꜥn*], with repulsing (or perhaps 'traversing,' *ꜥnꜥn*) the Ha-nebu or 'Island Lords,' a vague term for the nations of the Aegean. CT spell 785 offers a seemingly related formula: "O mighty of magic [i.e., the deceased]...the Gods, the lords of all things, circulate about you in your name of Him who goes round about the Isles," that is, the

Ha-nebu, with the injunction a couple of lines later to "be a spirit, O Baboon." The formula from the Book of the Celestial Cow perhaps implies, therefore, a circuit around the Mediterranean and thus through many foreign lands, perhaps related to the idea that Thoth "made different the tongue of one country from another," (Bleeker 1973, 140).

The general significance of the myth recounted in the Book of the Celestial Cow is that before Re's withdrawal from the mortal realm, access to Re's spiritual illumination was universal and immediate for mortals; after his withdrawal, this illumination is dependent upon their own wisdom and virtue. Mortals will require knowledge in this new order, and so Re charges Thoth with writing down the things that are in the netherworld. The typical example of this genre is the New Kingdom Amduat book (for this class of literature in general see Hornung 1999). These books are accounts of Re's nocturnal journey through the netherworld, or duat, which is divided into the hours of the night. As the boat with Re and his entourage enters each hour, the divinities, potencies and souls who reside in that hour are illuminated and interact with the boat. The partially illuminated space of the netherworld effectively embodies the withdrawal of Re from total presence, and the duat in this respect is not solely to be understood as a space of the dead, but as a particular perspective upon the world as such. The climax of Re's journey is his rendezvous with Osiris at or near the middle of the night. In these books, Re's illumination of the netherworld is the engine of the Osirian resurrection and its power supply. In this, we see yet another aspect of the great Egyptian theological project of uniting the interests of the mortal individual, society, and the cosmos, and as the patron of such texts Thoth is a constant presence underlying the operations described in them.

A large body of difficult-to-classify speculative literature in ancient Egypt was attributed to Thoth's authorship. In the hands of bilingual Egyptian priests, these texts were surely to some degree the inspiration for the Greek literature known as the 'Hermetica,' which date from the first through the third centuries CE. It is hazardous to attempt to be more specific about doctrines common to the Egyptian speculative literature and the Hermetica, however, because only fragments of this genre of Egyptian literature survive. The most significant surviving work of this kind, although it too is a tissue of fragments, is a Demotic text that has been dubbed the 'Book of Thoth' although its actual title does not survive (see Jasnow and Zauzich 2005). Much of it is hopelessly enigmatic, but it takes the form of an initiatory dialogue between Thoth, called 'He who praises knowledge', and a disciple, 'The one who loves knowledge' or 'who wishes to learn'. Occasionally joining the dialogue is Osiris, named by an epithet that could variously be translated as 'He who has judged upon his back' (i.e., lying upon his bier), 'He who is upon his mound,' or 'He who wears the *atef* (the distinctive Osirian crown). Prominent roles are also accorded to Seshat and to Imhotep, the latter as an initiator into the mysteries of Thoth. The dialogue is wide-ranging, including discussions of the tools and craft of the scribe, the nature of language and its origins, the art of interpreting sacred texts, cosmogony, the netherworld, and animals, both sacred and mundane. Symbols and concepts from the afterlife literature are deployed throughout the text, although the 'Book of Thoth' is clearly not itself funerary. Sadly, the state of the text is such that it is far easier to say what subjects are discussed than just what is said about them.

One suggestive passage in the 'Book of Thoth' may shed light on the relationship between this book and the afterlife literature. At one point (Jasnow and Zauzich, p. 306, 309-310), the aspirant ('the one-who-[loves/desires]-knowledge') recounts having received from certain animals certain items that are identified with parts of a boat. This procedure appears to be the inverse of one in the ferry-boat spells from the afterlife literature (e.g., CT spells 395-403, BD 98-99). The ferry-boat spells take the form of an elaborate dialogue between the deceased and a celestial or netherworld ferryman. The ferryman quizzes the deceased, sometimes in very cryptic terms, about his/her ritual or magical qualifications, intentions, and esoteric knowledge, to which the deceased responds in equally cryptic or ritualistic fashion. Particularly noteworthy about these spells are the lengthy recitations of the parts of the boat and their identification with diverse deities or divine potencies. A statement usually introduces these recitations to the effect that the boat has been disassembled, which requires the deceased to magically construct the boat, part by part, out of the images and attributes of the Gods as known to him/her. The 'vehicle' for the deceased therefore is to be constructed out of his/her knowledge of myth and iconography as well as his/her grasp of its significance. This understanding is manifested in the ability to apply this esoteric knowledge to the practical purposes symbolized by the construction of the boat. The ferry-boat spells therefore represent in some sense the deceased's appropriation for him/herself of the religious imagery and narratives taught to them. This is but one of the manifold expressions in the Egyptian afterlife literature of the fundamental theme of the resurrection as being accomplished through the summoning forth of the deceased's own initiative or volition from out of the inert passivity of death. The passage in the 'Book of Thoth' seems, in turn, to suggest that books such as this were intended to equip the living, through instruction, with the 'parts' to construct the ferry-boat after death.

Although he stands apart from the familial organization of the 'Children of Nut', i.e., Osiris, Isis, Seth and Nephthys, due to his extensive involvement on behalf of Osiris and Horus, Thoth is sometimes regarded as being among their number. Thus in BD spell 1, Thoth states, "I am one of these Gods, the children of Nut, who slay the enemies of Osiris and keep the rebels away from him. I belong to thy people, Horus. I fought on thy behalf; I intercede in behalf of thy name." In BD spell 175, however, in a dialogue with the primordial monad Atum, Thoth shows that he is not exclusively identified with this divine family circle.

In this spell, Atum complains to Thoth, "O Thoth, what is to be done with the Children of Nut? They have made war, they have stirred up turmoil, they have committed wrongs, they have started rebellions, they have made carnage, they have put under guard…Give thou effective help, O Thoth." Atum, as representing the most primordial, precosmic class of Gods, laments the disorder generated by all sides in the conflicts associated with the children of Nut, without preference. Thoth responds to Atum, "Thou shalt not experience wrongs…Their years have been shortened, their months have been brought near, since they have made a mockery of secrecy in all that thou hast done." The operator of the spell proceeds to affirm, "I am thy palette, O Thoth; I have brought thee thy water-bowl. I am not among these who betray their secrets." In this fashion, the operator, with the help of Thoth, identifies him/herself with a principle prior to the cosmic principles themselves, which are conceived here as betraying the 'secrecy' or latency of the precosmic state. Elsewhere, Thoth is called "the one with whose word Atum is content," (Bleeker 1973, 119). Thoth is also distanced somewhat from the drama of the Children of Nut in PT utterance 218, in which Seth and Thoth are called "brothers who did not mourn" Osiris.

BD spell 175 is a spell "for not dying again." In it, after the colloquy with Thoth discussed above, Atum engages in a dialogue with the deceased, who questions him about the netherworld, "the silent land, which has no water and no air and is very deep and very dark and all is lacking," including food, drink and sexual pleasures. Atum replies that he has granted blessedness and quietness of heart in place of these things, and that at any rate "thy face sees, and I will not suffer thee to choke." The deceased is then granted a vision of Atum face-to-face. The exchange is significant in that all of the necessities and amenities of life which are magically procured for the deceased throughout the afterlife literature are here dispensed with, not in contradiction to other parts of the *Book of the Dead*, but in accord with the peculiarly primordial bond affirmed here between the deceased and Atum. The significance of Atum's private remarks to Thoth at the beginning of the spell is the establishment of this bond.

The Children of Nut, or three of them at any rate (Osiris, Isis and Nephthys), represent throughout the rest of the *Book of the Dead* all that is hoped for on behalf of the deceased in the other world; and indeed, throughout the dialogue the deceased is, as in the rest of the Book of the Dead, designated as 'Osiris.' But Atum explains that he shall someday return everything into the abyss as it existed before the emergence of the cosmos, after which "I [Atum] shall survive together with Osiris [i.e., the deceased], after I have assumed my forms of other snakes which men know not and Gods see not." This is perhaps not to be regarded as an apocalyptic prophecy but rather as demonstrating the ability of Atum (and therefore the operator who successfully identifies with him) to set himself apart from all that is and to subsist unsupported, as it were, in and through the abyss. The destruction of the cosmos spoken of by Atum is not to occur in the distant future but is rather, in a sense, immediate for the deceased. From an undeniable perspective the end of the world has for him or her already in fact taken place. This acosmic condition of the deceased creates, in effect, a kinship with the precosmic Atum. In this spell Thoth's knowledge, insofar as it transcends the sphere of the 'Children of Nut,' is as a result able to secure for the deceased or the operator a stable identity on a plane of being more primordial than that on which the Osirian drama plays out.

The primordial nature of Thoth is particularly emphasized on other occasions. In PT utterance 534, in a series of formulae designed to repel ordinarily beneficent deities in case they come with 'evil' intentions for the deceased, i.e., contrary to the deceased's will, the formula to be used against Thoth is that he is "motherless." Sometimes Thoth's origins are too primeval to speak of his having parents; thus in BD spell 134, Thoth is referred to as "son of the stone, who came forth from the twin eggshells [lit., 'female stones']." A tradition of local importance at Armant, however, identifies the Goddess Raettawy ('Re [fem.] of the Two Lands', i.e., of the idealized North and South of Egypt as representing the totality of the ordered cosmos) as Thoth's mother. This may merely underscore the close relationship between Thoth and Re, however. In her capacity of mother of Thoth Raettawy bears the epithet *Snk(t)-Nt*, or "Nurse of Neith," (el-Sayed 1969, 73ff). Thoth is sometimes called "son of Neith" and Neith "divine mother of Thoth." Some texts add that Raettawy created Thoth "for Horakhty," the solar form of Horus closely associated with Re, or refer to her as "Raettawy, the wet-nurse who nurses her heir, she is *Snk(t)-Nt* beside Re." It is also stated that she brought Thoth forth "in the *sha'ê*," the great pool at the beginning of the universe, and that she "shines in the Nun [i.e., the precosmic abyss] with Shu," all of which serves to convey that Thoth's origins lie in the earliest discernible moments of cosmogenesis.

Thoth is placed in relation to Neith in the "Conflict of Horus and Seth." The assembled Gods summon Banebdjedet to aid them in their deliberations. Banebdjedet advises a letter be sent to Neith and that the Gods abide by her decision. Thoth drafts the letter, to "Neith the Great, the divine mother, who shone on the first face, who is alive, hale, and young," (Lichtheim, vol. 2, p. 215). Neith responds, in her own letter, that the office of Osiris should be given to his son Horus, and that Seth should receive in compensation Anat and Astarte as wives. The assembled Gods agree with Neith's decision, although they are unable to implement it straightaway. Neith is obviously accorded an exalted status by the assembled Gods, but her distance from them is signified by the necessity of a letter and hence Thoth's intervention. The myth thus illustrates an important aspect of Egyptian religious thought, namely the hierarchical structure of the pantheon, with powers distributed on several relatively autonomous planes. This relative autonomy is also demonstrated by the impossibility of simply putting Neith's judgment into effect without further ado.

Thoth's role in cosmogenesis was probably also expressed in the cosmogony that originated in his cult center of Hermopolis. This cosmogony prominently features a group of eight Gods — four Gods and four Goddesses; indeed, the city's Egyptian name was Khemennu, literally 'Eight City.' They represent a stage of the cosmos prior to the appearance of determinacy, and in addition to being referred to as 'the Eight' or Ogdoad, are known as the *Hehu*, or 'infinites,' often translated 'Chaos-Gods.' They are (with some variation) Nun and Naunet, 'the Abyss;' Heh and Hauhet, 'Infinity/Formlessness;' Kek and Kauket, 'Darkness;' Amun and Amaunet, 'Hiddenness.' By giving the central roles to such entities, this cosmogony clearly emphasized the nature of substance itself rather than other possible creative principles. The stages in the Hermopolitan cosmogony are typical of most Egyptian cosmogonies: solidity appears amidst the watery abyss, in the form of a primeval mound of earth, followed by the advent of light (in the Hermopolitan cosmogony, at a mythical place known as the Isle of Flames, *Iu-Neserser* — cp. *neseret*, the divine flame wielded by the 'Eye of Re'). The Hermopolitan cosmogony is distinctive, however, in its account of this process through the immanent transformations in the underlying substance of what is.

In accord with their manifest attributes of indefiniteness and inertness, the Ogdoad often seem to have the quality of transitional creators or 'proto-demiurges'. This idea is expressed in the symbolism of a primordial egg or lotus, their proximate creation, an intermediate creation or matrix of transformation, a vessel in which the subsequent stages of cosmogenesis can, as it were, incubate. The lotus or egg may be created by the Ogdoad, or merely fertilized by them, or it may simply embody the moment at which they come to be in a determinate place, this determinacy being itself a stage in the cosmogenesis. A text from Edfu (I, 289) states that the Ogdoad, "the august ones who came into being before the Gods…were engendered in the Nun [the precosmic abyss], and born in the flood." A second stage of the creation involves the emergence of the radiant lotus and the activity of Shu, from whose thought Thoth is begotten in the form of an ibis. It is said of Thoth that "his work is to create life," and the notion of a transition to a new level of cosmic organization perhaps underlies what follows, in which it is said that "the God completed his first creative plan, and did not let it be known. He buried the Ancestors [the Ogdoad] after the completion of their span of life." Inasmuch as the members of the Ogdoad preexist the first real event in the cosmos, namely the advent of light, they could be regarded from a viewpoint within the constituted cosmos as being, in a peculiar sense, deceased, and they did indeed possess a necropolis cult at Djême (Medinet Habu). The notion that the members of the Ogdoad were in some sense 'deceased' expresses their incorporation into the framework of the evolved cosmos as passive or inert elements. Another text from Edfu (II, 51) states of the Ogdoad that "[t]heir time on earth was completed…His majesty [Re] gave command that their bodies should be interred in the place where they were."

Seshat is the divine patroness of scribes — her name means 'the Scribe' or 'the Writer' — and is closely linked to Thoth. Egyptians distinguished conceptually between "words" (*mdw*) and "writing" (*drf* or *sesh*). Thoth, although ultimately responsible for both, is associated more strictly with the former and Seshat with the latter (Saleh 1969, 24). Seshat is regarded as the inventor both of writing, of reckoning, especially in the archaic form of notching palm-leaf stalks, and measurement in general — she "reckons all things on earth" (Edfu I, 291). She has special functions in relation to kingship. Seshat records the royal name at birth and writes it on the leaves of the sacred *ished*, or persea tree, at Heliopolis, records the royal titulary at the coronation, grants the king *sed*-festivals commemorating his accession and renewing his sovereignty, keeps count of the spoils he brings back from foreign lands, and marks his lifespan by notching off years on the palm-stalk, an image augmented by a symbol signifying a limitless quantity, indicating that the king's reign is eternal. In temple foundation scenes, Seshat holds the string used to mark out the structure's perimeter. This ritual, called the "stretching of the cord," expresses her grasp of all the subtle forces that must be harmonized in order for the sacred structure to fulfill its function. In general, Seshat guarantees that rituals of all kinds are performed according to the instructions in the holy books. In Egyptian thought, the concept of fate (*shai*) is always imagined in connection with writing, and hence Seshat is a Goddess of fate as well, which in Egyptian theology paradigmatically involves reckoning the lifespan. The divine command is written down, not as a mere record, but to render it concrete, and the writing of it is inseparable from its enforcement.

At Esna Seshat is depicted holding a net with Khnum, the artisan of living bodies, and she was associated with a 'House of the Fish-net' at Hermopolis; a 'House of the Net' was also part of the temple complex of Neith at Saïs. These epithets just may allow us to elucidate some of the significance of Thoth's association with the ibis, a carnivorous wading bird. The symbolism of the net in Egyptian theology extends from the dangerous nets in the netherworld, whose fishermen threaten to net the soul (CT spells 477-480, BD spell 153) to the depictions of fishing and fowling that decorate the walls of tombs. The fragmentary hieratic text known as 'The Pleasures of Fishing and Fowling' (in Caminos 1956) provides a literary depiction of the king's enjoyment of such activities. In a passage from the 'Book of Thoth', the aspiring initiate, "the one who loves knowledge," questioned about whether he has crossed certain bodies of water — perhaps in the sense of netherworld ferryboat spells like BD spell 99—states in reply, "I have caught their fish. I have trapped the best of their exotic birds," (L01.5, 10/13).

A wide-ranging symbolic value is attached, in particular, to fish and fishermen in Egyptian thought. In CT spell 158/BD spell 113, "for knowing the souls of Nekhen [Hierakonpolis]," the hands or arms of Horus are cut off by Isis and thrown into the water, becoming fish, thus acting as the God's operative 'limbs' in the world. The symbolic images of fishing in tombs and references in the afterlife literature to fishermen and fish-nets which threaten the deceased imply an identification between fish and mortal souls as such, and a concern that one be fisher rather than fish. In this respect it is worth noting that the Egyptian word for corpse, *khat*, incorporates an Oxyrhynchus fish, and that the word *mehyt*, 'fish,' can also mean 'drowned,' and is a term used of Osiris when he is cast into the Nile. Fish consumed the detached phallus of Osiris, requiring Isis to craft a magical substitute in order to conceive Horus. There may be a reference to this myth in the "Lamentations of Isis and Nephthys," where Nephthys addresses Osiris, asking him to "come to Djedet, O lusty bull...O lover of women, come to Hatmehyt," (Lichtheim vol. 3, 119). Hatmehyt here is the district whose eponymous Goddess was 'Foremost of the Fishes.' The sexual terms in which the appeal is posed suggest that Hatmehyt's role seems to be to receive the phallus of Osiris on a 'physical' plane while Isis receives it on a 'metaphysical' one.

BD spell 78, "Spell for Assuming the Form of a Divine Falcon," i.e., Horus, appeals to Geb for 'authority' (*hu*), and wishes that "the Gods of the netherworld be afraid of me...when they see that thy [Geb's] catches of fowl and fish are for me," alluding perhaps to lordship over other, subordinate souls caught in the nets. In BD spell 65, for "going forth by day and overcoming the enemy," the deceased says to the Gods, "If thou dost not let me go forth against that enemy of mine and triumph over him in the Council of the great God in the presence of the great Ennead, then Hapi [God of the Nile's annual flood] shall ascend to the sky to live on *ma'et*, and verily Re shall descend into the water to live on fish." The state of injustice and disorder that would exist if the deceased were not allowed to prevail over his/her enemy is here symbolized by the inversion of the natural order. Injustice for the deceased would mean that the Gods, rather than 'living on' justice, *ma'et*, 'live on' the helplessness of mortal souls, which is what the spell affirms is not the case.

In CT spell 474 (BD spell 153), Mahaf, who is usually cast as the netherworld ferryman, is instead the leader of the 'fishermen' who threaten to trap the deceased in their nets. This reversability of Mahaf's function is important for understanding the significance of ferry-boat and fishermen alike. The fishermen spells (represented by CT spells 473-481) are similar to the ferry-boat spells inasmuch as they involve a more or less detailed identification of the parts of the fishing-boat and the net with a series of deities or mythic images. They differ, however, from the ferry-boat spells in that there is no dialogue between Mahaf and the deceased, or between the deceased and any of the 'fishermen,' due to the adversarial relationship. Here, the ability to appropriate esoteric knowledge to one's own purposes is demonstrated, not in the ability to constitute a vehicle, but to transform something hostile into something beneficent. BD spell 153 contains a version of the 'fish-net' spells from the Coffin Texts, with references to Shesmu's participation, but differs from the Coffin Texts version in not only allowing the deceased to escape being caught by the 'fishermen,' but indeed to become one of them.

In addition, the pen was in Egyptian most commonly thought of as a reed. In the "Book of Thoth," the student asks "What is writing?" and "the one-of-Heseret" — a district of Hermopolis; hence a common title of Thoth's — responds "Writing is a sea, its reeds [ꜥ.w] are a shore," (B02, 4/12-13; Jasnow & Zauzich vol. 1, p. 204). Later, the student asks "What is the shape of the papyrus plant, O excellent of love?" and "the one-of-Heseret" responds, "They have named it the ꜥ-plant, namely the ꜥ-plant of life, which the land of mooring will touch it (the brush)," (the relative clause at the end is unclear) (B02, 6/2-3; J & Z v. 1, p. 226). Here the author plays on some different meanings of ꜥ as brush, but also 'shore' and 'well-being,' reaching the shore or a place of mooring being a typical Egyptian symbol for achieving happiness. The marsh, transitional space between the land and the water, the fixed and the indeterminate, is itself a constant symbol in Egyptian thought for the obscure sources of creativity. The *duat* or 'netherworld' of souls is, concretely, the marshes from which the sun rises as it is born from Nut each day. We recall as well the significance of the green papyrus, the omnipresent marsh plant, to the symbol of the *wedjat*, and which is also present in the name of Wadjet, the uraeus-cobra and 'Eye of Re,' executor of the solar will, which is simply to live and to flourish. The ibis, akin to the writer, frequents this ambiguous space, the medium of the creative will, bringing forth into determinacy the ephemeral beings within it.

Bibliography

Allen, T. G. 1974. *The Book of the Dead or Going Forth by Day*. Chicago: University of Chicago Press. [BD]

Bleeker, C. J. 1973. *Hathor and Thoth*. Leiden: E. J. Brill.

Boylan, Patrick. 1922. *Thoth, the Hermes of Egypt*. Oxford: Oxford University Press.

Butler, Edward. 2009. "The Book of the Celestial Cow: A Theological Interpretation." *Eye of the Heart: A Journal of Traditional Wisdom*, No. 3, pp. 73-99.

Cerny, Jaroslav. 1948. "Thoth as Creator of Languages." *Journal of Egyptian Archaeology* 34: 121-122.

Faulkner, R. O. 1969. *The Ancient Egyptian Pyramid Texts*. Oxford: Oxford University Press. [PT]

Faulkner, R. O. 1973-8. *The Ancient Egyptian Coffin Texts*. 3 vols. Warminster: Aris & Phillips Ltd. [CT]

Jasnow, Richard and Karl-Theodor Zauzich. 2005. *The Ancient Egyptian Book of Thoth*. Wiesbaden: Harrassowitz Verlag.

Piankoff, Alexandre. 1955. *The Shrines of Tut-Ankh-Amon*. New York: Bollingen.

el-Sayed, Ramadan. 1969. "Thoth n'a-t-il Vraiment pas de Mère?" *Revue d'Égyptologie* 21: 71-76.

West, Stephanie. 1969. "The Greek Version of the Legend of Tefnut." *Journal of Egyptian Archaeology* 55: 161-183.

Appendix B
A Pagan's Inspirational Romance
by Mary K. Wilson, CEO Jupiter Gardens Press

In the field of Inspirational Romance, the only game in town, so to speak, is the Christian Inspirational Romance. And while I have no quarrel with this sub-genre of romance, there seems to be little out there for pagan readers who are looking to have their spirituality mixed with their romance. At Jupiter Gardens Press, which specializes in metaphysical fiction and nonfiction, as well as romance, and as a pagan woman, we offer pagan readers the spiritually-themed romance they want.

The traditional inspirational romance is considered a sweet romance, where a chaste kiss may be all the sexual content shown in the course of the story. Because inspirational romances are geared towards Christian readers, it's quite common for the sex act to only take place after marriage, and there's plenty of references to God and the Bible. There's been some talk of more erotic Christian Inspirational Romances, which feature the values of more modern Church goers, but in reality, when the phrase "inspirational romance" is said in romance circles, it's the conservative, nary a kiss, but plenty of talk about God, books that dominate the scene. So that's where I started.

Sweet Pagan Inspirational Romances

When I started writing my pagan inspirational romances as Mary Caelsto, I wanted to offer a clear alternative. For me, writing pagan inspirational romances provides me with an opportunity to show that strong faith runs through all spiritual traditions and to provide a showcase for the rituals and fundamental beliefs of paganism. My romances are considered "sweet," because other than the occasional kiss, most intimate encounters happen behind closed doors. Though there isn't the taboo on sex outside of marriage, because of course, all acts of love and pleasure are Her rituals.

When looking to publish pagan inspirational romances through *Jupiter Gardens Press*, I want a book that will appeal to both segments of the reading public: romance readers and pagans. Most pagans I know want fiction which accurately showcases their beliefs, so to me, accurate and well-researched books are a must. There is no one true way, and honestly, I would love to see books which feature different traditions or paths. For example, I would love to see characters who follow a strict Wiccan Tradition. The main goal is that someone reading the book will not be exposed to any mistruths and will come away having learned a little something about the characters' spirituality.

Romances must come with a happy ever after, or a happy for now ending. In the sweeter books, I believe a happily ever after is a must! This means the characters' relationship must unfold throughout the book and come to a believable and comfortable resolution. Spiritual conversion or adaptation can happen during the course of the book, but obviously the more contrast between how the characters begin the story and how they end, will impact how quickly the story can unfold.

When it comes to the sweeter books, the romance reader wants a strong story, one with emotional depth. Through every single moment, whether each one is happy or sad, the reader wants to feel along with the reader. That's the key for romance: the emotion.

Sensual and Erotic Pagan Inspirational Romance

When it comes to giving the reader more than a glimpse into the characters' sexual chemistry, it's vitally important to share the emotion with the reader. Sensual and erotic romance relies on the emotion to tie the sexual content into the plot. The very definition of an erotic romance is one in which the sexual content is such an important part of the story that it cannot be removed without harming the story. As the characters discover and explore their feelings, the sex becomes a part of that journey.

To me, part of the beauty of publishing pagan inspirational romance with definite sexual content is the fact that sex itself is beautiful. Through the story the characters' emotions and spirituality become intertwined with the sensual content, and this makes for a story which shows that sex doesn't have to be handled off the page as it is in the sweeter inspirational romances. The readers expect, even want, to see the sexual interactions between the characters.

The elements you'd expect in a romance novel are here, too, including the happy ending. Depending on the length of the work, and the characters' emotional journeys, the endings for these books may tend toward the "happy for now" end of the spectrum, rather than a "happily ever after." This also feeds the reader's need for a sequel, and many readers love revisiting their favorite couples again and again, even after the "happily ever after" is reached.

Expressing The Joy Of All Relationships

During a conversation about different spiritual traditions having their own "inspirational romances," an author asked me about erotic romance, and more specifically a pagan erotic gay male romance. I was ecstatic and when she sent the manuscript, I contracted it. Our romance imprint, *Pink Petal Books*, published the book, *Shell Shocked*, by Angelia Sparrow and Naomi Brooks. To me, this very honest story about a veteran with PTSD and a disabled man who lost his legs in a tragic accident who shared his pagan faith with his partner, was perfect both as a romance and as a pagan inspirational story.

The inclusive nature of paganism easily lends itself to having spiritual, inspirational stories involving all types of relationships. In addition to monogamous heterosexual, homosexual, and transsexual relationships, polyandrous and open relationships have a home within the body of "pagan inspirational romance." These types of stories already exist within the romance genre. Erotic gay male and ménage romances are some of the hottest selling sub-genres. There's no reason to believe readers wouldn't welcome these stories with an overlying pagan spiritual theme.

Of course, the wide variety of beliefs, as well as the inclusive nature of the pagan faith, means that there is no clear way to label pagan inspirational romances. This is a boon to authors who can write the story of their spiritual heart without worrying about how their faith may, or may not, fit into pre-defined guidelines established by a publisher looking to satisfy the broadest possible cross-section of a specific religious tradition.

This also means that many novels may not be specifically marked in the inspirational category, so they might be difficult to find. You'll have to look for them, read the blurbs, and perhaps visit the author's website. To my knowledge, we're the only publisher labeling our books as pagan inspirational romance.

Conclusion

If you're looking to write, or publish, pagan inspirational romance, it's important to remember that they are romances first and foremost. The romance reading community is very close knit and very vocal. Releasing a book that doesn't provide that emotionally satisfying conclusion, even in a "happy for now" ending, will quickly alienate readers. They want the emotional journey that comes with two individuals finding each other, working through their problems and coming together, if not forever, then at least in agreement that they'd like to continue to stay together.

However, the spiritual content cannot be layered onto the story. It has to be who the characters are or will become. And when you're dealing with matters of spirituality, it must come from the heart — the characters' hearts. Religious acceptance, such as in my book *This Divine Night*, which deals with a Christian man and a Pagan woman, must come from the character's motivations. The acceptance, or even a religious conversion, can't feel tacked on like an "after school special" lesson. If it does, the spiritual reader will feel cheated.

Publishers also need to understand the unique marketing of these books. There's room for them within both the romance and the pagan/Wiccan community, if the outreach is done. But again, just as with the characters, it must be sincere. And the publisher must be willing to find and cultivate a market for these books, not just accept that the general romance audience will embrace them. This has been true for all new genres of books, such as with the erotic romance market in the mid-1990's. Once hard to find, a few niche publishers began producing the hotter books readers wanted until eventually erotic romance made its way into well established publishers and now is seen on bookstore shelves. For the most part, erotic romance is an accepted part of the romance genre. We can hope that eventually, pagan inspirational romance is seen in much the same way.

As an author and a publisher, I find pagan inspirational romances to be fascinating both to publish and to read. Not only do they shed new light on my faith, but they also showcase the variety we have within our spiritual community. United by the romance guiding the story along, a pagan inspirational romance shows that not only does it hold true to its inspirational roots, but it also shows us the beauty and the power of love.

Appendix C
The Green Man and the Fool: Pagan Archetypes in the Fiction of Laurie R King
by Literata

Laurie R. King is an acclaimed novelist who draws on her background in comparative religious studies to weave together fiction that touches on spiritual truths. Her works of mystery and suspense include religion as an essential part of life, and she writes fascinating characters from a dazzling array of religions. Her richly detailed evocations of two archetypes familiar to many Pagans highlight ways those archetypes and other Pagan attitudes may provide healing in the face of difficult social issues.

The heroines of King's two series are a good example of the rich diversity of detail she works with. Mary Russell is a Jewish feminist in 1920s England who takes her theology as seriously as her detective work. In contrast, Kate Martinelli, a lesbian cop in present-day San Francisco, is a lapsed Catholic who constantly finds herself face-to-face with curious parts of that city's riotous mélange of cultures and religions.

In one novel, Russell spends quite a bit of time teaching a Christian minister about the feminine aspects of Jehovah in the Old Testament, a subject which was incidentally the topic of King's own master's thesis. Another work describes many different responses of women to patriarchy and especially domestic violence, using the goddess Kali as a theme, and Martinelli has to struggle with which ways of channeling women's rage into acts against men are actually laying the groundwork for future healing and rebirth, and which are unacceptable because they are solely destructive.

In two of her most interesting works from a Pagan point of view, King's two very different heroines encounter characters who have consciously reconstructed themselves in archetypal roles: One is the Fool who sows humor and chaos in the midst of a social order grown rigid and unjust, and the other is the Green Man, the living spirit of the vegetation god who cannot be repressed, in spite of all the industrialization humans bring to bear on the natural world.

These characters encounter complex situations and challenging choices about how to right wrongs and bring healing to people and societies in desperate need. Their responses and the nature of their archetypes exemplify qualities that contemporary Paganism can provide, from valuing playfulness and creative chaos to a deep connection with nature that makes us aware of the interconnectedness of all life.

The Fool

King's murder mystery *To Play the Fool* is set in San Francisco in the mid-1990s. Rational, reasonable homicide cop Kate Martinelli finds herself flummoxed by a mystical, mysterious man who has chosen to become a Fool, a role described in the book as:

> "...the mirror image of the shaman. The shaman's mythic voyage takes him from insanity into control of the basic stuff of the universe; the Fool goes in the other direction, from normality into apparent lunacy, where he then lives, forever at the mercy of universal chaos."[1]

The idea of apparent lunacy, or Foolishness, and its relationship to chaos are similar to the attributes of the Fool card in Tarot. King wrote her bachelor's thesis on the idea of the holy fool, finding examples of the archetype in the apparent foolishness of Zen practices and in Native American Trickster stories. Although this character is Christian, and draws on predominantly Christian ideas and tropes, he is also a true example of the Tarot archetype, treading his chosen path heedless of the potential for a fall.

King's depiction shows how the quixotic, mercurial personality behind the Foolishness can actually be working with purpose. The Fool defies all conventional ideas of cause and effect but still makes tremendous changes in the world around him and in the consciousness of others. Although his methods are different, he shoulders the same burden of righting and healing the world as the shaman.

In King's story, the character made a choice to take on the persona of a Fool because what he had regarded as wisdom led to a terrible disaster. As a result, he surrendered his words -- which he saw as the root of the disaster -- and spoke only through quotations. At the same time, he relinquished his normal role in society and committed himself to the sheer Foolishness of caring for the homeless, the dispossessed, and the needy. As King writes:

> "There is no place for the Fool in the modern world of science and industry. The Fool speaks a language of symbols and Divinity. ...there is an entire population living, as it were, on the edge, who feel as powerless as children and cling, therefore, to alternate possibilities. They believe in the possibility of magic, the reality of

Saints, and would not be surprised at the existence of miracles. The Fool is their representative, their mediator, their friend."[2]

The Fool's deliberate distance from his former self and the non-Foolish world comes by choice, but it is still similar to the dichotomy between the people he ministers to and the more settled population of the city. He spends much of his time among those who, for reasons ranging from disability to deliberate disconnection, have fallen through the cracks in urban society. His Foolishness, in which he empties himself of his own concerns, making himself almost the absence of self, lets him fit in to fill the lacunae in the lives of those who themselves live in the interstices.

In his service to others and emptiness of self, the Fool becomes a mirror-image in another way as well. Along with his words, he has in some ways relinquished his will; he often reflects others back to themselves and lets their words and actions drive his interactions with them. At the same time, he does make choices, and has a tremendous impact on others. Even though he speaks in quotations, one observer points out that he's strangely impressive, because "when he says a thing, he means it down to his bones."[3] In a way, his surrender to chaos and to the will and words of others becomes his means of expressing the truth and effecting healing one might describe as almost magical.

The Green Man

The issues of will, choice, and responsibility are featured again in the self-transformation of a World War I veteran in 1920s England, where King sets her suspense novel *The God of the Hive*. The traumatic experience of the trenches and the horror of industrialized warfare drive an officer to abjure his previous identity and recreate himself in the image of the Green Man. He retreats to the woods, living a life of utter simplicity, until King's heroine Mary Russell accidentally finds herself in his domain and desperately in need of help.

Russell is well aware of the ancient pagan sources of the Green Man imagery: "[He] was often shown as a face with branches bursting from his mouth and nostrils and twining about his head in the exuberance of life: a divine creature, speaking in leaves."[4] She compares him to Ariel from *The Tempest*, to Puck from *A Midsummer Night's Dream*, and to a wood sprite, but most of all she sees the character as John Barleycorn, another aspect of the vegetation god who dies and lives again.

As she struggles through her own confrontation with science and industrialization in the service of evil, the contrast between the Green Man and her opponents becomes a touchstone in Russell's quest. Like the Fool, the Green Man's interest in nature and his inherent playfulness separate him from normal society. Russell finds his "madness" compelling: "If the unseen threat was an approaching thunderstorm that raised one's hair into prickles, [the Green Man] was a bucket of water atop a half-open door: an unsubtle but refreshing distraction."[5]

Like the Fool, he is an embodiment of a particular kind of creative chaos. His is the irrepressible spirit of life that pervades the green and growing world, never fully under the control of those who would simplify matters down to purely scientific concepts that can be mechanized and industrialized.

The Green Man chose to recast himself after a disaster, as the Fool did, but the Green Man's disaster was not purely personal; it was the horror and seemingly meaningless death and destruction of the First World War that shook him out of his previous self. As far as he was concerned, his identity as part of an aristocratic family was an example of the European mindset that brought about World War I.

To get away from that system, he not only gave up his role as an officer, but his whole identity. After his self re-creation, he hesitates to take a role of command or direction in his subsequent relationships, letting himself be swayed by the currents around him.[6] Although the Green Man usually speaks freely, when it comes to talking about his former life and former self, or things connected with it, like family, he finds it almost physically impossible to force out the words.[7] Otherwise, he tends to play with words and symbols as he does with everything else: One of his particularly nonsensical but unexpectedly effective acts is preceded by the observation, "Who says a funeral has to be funereal?"[8]

In spite of his flight from his past, a symbolic connection with part of his traumatic transformation drives him to leave his nature retreat and plunge with Russell into the heart of London, the densely urban center of much of the industrialization he has come to loathe. When he sheds his woodland attire and prepares to go into the city, Russell describes him as having transformed into "the Grey Man," the office-working city inhabitant who is indistinguishable from his fellows.[9]

In this guise, he struggles to understand his sense of alienation. The mechanization and industrialization that drove killing to new depths of meaninglessness in the trenches have infiltrated the civilian city as well, and not just in the form of telephones and automobiles, but in the transformation of the citizens themselves, who have been reduced to cogs fitting neatly into the vast urban machine of the modern city. In spite of the superficial changes, though, the Green Man obviously does not conform to these expectations, continuing to be a force unto himself, the Lord of Misrule who puts things upside down, but as it turns out, that may be the only way to get them right side up.[10]

The Green Man emerges from his archetypal personality enough to go back into the city, but once there, his deeper struggle is not just with appearances but with individuality and will. He struggles with how to assume responsibility again, how to direct his will to make choices that can affect the tremendous inertia of the system set in motion against Russell. Eventually, he realizes that surrender is also an action, and that the only way to confront a villain whose schemes are as mechanical as clockwork is with the very chaotic spirit of irrepressible, irreducible life, which will always find a way around merely technological attempts at subjugation.

Intersection

At first, the Fool makes similar choices: He is willing to offer up his body to be beaten and even to allow himself to be imprisoned, seeking only new ways to carry out his Foolishness in these different circumstances. Eventually, though, he must emerge from behind the mask of the archetype he has chosen. He is forced to act on his own will, and to speak in his own words, only when he is confronted with how his retreat has allowed others to be hurt; he would not do so to save himself.

Paradoxically, the Fool who exists to challenge social order finds himself on this occasion allied with the forces of justice to protect even the homeless whom society usually disregards. By temporarily breaking free of his role, he stays true to the spirit of the ministry he has chosen.

In contrast, the Green Man's confrontation with his issues leads him further into the archetype of the vegetation god, taking up the mantle so fully that, like John Barleycorn, he sees self-sacrifice as the perfect act of will, the surrender that is also a success. The final confrontation takes place at the foot of Big Ben, a literal example of the way clockwork has come to dominate the modern city. Instead of going into the tower, though, the Green Man commits himself to the river Thames that flows through the heart of the city, an inexorable current of the nature that even the technocrats cannot conquer.

His sacrifice is something so illogical that it entirely confounds the villain's meticulous planning. It is an act of sheer foolishness to a mechanical mind, but it makes perfect sense in the natural world, and here the two archetypes meet.

In the end, the Green Man chooses to re-envision the city as something organic, a hive rather than a machine, and he acts on the basis of that vision; with his action, he helps make that vision real, and restores life to what might have been damaged or destroyed by systematized, industrialized approaches.

[166]

Similarly, the Fool goes out into his city again at the end of his story, resuming his mission to the people who don't fit smoothly into the urban mechanism and treating them as fully human in their own right, even when they can't or won't fit in. Both characters use their choices to move people to treat each other just a little more humanely. May we do as much with our wills and our words when we take our turns playing these roles and embodying these archetypes.

Notes

[1]King, Laurie R. *To Play the Fool*. New York: St. Martin's Press, 1995, p 128.
[2]King, *To Play the Fool*, p 106.
[3]King, *To Play the Fool*, p 197.
[4]King, Laurie R. *The God of the Hive*. New York: Bantam, 2010, p 48.
[5]King, *The God of the Hive*, p 189.
[6]King, *The God of the Hive*, p 263.
[7]King, *The God of the Hive*, p 165.
[8]King, *The God of the Hive*, p 266.
[9]King, *The God of the Hive*, p 178.
[10]King, *The God of the Hive*, p 283.

Appendix D
Select Timeline of Pagan and Polytheist Literature and Related Texts

At Saqqara, the *Pyramid Texts* are carved into the walls of the Pharaohs' burial chambers and sarcophagi, protecting the deceased ruler and guiding him to the afterlife. The *Pyramid Texts,* circa 2400 BCE, are the oldest surviving religious texts in the world.

Enheduanna (2285-2250 BCE) composes the *Sumerian Temple Hymns* and *The Exaltation of Inanna.* Clay tablet copies of her poems have been found which date to hundreds of years after her death, testament to Enheduanna's continuing importance and influence.

The earliest tales about Gilgamesh date to around 2150 BCE. The "standard" edition of *Sha naqba īmuru* (aka *He Who Saw the Deep*) or *Shūtur eli sharrī* (*Surpassing All Other Kings*), known to modern readers as *The Epic of Gilgamesh,* dates to roughly 1300 BCE.

Sometime between the 18th and 16th centuries BCE, the *Enûma Eliš* is composed. The version of the Sumerian creation epic known today was dug out of the ruins of the Library of Ashurbanipal at Ninevah in 1849 CE.

The Rigveda is composed in the north-western region of modern India between 1700 and 1100 BCE. It is the world's oldest, continuously-used religious text.

Shī Jīng (aka *The Book of Songs* or *The Book of Odes*) is composed between the 11th and 7th centuries BCE. According to traditional lore, the three thousand songs which originally comprised *Shī Jīng* were collected from throughout Han China, then edited down to three hundred by Confucius.

Between 1550 and 50 BCE, various texts known as *The Book of Going Forth By Day* (or *The Book of Emerging Forth into the Light*) are used throughout Egypt. There is no one canonical text. The first modern edition appeared in 1805 CE, though the first translated portions did not appear until 1822. (Really, there's lots more to the story. Go find a good book on the subject.)

Around 1400 BCE, clever scribes invent the Ugaritic alphabet. Over the next several hundred years, a number of poetic epics are written, including the *Legend of Kirtu,* the *Legend of Danel,* and the Ba'al tales. Clay tablets containing fragments of these poems are rediscovered in the 1930s CE and cause much consternation in the field of Biblical Studies.

Sometime during the eighth century BCE, *The Iliad* and *The Odyssey* are composed and eventually written down.

Sometime between 750 and 650 BCE, Hesiod composes *The Theogony* and *Works and Days*. He may also have written the *Catalogue of Women*. He probably did not write *The Shield of Heracles* (sorry).

Over the course of the seventh and sixth centuries BCE, the oral *Homeric Hymns* are written down.

Sometime during the fourth or third centuries BCE, Lao Tzu writes down the Taoist tenets which will become known as *Tao Te Ching* (aka *The Classic of the Way and Its Power or Virtue*). Then he disappears.

Roman poet Publius Vergilius Maro (aka Virgil) pens *The Eclogues*, *The Georgics* and *The Aeneid* between 42 and 19 BCE. He dies before completing *The Aeneid*, leaving the job of editing it to his two assistants.

By the year 8 CE, Publius Ovidius Naso (aka Ovid) has completed *Metamorphoses*.

Sometime between 159 and 189 CE, Lucius Apuleius writes *Metamorphoses*, aka *The Golden Ass*. It is the only ancient Latin novel to survive intact..

Around 177 CE, Greek philosopher Celsus pens *The True Word* (aka *On the True Doctrine*), the first comprehensive pagan critique of Christianity. It only survives because Christian theologian Origen includes it in a near line-for-line refutation, *Against Celsus*.

Flavius Claudius Julianus Augustus, aka Julian the Apostate, writes *Hymn to the Mother of the Gods* and *Hymn to King Helios* in 362.

The *Devi Mahatmya* (aka *Glory of the Goddess*), traditionally attributed to the poet Markandeya, is composed between 400 and 500 CE.

The *Táin Bó Cúailnge* is composed sometime during the sixth century CE in Ireland.

Around the year 711 CE, Empress Gemmei commissions Ō no Yasumaro to compose *Kojiki* (aka *Record of Ancient Matters*), which chronicles the creation of the four main islands of Japan and of the kami. Along with *Nihon Shoki*, it is the inspiration for much of traditional and modern Shinto practice.

Sometime between the 8th and 11th centuries, *Beowulf* is composed by an unknown Anglo-Saxon poet. It survives into the modern era on one single fire-damaged manuscript, the Nowell Codex. (Makes one wonder what else has been lost.)

In 13th century CE Iceland, the *Poetic Edda* and *Prose Edda* are composed, drawing material from much older oral and written sources. Snorri Sturluson wrote the *Prose Edda*; he did not write the *Poetic Edda*. Lots of people get that wrong.

The oldest surviving manuscripts of the *Nibelungenlied* date to the 13th century, loosely based on historical events and heroic motifs from the 5th and 6th centuries. Thirty-five manuscripts in varying states of completion are known, and they are all different from one another.

By 1405, Venetian-born Christine de Pizan has completed her two most well-known works: *Le Livre de la Cité des Dames* (aka *The Book of the City of Ladies*) and *The Treasure of the City of Ladies*. Goddesses (recast as clever queens and maidens) are praised as models of womanhood.

In 1484, Marsilio Ficino -- astrologer, vegetarian, Catholic priest, humanist philosopher and magician -- completes the first translation of Plato's works from Greek into Latin. He goes on to translate the *Corpus Hermeticum*, and the works of Porphyry, Iamblichus and Plotinus, setting the stage for a Renaissance era rebirth of NeoPlatonism.

In 1487, *Malleus Maleficarum* (*The Hammer of the Witches*) by Heinrich Kramer, an Inquisitor of the Catholic Church, is published in Germany. Guttenberg's printing press allows the book to spread to every corner of Europe by the end of the 16th century. Ironically, Kramer is denounced by the Inquisition in 1490.

In Lyon, poet Pernette du Guillet (1520-1545) writes dozens of Neo-Platonist-inspired poems, including the mythological *Élégies*.

In the mid-1500s, Portuguese poet Luís Vaz de Camões pens *Os Lusíadas (The Lusiad)* , a fantastical celebration of Portuguese voyages of discovery. The Gods of Rome feature prominently.

1564-1616. Shakespeare. Pay particular attention to *A Midsummer Night's Dream*, *MacBeth*, and *The Tempest*.

In 1701, Dominican Friar Francisco Ximenez begins transcribing from Quiche the Mayan text which will become known as *Popol Vuh*. In 1855, the text is rediscovered by Abbot Charles Etienne Brasseur de Bourbourg, who "borrows" it before returning to France. The whole story of *Popol Vuh*'s survival and introduction to the modern world is quite convoluted and interesting; read up on it.

In 1812, Wilhelm and Jacob Grimm publish *Kinder-und Hausmärchen (Children's and Household Tales)*. Over three decades and seven editions, the tales will be much changed and made more "suitable" for children. Between 1832 and 1854, Jacob Grimm also releases his three-volume *German Mythology*.

In 1821, Romantic poet Percy Bysshe Shelley raises an altar to Pan. Read his literary canon for more appearances by the old Gods and Goddesses.

In the mid-19th century, Lady Charlotte Guest releases the first English translation of several medieval Welsh tales, which will come to be called the *Mabinogion*. Some of these stories may date back as far as the 1000s.

Boston banker and amateur mythologist Thomas Bulfinch releases *The Age of Fable, or Stories of Gods and Heroes* in 1855.

Drawing upon Finnish and Karelian folk traditions and mythology, Elias Lonrot crafts *The Kalevala* in the mid-1800s CE. It goes on to become the Finnish national epic.

In 1890, Sir James George Frazer publishes *The Golden Bough*. If possible, read an unexpurgated version of the text.

Aleister Crowley publishes *The Book of the Law*, the central text of Thelema, in 1904.

Margaret Murray releases *The God of the Witches* in 1931. Immensely influential, it will prove divisive in both academic and Pagan circles.

Poet Robert Graves publishes *The White Goddess: A Historical Grammar of Poetic Myth* in 1948. While its historical veracity is highly suspect, the book's mythological and poetic insights are profound.

Joseph Campbell releases *The Power of Myth* and Mircea Eliade publishes *Le Mythe de l'eternel retour: archétypes et répetition* (aka *The Myth of the Eternal Return*) in 1949.

Gerald Gardner publishes *Witchcraft Today* in 1954.

Between 1954 and 1955, JRR Tolkien publishes the three volume *The Lord of the Rings*. He is supported in this endeavor by his good friend CS Lewis, author of *The Chronicles of Narnia*.

In 1961, Robert Heinlein publishes *Stranger in a Strange Land*. Church of All Worlds, founded in 1968, will draw heavily on the text, going on itself to influence the broader, nascent Pagan movement.

Published in 1972, Ivan Efremov's *Таис Афинская* (aka *Tais of Athens*) is a fictionalized account of the life of the famous hetaera, lover of Alexander the Great, wife of Ptolemy Soter, and initiate into the mysteries of Astarte.

Marion Zimmer Bradley, an ordained Gnostic Catholic priest, releases *The Mists of Avalon* in 1982 and *The Firebrand* in 1987.

Kim Chernin publishes *The Flame Bearers* in 1986, about a Jewish sect of female healers and Goddess worshippers.

In 1989, the first issue of *The Sandman* is released by *DC Comics*. (Too much Gaiman stuff to list here. Just check his homepage or the shelves of your local library.)

Our Contributors

Quincy Allen started with the intention of becoming an author. Unfortunately, he was waylaid by bandits early on who were armed with the age-old phrase "So you wanna be a starving artist the rest of your life?" He ended up a slave to the IT grind for 17 years, maintaining his sanity with motorcycles. In spite of the slavery, there was always writing and the dream of becoming an author.

Now in the midst of a mid-life career change, he's been published in *Short, Fast and Deadly* and written two episodes for the Internet radio show *RadioSteam* scheduled to air in Q1 of 2011. He's also working on editing several anthologies and works part-time as a Tech-Writer to pay the bills (and eat).

The mission now is to write a short story here, a blog there and the occasional novel manuscript. If all goes well, he'll be writing till the day he dies, earning at least enough to keep a roof over his head and his mouth full of sushi. He still rides motorcycles to maintain his sanity, and for those who don't know, $5 of gas is worth about $1,500 of psycho-analysis.

Amanda Sioux Blake is the keeper of the Temple of Athena the Savior, Alexandrian Tradition. She is the author of *Ink In My Veins: A Collection of Contemporary Pagan Poetry*, and *Songs of Praise: Hymns to the Gods of Greece*, as well as the forthcoming *Journey to Olympos: A Modern Spiritual Odyssey*.

A self-labeled history geek, she has taught classes on Greek Mythology and contacting your spirit guides at her local chapter of Spiritual Frontiers Fellowship International. She is currently teaching "Olympos in Egypt," an introduction to the unique hybrid culture and spirituality that grew up in Alexandria, Egypt in the Hellenistic Age, sponsored by the Temple. Visit her blog at templeofathena.wordpress.com, or email her at starsong_dragon @yahoo.com. She also runs an online t-shirt store, Otherworld Creations, specializing in Pagan and fantasy designs, at cafepress.com/other_world.

Rebecca Buchanan is the Editor in Chief of *Bibliotheca Alexandrina*. She is also the editor of *Eternal Haunted Summer*, a Pagan literary ezine. She has been previously published in *Datura: An Anthology of Esoteric Poesis* (Scarlet Imprint), *Luna Station Quarterly*, *Cliterature*, *Hex Magazine*, and *Bards and Sages Quarterly*, among other venues.

Edward P. Butler received his Ph.D. in Philosophy from the New School for Social Research in 2004 for his dissertation "The Metaphysics of

Polytheism in Proclus." More information about his work is available at henadology.wordpress.com.

Brandon Cracraft lives in the historic district of Tucson, Arizona with his partner and a black cat. His home is over a hundred years old. His short stories have appeared in several anthologies including *Monster Party* and *Attack of the Fifty Foot Book*. He has also written plays, screenplays, and articles. His fiction is set to appear in the comic book anthology, *Life After the So-Called Space Age*.

John Drury received his college degree with a double major in History and Political Science, and a minor in Classical Studies. His history focus was on the Greco-Roman-Byzantine period. Years later, he found his way back to the Gods. John is an initiate and priest in the Tradition of the Witches circle, and is editor of *Megaloi Theoi: A Devotional Anthology for the Dioskouroi and Their Family* (Bibliotheca Alexandrina).

Star Foster is managing editor for the Pagan Portal at Patheos.com, a multi-faith religion and spirituality website. A Southern Witch training in the Ravenwood tradition of her native Georgia, she admits to reconstructionist tendencies and occasional crankiness.

Teresita Garcia is a former elementary school teacher turned writer. She has published under the pen name Theresa Newbill in various ezines and print magazines and has received numerous awards for her writing. Her book *The Open Diary of a Witch* (a magical, autobiographical journey through poem and prose) is available at Hedge-Witchery Books UK: www.hedge-witcherybooks.com/page18.htm.

Steven Gepp is an Australian, married with two children, two university degrees, and a resumé that looks like a list of every job you could ever have without really trying. He is also a performance acrobat and professional wrestler. He has had a few short stories and poems published and has been writing for twenty-five years. A dull life.

Ashley Horn is a priestess of Artemis and devotee of Thoth. She is also a writer of adolescent fantasy fiction. She lives in southeastern Michigan with her wife, Mary, and passes time doing outreach for both the Pagan community, and for lesbian, gay, bisexual, and transgender rights groups.

Jason Ross Inczauskis is currently completing his Masters degree and is residing close to Chicago, Illinois. He lives in a small apartment with his love, Tabitha, his pet plant, Audrey the Immortal, and more books than you can shake a stick at. He is a fairly recent convert to Hellenismos despite a long-held fascination with the Greek Gods. When asked about his spiritual path, he may refer to himself as a Hellene, a Hellenic, or Greek Pre-Orthodox, depending on who's asking and his mood at the time, though he always follows it with the caveat: 'but not a very good one.' He has worshipped Athena for many years, but now honors the other Hellenic deities as well.

K. A. Laity writes so much that she had to create some pseudonyms [C. Margery Kempe & Kit Marlowe] to keep her colleagues from thoughts of murder. A tenured medievalist at a small liberal arts college, she mostly tries to find ways to avoid meetings in order to write more. Find her on Facebook or follow her on Twitter to hear the latest news, or check her site at www.kalaity.com.

Erynn Rowan Laurie is many things: professional madwoman, poet, ritualist, dreamer. She is the author of *A Circle of Stones: Journeys and Meditations for Modern Celts* and *Ogam: Weaving Word Wisdom* as well as many published poems and articles. Much of her work in the last twenty years has been focused on the art of filidecht, sacred poetry in the Gaelic tradition. Her website is The Preserving Shrine: www.seanet.com/~inisglas.

Gerri Leen is celebrating the release of her first book, *Life Without Crows*, a collection of short stories published by *Hadley Rille Books*. She has over fifty stories and poems published in such places as: *She Nailed a Stake Through His Head*, *Sword and Sorceress XXIII*, *Return to Luna*, *Sniplits*, *Triangulation: Dark Glass*, *Footprints*, *Sails & Sorcery*, and *Paper Crow*. Gerri lives in Northern Virginia and originally hails from Seattle. Visit www.gerrileen.com to see what else she's been up to.

An author, essayist and poet, **Alison Leigh Lilly** explores the interplay of aesthetics, theology, social and personal ritual, ecology, conservation, ethics and social justice in the contemporary Western political and spiritual landscape, with particular focus on nature-centered and Pagan traditions. She is the creator and writer of the popular spirituality blog, Meadowsweet & Myrrh, where she shares social commentary, philosophical contemplations and personal reflections from a place of connection, longing and curiosity about the sacredness of ordinary life, and our place in a Spirit-infused world.

Her work has appeared in a number of journals and magazines, both in print and online, as well as on websites such as Patheos.com and The Wild Hunt. A former columnist for PaganPages.org and contributing editor at *Earth Mysteries, LLC*, she currently writes regularly for No Unsacred Place and

Pagan+Politics with the Pagan Newswire Collective, as well as sharing musings and news on her own blog. Her author website can be found at alisonleighlilly.com.

Literata is a Wiccan who studies theaology and enjoys developing poetry and rituals. Her work appears in the anthology *Anointed: A Devotional Anthology for the Deities of the Near and Middle East*, *CIRCLE Magazine*, the group blog at the *Slacktiverse*, and in the e-zine *Pagan Pages*. On her blog, *Works of Literata*, she reflects on her relationships with nature and divinity and reviews Pagan and Wiccan books. She is also writing her Ph.D. dissertation in history and enjoys travel and spending time with her husband and four cats.

P. Sufenas Virius Lupus is one of the founding members of the Ekklesía Antínoou – a queer, Graeco-Roman-Egyptian syncretist reconstructionist polytheist group dedicated to Antinous, the deified lover of the Roman Emperor Hadrian, and related deities and divine figures – as well as a contributing member of Neos Alexandria and a practicing Celtic Reconstructionist pagan. Lupus' writings are available in several Bibliotheca Alexandrina devotional volumes, including those for Artemis, Isis and Serapis, Hekate, Zeus, and Pan, a sole-authored book of poetry, *The Phillupic Hymns*, and *The Syncretisms of Antinous*. Lupus' poetry has also appeared in the *Scarlet Imprint* anthology *Datura: An Anthology of Esoteric Poesis*, and fiction in *Misanthrope Press' Etched Offerings: Voices from the Cauldron of Story*. An essay by Lupus also appears in the anthology edited by Lee Harrington, *Spirit of Desire: Personal Explorations of Sacred Kink*.

J.D. Revezzo can't remember the first time she fell in love with the Arthurian tales, but it seems she's always told stories. That early influence was later bolstered by her college studies pursuing literature and art history degrees at the University of South Florida, and by devouring the works of everyone from her favorite musicians to many authors from the Science Fiction and Fantasy genres such as Michael Moorcock, Melanie Rawn, and the late Sir Arthur C. Clarke, and the works of Virignia Woolf and Tom Harris. Her short fiction has been published (under various pseudonyms) in *Eternal Haunted Summer*, *Twisted Dreams Magazine*, and *Crossed Genres'* "Posted stories for Haiti relief" project, while her non-fiction has been included in *The Scarlet Letter*. She has also, on occasion, edited the popular e-zine *Nolan's Pop Culture Review*.

She is a Pro member of the Romance Writers of America, and a member of The Tampa Area Romance Authors, and the Fantasy, Futuristic and Paranormal Special Interest chapter of the RWA.

Michael Routery is a writer, poet, and educator living in northern California. His writing can be found in a variety of publications, including *Datura*, *Beatitude 50*, and the Bibliotheca Alexandrina anthologies: *Written In Wine*, *Bearing Torches*, *Unbound*, and *Out of Arcadia*. Michael is a long time pagan. He can be found online at finnchuillsmast at wordpress.

K.S. Roy (also known as Khryseis Astra) is an artist, astrologer and writer living in Western Pennsylvania. She is particularly devoted to Hekate, Hermes, Persephone, Apollon and the Muses but also honors the rest of the Theoi as a practitioner of Hellenismos. She is the Graphic Designer for He Epistole, a Hellenic Polytheist newsletter issued by Neokoroi, and is currently at work on a new devotional art series for the Theoi.

Eric Scott was raised in St. Louis by Coven Pleiades, a Wiccan group based in the Alexandrian tradition. His fiction and memoir explore the joys and doubts of being a second-generation Pagan in the modern world. He holds an MFA in Creative Writing from the University of Missouri - Kansas City. His work has appeared in or is forthcoming in *Ashe! Journal*, *Kerouac's Dog Magazine*, *Caper Literary Journal*, and *Witches & Pagans*. He is also a Contributing Editor at *Killing the Buddha* and writes the column "Family Traditions" at Patheos.com. He used to sing in a Taoist glam rock band and occasionally paints elaborate metaphysical diagrams on his bedroom walls.

Diotoma Sophia agrees with the original Diotima that the western world has invested far too much energy into separating the inseparable duo of mind and heart. Diotima has written widely on a number of subjects, including essays, fiction and poetry. Her two latest books have been published by the Bibliotheca Alexandrina: *Dancing God*, a collection of poetry, and *Goat Foot God*, an examination of the Great God Pan. She is also the editor of *Out of Arcadia: A Devotional Anthology in Honor of Pan* from the same publisher.

Melia Suez is an eclectic Hellenic Pagan dedicated to Zeus. She discovered writing when she discovered this spiritual path. Her works are a tribute not only to the chosen subject, but also to Hermes. Her blog is 4ofwands.wordpress.com. She is also the editor of *From Cave to Sky: A Devotional Anthology in Honor of Zeus* (*Bibliotheca Alexandrina*).

Jhenah Telyndru is the founder of the Sisterhood of Avalon, the Director of the Avalonian Thealogical Seminary, and facilitates pilgrimages to sacred sites in the British Isles. She is the author of *Avalon Within: A Sacred Journey of Myth, Mystery and Inner Wisdom* (*Llewellyn* 2010), a contributing author to several Pagan annuals and compilations, and has had her writing published in

SageWoman, *PanGaia*, *Witches and Pagans*, *The Beltane Papers*, and *Circle Magazine*. Jhenah is the creator of a unique system of trance journey postures found on the DVD *Trancing the Inner Landscape: Avalonian Landscape Postures*, and has produced a spoken word album of guided meditations entitled *Journeys to Avalon: Immrama to the Holy Isle*. Jhenah holds a Bachelor's degree in archaeology and is currently a second year student at the University of Wales Trinity Saint David, where she is earning her master's degree in Celtic Studies. She welcomes your contact through her website: ynysafallon.com.

Mary K. Wilson lives in Iowa with her partner and a menagerie of animals, including opinionated parrots, a horse who lives the life of leisure, and a cat who was a dog in a past life. She began *Jupiter Gardens, LLC* and *Jupiter Gardens Press* in 2009, though she's been writing for over two decades and has had numerous articles published in pagan magazines and newsletters. As Mary Caelsto she writes pagan inspirational romance and spiritual nonfiction, including a book on Animal Reiki. You can learn more about Jupiter Gardens Press at jupitergardens.com and Mary's writing at marycaelsto.com

About Bibliotheca Alexandrina

Ptolemy Soter, the first Makedonian ruler of Egypt, established the library at Alexandria to collect all of the world's learning in a single place. His scholars compiled definitive editions of the Classics, translated important foreign texts into Greek, and made monumental strides in science, mathematics, philosophy and literature. By some accounts over a million scrolls were housed in the famed library, and though it has long since perished due to the ravages of war, fire, and human ignorance, the image of this great institution has remained as a powerful inspiration down through the centuries.

To help promote the revival of traditional polytheistic religions we have launched a series of books dedicated to the ancient gods of Greece and Egypt. The library is a collaborative effort drawing on the combined resources of the different elements within the modern Hellenic and Kemetic communities, in the hope that we can come together to praise our gods and share our diverse understandings, experiences and approaches to the divine.

A list of our current and forthcoming titles can be found on the following page. For more information on the Bibliotheca, our submission requirements for upcoming devotionals, or to learn about our organization, please visit us at **neosalexandria.org**.

Sincerely,

The Editorial Board of the Library of Neos Alexandria

Current Titles

Written in Wine: A Devotional Anthology for Dionysos
Dancing God: Poetry of Myths and Magicks by Diotima
Goat Foot God by Diotima
Longing for Wisdom: The Message of the Maxims by Allyson Szabo
The Phillupic Hymns by P. Sufenas Virius Lupus
Unbound: A Devotional Anthology for Artemis
Waters of Life: A Devotional Anthology for Isis and Serapis
Bearing Torches: A Devotional Anthology for Hekate
Queen of the Great Below: An Anthology in Honor of Ereshkigal
From Cave to Sky: A Devotional Anthology in Honor of Zeus
Out of Arcadia: A Devotional Anthology for Pan
Anointed: A Devotional Anthology for the Deities of the Near and Middle East.
The Scribing Ibis: An Anthology of Pagan Fiction in Honor of Thoth

Forthcoming Titles

Megaloi Theoi: A Devotional for The Dioskouroi and Their Families
Queen of the Sacred Way: A Devotional Anthology in Honor of Persephone
Harnessing Fire: A Devotional Anthology in Honor of Hephaestus
Guardian of the Road: A Devotional Anthology in Honor of Hermes